Praise for *Anything but Plain*

"Readers will be won over by the delightful leads, and the nuanced treatment of Lydie's ADHD and crisis of faith brings depth to the narrative. This is another winner from Fisher."

Publishers Weekly

"Do you ever get your hands on a novel and know, before you've ever read a single page, that it's going to be a fantastic read? That's what happened to me when Suzanne Woods Fisher's latest release, *Anything but Plain*, arrived. I knew it would be wonderful and I was not disappointed!"

Destination Amish

"*Anything but Plain* by Suzanne Woods Fisher is a heartbreaking yet beautiful Amish journey. . . . I love how Suzanne Fisher tackled so many themes beautifully in this novel. I laughed and cried so much. This is definitely an emotional read."

Urban Lit Magazine

Praise for *A Season on the Wind*

"Woods Fisher uses the intriguing arts and sciences of birding and wildlife photography to reveal unexpectedly rich truths about pain, healing, and spiritual connection within the natural world. She approaches subjects of depression and suicide with compassion, and her thematically compelling storytelling will inspire discussion. Woods Fisher's relatable characters bring to life the experience of birding as a passion, a career, an escape, and most revealingly, a way of understanding life both in its patterns and its unpredictability."

Booklist

"*A Season on the Wind* is Suzanne Woods Fisher's newest Amish fiction book, and it truly is a wonderful read!"

Interviews & Reviews

"This is a delightful Amish story. . . . The story is one of love and forgiveness and discovering one's true self. You will be uplifted and inspired in the reading."

Evangelical Church Library

Lost *and* Found

Novels by Suzanne Woods Fisher

LANCASTER COUNTY SECRETS

The Choice

The Waiting

The Search

SEASONS OF STONEY RIDGE

The Keeper

The Haven

The Lesson

THE INN AT EAGLE HILL

The Letters

The Calling

The Revealing

AMISH BEGINNINGS

Anna's Crossing

The Newcomer

The Return

THE BISHOP'S FAMILY

The Imposter

The Quieting

The Devoted

NANTUCKET LEGACY

Phoebe's Light

Minding the Light

The Light Before Day

THE DEACON'S FAMILY

Mending Fences

Stitches in Time

Two Steps Forward

THREE SISTERS ISLAND

On a Summer Tide

On a Coastal Breeze

At Lighthouse Point

CAPE COD CREAMERY

The Sweet Life

The Secret to Happiness

The Moonlight School

A Season on the Wind

Anything but Plain

Lost and Found

Lost *and* Found

SUZANNE WOODS FISHER

Revell

a division of Baker Publishing Group
Grand Rapids, Michigan

© 2023 by Suzanne Woods Fisher

Published by Revell
a division of Baker Publishing Group
Grand Rapids, Michigan
www.revellbooks.com

Printed in the United States of America

Library of Congress Cataloging-in-Publication Data
Names: Fisher, Suzanne Woods, author.
Title: Lost and found / Suzanne Woods Fisher.
Description: Grand Rapids, Michigan : Revell, a division of Baker Publishing
    Group, [2023]
Identifiers: LCCN 2022060121 | ISBN 9780800739522 (paperback) | ISBN
    9780800745059 (casebound) | ISBN 9781493443482 (ebook)
Subjects: LCGFT: Christian fiction. | Novels.
Classification: LCC PS3606.I78 L67 2023 | DDC 813/.6—dc23/eng/20230105
LC record available at https://lccn.loc.gov/2022060121

Scripture used in this book, whether quoted or paraphrased by the characters, is taken from the King James Version of the Bible.

This book is a work of fiction. Names, characters, places, and incidents are the product of the author's imagination or are used fictitiously. Any resemblance to actual events, locales, or persons, living or dead, is coincidental.

Published in association with Joyce Hart of the Hartline Literary Agency, LLC.

Baker Publishing Group publications use paper produced from sustainable forestry practices and post-consumer waste whenever possible.

23 24 25 26 27 28 29   7 6 5 4 3 2 1

Uniformity is not the same thing as unity.

DAVID STOLTZFUS,
bishop to the Old Order Amish
church of Stoney Ridge

Meet the Cast

Micah Weaver—(age twenty) Has developed a reputation in the bird world for his remarkable ability to spot and identify birds, especially rare birds. Started a business as a field guide for avid birders. When not birding, he repairs shoes at the Lost Creek Farm Shoe Repair Shop.

Trudy Yoder—(age seventeen) Avid birder, works at the Bent N' Dent store. Rather fond of Micah Weaver.

David Stoltzfus—Amish bishop to the little Amish church of Stoney Ridge, husband to Birdy, brother to Dok, son to Tillie Yoder Stoltzfus, father to many—both his own children and his flock.

Birdy Stoltzfus—Wife of David, mother to Noah and Timmy, passionate birder.

Dok (Ruth) Stoltzfus—The only doctor who makes house calls in Stoney Ridge. Sister to David, daughter to Tillie, wife to police officer Matt Lehman. While in her teens, Dok left her Amish up-bringing to pursue higher education and a medical career. Over time, she has been reunited with her family.

Tillie Yoder Stoltzfus—Mother to Bishop David Stoltzfus and Dok Ruth Stoltzfus. Known for being a teensy bit difficult to get along with.

Hank Lapp—Needs no introduction. You'll hear him coming.

Edith Fisher Lapp—Hank's wife. Best to stay out of her way.

Billy Blank—(age twenty-one) Young Amish goatherd. Fainting goats, to be specific. (No one understands why.)

Shelley Yoder—(age twenty) Trudy's older sister. Ran away from home in *A Season on the Wind* to pursue a singing career in Nashville.

Zeke Lehman—Bishop of the Beachy Amish church (read Author Note in the back if you'd like to know more about the Beachy Amish).

Dave Yoder—Amish farmer, father to Trudy and Shelley, husband to Bonnie.

Titus and Alice Gingerich—Swartzentruber farmers in Tennessee (read Author Note in the back if you'd like to know more about the Swartzentrubers).

Tattooed woman—Runs the tiny city hall of Stoney Ridge. President of the local Audubon Society. Has political ambitions. Mo McIntosh is her actual name. She wants you to remember it.

Birder's Glossary

accidental: a bird that shows up where it shouldn't (aka casual)

bins: slang for binoculars

casual: birds that fly from wherever to a wrong place (aka accidental)

chase: to chase after a reported rarity

chick: newly hatched baby bird

clutch: eggs in a nest

dip: a rare bird that a birder missed seeing

fledgling: a young bird with wing feathers large enough for flight

irruption migration: when a species migrates to an area in large numbers based mainly on food supply

lifer: a first-time sighting for a birder

LBJs (Little Brown Jobs): a blanket term for bland songbirds that are difficult to distinguish

nemesis bird: a species that constantly eludes a birder

jinx bird: a relatively common bird that has managed to elude a person's life list despite repeated attempts on their part to find that species

rookery: a breeding colony

snags: dead trees

spark bird: a species that triggers a lifelong passion for birding

twitcher: a hard-core birder who goes to great lengths to see a species and add it to his or her list

vagrant: straying well outside of the regular ecological range

whitewash: excrement outside of nest

1

The horse knew the way to the Bent N' Dent store so well that David Stoltzfus only had to hold the buggy reins loosely in his hand, his mind free to wander on this warm August morning. To ponder, to mull, to consider. Mostly, to fret.

David couldn't fathom how quickly things had changed in Stoney Ridge. His horse turned right on the narrow country road that led to the store, and the summer sun hit him right in the face, making him squint. Normally, on the pleasant drive into work, he could hand off his burdens of worry to the Lord and arrive at the store with a lightened heart. Not today. It was only eight in the morning and that familiar heaviness he'd been experiencing lately weighed him down. It was weighing the whole church down.

Last evening, Gideon Smucker had come to his house to tell him that he and Sadie were moving their large family to Ohio. That would be the third family to move away in the last few months.

Losing the Smucker family was a particularly hard blow. Gideon was a beloved schoolteacher, one of the few male career teachers among the Amish. Sadie baked goods and sold them at a bake stand at the farmers' market. But they just couldn't make ends meet any longer, Gideon told David, not after . . . Stroking his beard, he had paused. "Well, you know."

David knew. They couldn't make ends meet after the Beachy

Amish church had moved into Stoney Ridge last year. The Old Order Amish felt squeezed out . . . by another Amish church. "Is your mind settled? Couldn't we consider some options to help you stay put? You and Sadie, and your children, you're all greatly loved here."

"I already accepted a position at a school in Millersburg. For this fall term." His face scrunched up. "I'm sorry about the short notice."

David felt as if he'd been punched in the gut. It was late August. School would be starting soon. Who could replace Gideon? The church population had dropped so much in Stoney Ridge that they'd whittled down to one school, one teacher. It was a full classroom of pupils, but there wasn't a teacher waiting in the wings. When Gideon had been hit by the flu last winter, David's wife Birdy had substituted for him. His mind started racing, mentally scanning through the church for possible teachers, coming up empty. "I'm hopeful . . . you have someone in mind to take your place? A recent graduate?" Anyone? Even to his own ears, it sounded like a desperate plea.

Gideon didn't meet his gaze. Or maybe he couldn't. "I wish I did. It doesn't feel right to leave you in a tight spot. Some of the youth are needed at home, but most are working out. They can make more money working out . . . and lately that seems to be the only thing that matters." Gideon hesitated, as if reluctant to say more. "Honestly, we don't want to move. We love Stoney Ridge. But it isn't just about making ends meet." He rose from the rocking chair and walked to the top of the porch steps, then turned back to face David. "Sadie and I have prayed over our children since the day they were born. Our heart's desire is that they would join our church. If we stayed . . ."

Another long pause. "If you stayed," David prompted.

"If we stayed, we're worried our children would lean to the Beachy Amish. I see it in the classroom among the upper grades. I hear the pupils talking about cell phones and computers. I see

14

what such temptations are doing to the Old Order children." He raked a hand through his hair before plopping on his hat. "Two years ago, it wasn't that way. It feels like . . ."

David filled in the missing words. "It feels like someone's opened a Pandora's box."

"Yes. Exactly." Gideon's eyes lit. "Sometimes I think it would be easier if it was an Englisch church that moved in. More separate, more distinct. To our youth, the Beachys look mighty tempting." He adjusted his hat brim. "Funny thing is, I can understand the attraction. Maybe that's what has me worried. If I were a teenager, I'd be chomping at the bit to go to the Beachys. All their bells and whistles are mighty appealing."

Already, there'd been three Old Order youth who chose to be baptized as Beachy Amish. More to come, no doubt, attracted like bees to flowers. Parents were raising the alarm bell, spewing their worries at David. "They're tempting our children to the ways of the world" or "They're stealing them from us!"

Gideon started down the steps and stopped at the bottom to look back up at David. "This very morning," he said, "Sadie kept trying to water the garden with a bucket."

David settled back in the chair, waiting. Gideon had a round-about way of drilling home a point and it was usually worth the wait. But conversations with the earnest schoolteacher required more than a little patience. You could hurry speaking, but you couldn't hurry listening.

"She'd fill it to the top from the hose bib," Gideon said. "By the time she'd crossed the yard to get to the flower bed, half the water was gone. It took her the longest while to figure out the bottom of the bucket had a leak."

There was probably a point to this story, there usually was to Gideon's stories, but David wasn't sure what it might be.

"It occurred to me that you, my friend, are holding a leaky bucket."

David's eyebrows rose. "How's that?"

"More and more families are going to be leaving Stoney Ridge."

David pushed back and forth on the front porch rocker, back and forth. Gideon's warning wasn't a new thought. He could see what was coming.

"Pardon my bluntness, but you can't ignore this much longer." Ignore it?

From anyone else, that remark would've felt like a sharp elbow jab. David knew that many considered his leadership to be too passive, too accommodating. But from gentle Gideon, the advice was meant for his good. "The bucket is leaking," he said.

Gideon gave a nod. "The future of this church hinges on how you lead everyone, how you hold it all together. You know how that old saying goes. Aller Mann fer sich un der Deiwel fer die Iwwriche." *Everyone for himself and the Devil takes the rest.*

As David watched Gideon drive off in his buggy, he wished he had thought to remind him that he needn't worry about the church. The church belonged to God and God alone.

But Gideon knew that. He might be much younger than David, but he had a mature faith. His warning about the encroaching temptations of the world was worth heeding. As was his remark that David couldn't ignore this any longer.

The horse made a sharp right turn down the road that led to the store, tugging David out of his daze, back to the present. Somewhat. His mind kept returning to Gideon's warning. The Plain People weren't perfect. Not at all. But one thing they'd always done well was community. People took care of each other. They looked after each other. They had each other's back.

But a shift was in the offing.

It started over a year ago when a Beachy Amish church group moved to Stoney Ridge. To outsiders, they seemed similar to the Old Order Amish—head coverings for women, beards for men, no television or radio—though insiders knew the Beachy Amish leaned toward conservative Mennonites. Progressive, at least, compared to the Old Order ways. Others might call them liberal. The Beachy

Amish considered themselves to be moderate. Tractors in the fields, filtered internet and electricity in the houses and buggy shed.

Even though all Anabaptists could trace their roots to the Dutch priest Menno Simons, most Old Order Amish considered other denominations to be outside the sheepfold. David had a more generous outlook, based on the kindness and mercy of God he'd experienced. He liked to think that all Plain People had more in common—a love of God—than what separated them.

The horse stopped under the shade tree in front of the Bent N' Dent, its favorite spot to pass the time. David climbed out and gave him a few long strokes down his big neck before tying the reins to the hitching post. "I won't be long, old boy. Just opening the store and waiting until Trudy arrives for work."

He thanked God for Trudy Yoder, something he'd done daily for the last two months, since his mother had fallen and broken her hip and he was needed at home more often. Trudy was one of those rare employees who saw what needed to be done before it had to be pointed out to her.

He unlocked the door to the Bent N' Dent and went inside, closing the door behind him. The shades were drawn to keep the store as cool as possible during the long summer day ahead, and for a moment he could see nothing. He stopped, waiting for his eyes to adjust. It didn't take long to grow accustomed to the darkness—in less than a minute, the rockers by the cold woodstove emerged into sight, the shelves, the counter with the rusty-but-still-working register.

He paused, struck by the relevance. Gideon's remark that he couldn't ignore the situation much longer drifted once again through his mind. Discouraged, he took in a deep breath and let it go.

It didn't take long to grow accustomed to the darkness.

How good was that line? A smile tugged at the corner of his lips. There was a sermon in that sentence.

Today was the best day of Trudy Yoder's life. She knew that Micah Weaver's feelings for her were changing. She knew this because she had read it in his bird log. Read it from front to back cover and didn't even feel too terribly guilty about it. How else could she know what thoughts and feelings went through that silent head? He hardly ever talked. If he did have something to tell her, it was usually about birds.

Not that Trudy didn't appreciate hearing Micah's sightings. She was as dedicated to birding as he was, though not as gifted a guide. No one was. But she'd also come to a time in her life when she was ready for a little more than just bird-watching between them. And she'd been hoping and praying and waiting patiently for Micah to feel the same way.

So when she came across his bird log today—forgotten on the counter of the Bent N' Dent because Hank Lapp burst into the store to announce he'd seen something odd in the eagle aerie at Wonder Lake and Micah blew out of that store to go see for himself—she picked it up to go running after him to return it.

But then she thought twice.

She slipped Micah's bird log into her apron pocket and waited until the store emptied of customers and she was alone. David Stoltzfus had left the store in her hands today, and she was thankful, because if he were here, she wouldn't have been able to do what she did. She sat on a stool, took the bird log in her hands, and looked up. "Lord, forgive me in advance for this transgression. And thank you for understanding." Then she opened Micah's precious leather-sided bird log.

Micah carried it with him wherever he went, scribbling away in it throughout the day. Nervously glancing up at the door to see if any customers were coming, Trudy skimmed through the pages, as quickly as she could. Mostly, the entries were bird sightings. Which birds he'd seen and where, details he'd noticed. Things he already knew about them.

A dried flower slipped out of the log and she bent down to pick it up. She let out a loud gasp. She knew this flower! She'd picked it one spring day when she'd gone birding with Micah and happened upon a Scott's Oriole—an accidental. Pleased, she'd stooped to pick a bright yellow mustard flower growing in the grass to commemorate this rarity, and stuck it behind her ear. A funny look came over Micah, almost like he was seeing her for the first time. He leaned forward, closing the space between them, and everything started to fade away around them. For just a split second, she thought he was going to kiss her. Soooooo close. Then, as if he suddenly realized he was letting the excitement of finding the Scott's Oriole carry him away, he pulled back, pushing his hair from his forehead, rearranging the bent of his hat. The sweet, tender, romantic moment was over. She thought of it as their near-kiss.

Gently, she placed the dried flower back in the log, and that was when she saw the page was filled not with a bird log but with a poem he'd written. A poem! Who would've ever thought Micah Weaver had a poet's soul?

She did. She always knew that still waters ran deep in him. And then she realized the poem was about . . . her. *Me!*

LBJ (Trudy)

A sparrow, a little brown job
Hops along from bush to bush
Its song a constant chirping
Its chatter calls my attention
Its piercing trill tugs at me
Little Brown Job, Trudy
Overlooked, unnoticed, asking nothing
But sings like spring has come
Why do people cherish the rare and disdain
the common?

Her heart soared. Her hands shook. She thought she might stop breathing and faint dead away. A sparrow.

He thought of her as a sparrow.

Trudy believed that birds held special meanings, that they were symbolic of greater truths. She kept such thoughts to herself after Edith Lapp once told her that kind of thinking bordered on paganism. Assuming Edith was joking, Trudy had burst out with a loud laugh. Big mistake. Edith Lapp did not make jokes. Ever. Trudy sobered instantly, though she wasn't about to accept Edith's narrow thinking. What was so wrong about the Christian tradition of symbolism assigned to a bird? It wasn't as if she was making the bird into an idol to be worshiped. Nothing like that.

Besides, God loved birds. They were everywhere in the Bible, from beginning to end—from a dove sent out from Noah's Ark, to a raven delivering food to the mighty prophet Elijah, to a sparrow pointed out by the Lord Jesus himself. There were layers and layers of meaning to birds in the Bible. God described himself as an eagle, carrying the Israelites on its wings, under whose feathers they would find refuge. Birds held so many keys to what the Scriptures had to teach about God. Even Jesus said to consider the birds.

She hugged the bird log to her heart. So . . . Micah thought of her as a sparrow. Subtle praise, but nothing could have pleased her more. It was all she'd needed—solid gold evidence that Micah did, indeed, care for her, even a little, in the way she cared for him.

She reread the LBJ poem three more times, then carefully replaced the bird log on the counter where Micah had left it.

Best. Day. Ever.

———————

Micah Weaver fiddled with the dials of his bins until the lens focused in on what he thought was a small fuzzy gray head. He wouldn't have thought that Hank Lapp could be right about the eagle aerie—could be right about anything at all—but astonishingly, Hank was spot-on. There was definitely something weird inside the nest at Wonder Lake. Something alive, something that didn't belong with the two eaglets. The mother eagle flew in with a fish in her claws and started to feed the chicks.

"WHAT do you THINK it IS?"

"Shhhh! Try and k-keep your voice down."

"I AM!"

Micah and Hank were on the resting rock, watching the large stick nest from quite a distance, yet the eagle mother was startled by Hank's thundering roar and flew off. "Then stop t-talking. You scare every living thing when you start b-bellowing."

Hank looked hurt, which Micah felt a little sorry about, but at least he stopped his endless yapping as the mother eagle circled back in and flew back to the edge of the nest.

"WHAT do you THINK?"

"I think you're t-too loud."

Hank tried to whisper and it came out wheezy, like a patient with advanced tuberculosis. "But *what's* in the nest?"

"How should I know?"

"You're the GO-TO GUY. The FOWL expert." The eagle mother turned her head to glare at Hank, as if to say that if he kept bothering her babies, she might have to murder him.

Hank Lapp was a good man, but he was a loud and unaware good man. Still, it was hard to stay mad at him. "There's definitely something else in the n-nest that's alive."

"HOW could THAT be?"

"Shhhh!" But Micah shared Hank's bewilderment. "Maybe the parents brought back some k-kind of rodent to feed the eaglets."

"BUT its HEAD keeps POPPING UP like it's trying to be FED. NOT trying to GET AWAY from being EATEN ALIVE."

"Yeah. Yeah, you're right. Couldn't b-be a rat."

"I didn't think EAGLES ate up living THINGS. I thought they was SCAVENGERS."

"M-Mostly, you're right. They prefer easy prey. Fish, best of all. But those sharp t-talons can scoop up most anything." Micah squinted and peered through the binoculars. Not good enough. He

21

needed his spotting scope. "I'll come out at dusk t-tonight during feeding t-time. That way I can get a clear view."

"I'll COME too."

"No! No, I'll, um, let you know." Hank gave him a look of doubt. "I promise."

"Micah, does TRUDY ever hear from SHELLEY?"

"Shelley?" Micah froze. "Why w-would you ask th-that?" Shelley was Trudy's older sister. She'd left Stoney Ridge to pursue a singing career in Nashville, leaving Micah high and dry. He'd thought they shared a special bond. He was wrong.

"The other day, I thought I SAW her."

Micah lifted his eyebrows.

"Turned out to be a SCARECROW wearing a blond WIG."

Shelley Yoder? A scarecrow? The most beautiful girl in Stoney Ridge, in all the world over, and Hank Lapp called her a scarecrow. "You need g-glasses."

Hank squinted his good eye. "I SPOTTED your MYSTERY chick, didn't I?"

Micah tucked the bins in his back pocket. "Let's go."

As soon as the two parted ways at the fork in the bottom of the hill, Micah picked up his pace to get to Lost Creek Farm. He wished his sister Penny and her husband Ben were in town. Especially Ben. In one glance, he'd be able to identify that little gray-headed chick. Ben Zook was a highly skilled birder, an author who wrote books about rare birds. Ben and Penny had gone to Canada to work on a bird migration book. Following the birds, Ben said.

He'd picked a good year to go. The last few years had brought drought to Lancaster County and the sparse rainfall was taking a toll. Each year brought fewer migrating birds. Even the songbirds, those that normally didn't migrate, had reduced numbers. The birds knew to seek out new food sources.

Micah would've liked to tag along with Ben and Penny. Sadly, they hadn't invited him. Not only that, they'd left him with full responsibility for the Lost Creek Farm guesthouse, on top of his important field guide work *and* his boring shoe repair shop. As he arrived at Lost Creek Farm, he made a beeline to the repair shop and found his bird log on the ground, left leaning against the door, with a Post-it note stuck on it:

> *Micah, please see me at the store at your earliest convenience.*
> David Stoltzfus
> *P.S. You left your bird log on the counter.*

Micah reread it, tendrils of dread curling through his stomach. His mind raced through the last few days since church. Was iss letz? *What could be wrong?* Had something happened to Penny? To Ben?

At your earliest convenience.

That didn't sound like an emergency. Micah ruled out any concern about his sister and her husband.

At your earliest convenience.

What exactly did that mean? Like . . . should Micah drop what he was doing and get over to the Bent N' Dent? Or could it wait until tomorrow? He felt a flicker of uncertainty. Everyone knew the bishop didn't come calling for a chat. He came for a reason.

Micah glanced at the sun's position in the sky. Wonder Lake had early sunsets because of the ridge that surrounded it. There'd only be another couple of hours before it'd be dark. Too dark to see what was in the eagle aerie. Surely, David could understand this pressing need.

Yeah, of course he did. His wife Birdy certainly would. After all, there was a bird waiting to be identified! Yeah, absolutely. The bishop could wait. He scrunched up the Post-it note and tossed it on his desk. His full attention turned to the mission he was on: Grab his spotting scope and get back up that hill.

Twenty minutes later, Micah found a place on the highest part of the ridge to set up the tripod. He wanted to look straight down into the aerie rather than across from it on the resting rock, his typical place. He adjusted the dials and peered through the eyepiece. "Whoa." There it was. A much, much smaller head popped up. Disappeared. Popped up again. "Whoa, whoa, whoa." How could that chick—so clearly not an eaglet—avoid getting eaten by its larger nestmates? Because it seemed to be accepted as one of the gang. Healthy, active, hungry. Constantly begging for food.

He watched one of the eagle parents—most likely the father because it was smaller than the mother—fly to the edge of the nest with a fish in its talons. The larger eaglets reached up to commandeer the fish, moving to the edge of the nest and swallowing it in large chunks. He saw the chick bob up and down underneath its adopted siblings, grabbing whatever was dropped. The eaglets were probably four or five pounds. The chick was less than one pound. How could it survive on meager leftovers?

But then he saw the mother eagle fly in with something in her mouth. The chick aggressively grabbed morsels out of her beak. He nearly laughed out loud. This chick had gumption. As soon as the somewhat satiated eaglets realized more food was available, they swooped in and crowded out the chick. At that point, the chick resumed its begging.

Interesting. So that might be why the eaglets accepted this imposter sibling instead of killing it. Its constant begging brought them all benefits. These attentive parents supplied the nestlings well.

Man o' man. He wished Ben and Penny were here to see this natural phenomenon. Ben had shown him an article about how raptors form exceptionally strong bonds with their young. If these eagle parents were steadily feeding this chick, it was apparent that they had accepted it as one of theirs too.

Amazing. Just amazing.

But how did the chick get in the nest in the first place?

Micah straightened, staring at the stick nest, as big as a buggy. What a curious, remarkable thing he was observing. He had no answers for it. Not yet. But he would. Packing up his scope, he grinned. Trudy would be all over this bird mystery. She had a nose for research—especially bird behavior. Micah thought she gave birds way too many human qualities—like she believed those that mated for life were soulmates. And those that lost such a mate mourned. He was pretty confident that the only thing birds had on their minds was how to survive the day. Still, with Trudy's help, he hoped to figure out the whole story behind that little chick.

As he folded up the tripod, for some reason, an image of Trudy's older sister popped into his mind.

Why did Hank have to go and bring up Shelley's name? Micah hardly thought about her anymore. There was a time when she was pretty much all he thought about, mostly with how she'd left him, having played him for a fool.

It was a good thing Trudy didn't resemble Shelley in any way. You wouldn't even know they were sisters. Shelley was gorgeous. A head turner. A jaw dropper. Trudy . . . well, if Shelley were a Purple-crowned Fairywren, Trudy would be a House Sparrow. Plain, solid, reliable. Trustworthy. Good to the core. She was . . .

He didn't know. He wasn't sure what Trudy was to him. He'd always thought of her as a pesky little girl, more nuisance than anything else. This last year, they had met often to go birding. He found she was easy to be with, easy to talk to. She had more patience in the field than he did, which was considerable, and could outwait a bird like no one else. Somehow, songbirds knew to trust her. She could even entice chickadees to eat seed out of her hand.

But she was still just a girl to him, with wide owl-like eyes that appeared large and dark in her small, pale face.

Then came that day in March when she had spotted a Scott's Oriole. Typically, the Scott's Oriole was found in the southwestern United States and Mexico. This was only the second time the bird had been spotted in Pennsylvania, and the first time it had ever been recorded in Lancaster County. The first time Micah had ever laid eyes on one. It was a stunning little bird—yellow-bodied with distinctive white stripes on its wings. It was a noteworthy find, a lifer, and Trudy had tucked a flower behind her ear to celebrate. On that day, it dawned on him that she wasn't a little girl anymore.

It was the second time Trudy had noticed a rarity. She'd been the one who had first seen the White-winged Tern, though credit had gone to Micah. Correction. Micah *took* the credit. Stole it from her. His behavior still stung him, even after he made things right with Trudy. There was a code of honor among birders, and he'd broken it. She'd never accused him of stealing the claim, but then again, she said she had never noticed his stutter, either. Whenever he brought it up, she brushed it off as nothing. She was too easy on him.

A smile started slowly, then filled him, and he picked up his pace down the hill. He couldn't wait to tell Trudy about this eaglet imposter. The way Trudy would look at him, her delicate face so open, so earnest, so *on his side* . . . she always made him feel like he was something special. And he wasn't.

Man o' man. For a smart-as-a-whip girl who noticed everything, she sure missed some big things.

———

Trudy Yoder, Bird-Watching Log

Name of Bird: Scott's Oriole

Scientific Name: Icterus parisorum

Status: Low concern

Date: March 28

Location: Hiking in the hills

Description: Yellow-bodied, with black velvety plumage and white stripes on its wings. A standout even among a family of fabulous orioles.

Symbolism: Two fascinating facts about orioles make them a symbol of hope and resurrection. First, they're known to build nests in trees that have been struck by lightning. Incredible! Second, their nests are often built in the shape of the cross. (Isn't that just astounding? How would they know?!)

Bird Action: Serenading us from a tree branch.

Notes: It was a special treat for Micah and me to catch sight of a male Scott's Oriole right here in Lancaster County (a lifer for us both!). Even better than its stunning appearance, the Scott's Oriole is one of the first birds to start singing each day, well before sunrise. In fact, they're known for their lovely singing. The females are pretty, but it's the males that really shine.

Velvety black, bright yellow. Dazzling! Sparkling! Radiant!

Despite its breathtaking beauty, this little bird is tougher than it looks. It migrates all the way to Mexico, enduring cold temperatures and biting winds, to winter in the warm sunshine.

Sadly, while wintering in Mexico, the Scott's Oriole is a predator of beautiful Monarch butterflies. (I do so love Monarchs!) Setting aside that one little disappointing reality, there's everything to love in this songbird.

2

David Stoltzfus waited as long as he could, hoping Micah Weaver would stop by the store before closing time. He needed to get home for supper, though he wasn't at all eager to see his wife, Birdy. Not after Zeke Lehman, bishop of the Beachy group, had come to the store this afternoon to deliver news.

Zeke Lehman had sat in a chair across the desk in David's office and crossed one leg over the other, leaning back, a pleased look on his face. He was a charismatic man, full of big plans, blessed with the gift of persuasion. He had a way of making you feel like you were part of something big, something exciting. No wonder the members of his church were enthusiastically devoted to him. No wonder his church was growing by leaps and bounds. As Zeke told one amusing story after another, David found himself warming up to him, thinking that surely they'd be able to find ways to work out their differences.

And then came the news.

Zeke said he wanted David to hear this directly from him—he'd just received permits from the county to build a church along the banks of Wonder Lake. Actually, he didn't even call it Wonder Lake. That was a term the Old Order used for it. He called it a cow pond, which it was. "So right along the fence line of Lost Creek Farm, a road will be graded and built on top of the existing cow trail. The entire project will require a whole lot of tree clearing and land grading."

David had heard rumblings now and then about the Beachy plans to build a church, but he hadn't given much thought to it. "Why there?" His stomach twisted into a tight knot. "Of all places, why there?"

"Because of Hiram, of course."

Hiram Lehman, Zeke's older brother. Hiram Lehman had once owned a large dairy farm in Stoney Ridge. When he retired, he sold off his herd and let his farm fall into neglect. Not a churchgoer—any church, as far as David knew—he'd never been a terribly friendly neighbor to the Old Order Amish. Now and then, he'd come into the Bent N' Dent, but he certainly didn't linger, not like the other old men. Not like Hank Lapp, who had his own rocking chair next to the woodstove.

When Hiram died last year, he left his property to his brother Zeke, bishop of a church in central Pennsylvania. That was how the Beachy church came to Stoney Ridge in the first place. Zeke subdivided Hiram's expansive farm into multiple five-acre lots and sold them to families from the Beachy church who were willing to relocate. Many did.

The Old Order farmers had been disappointed. They would've liked an opportunity to purchase some of that land for their sons. It was the start of friction between the two churches, like an itch that couldn't get scratched.

But Wonder Lake? David never dreamed that particular piece of land would be built on. Not ever. Hard to get to, it seemed . . . forgotten. Abandoned.

"Apparently," Zeke said, "Hiram's wife loved that cow pond. Just loved it."

"Hiram's wife?" David didn't even know that Hiram had been married.

"Yes. Sweet little gal. Died years ago from some terrible flu." Zeke looked up at the ceiling. "Or was it a gall bladder problem?"

He cupped his hands over his knees. "Well, one or the other. She passed a long time back. She's the one who told Hiram it felt like church to her up there, like it was closer to Heaven. She talked about having a little chapel built there. She even drew up plans for it. She wanted a big, clear window at the back so others could see the natural beauty."

Seriously? David had hiked up to Wonder Lake with Birdy a few times and he didn't think it was all that impressive. It was a farm pond used by Hiram's dairy cows, tucked in a valley nestled between two ridges, with no actual road leading up to it. Only cow trails. Most everyone in Stoney Ridge had forgotten about the pond after Hiram's herd was sold. Then Penny Weaver and her brother Micah moved to Stoney Ridge. Avid birders, they'd discovered the little forgotten pond was home to all kinds of wildlife, including a bald eagle's nest that had been in active use for years and years.

"Yes, but . . ."

Zeke waited. And waited. "But what?"

"That lake . . . it's been a place for bird-watching. Birders love it up there."

Zeke's large head jerked up and down. "Yes, yes, and soon a place for everyone else to enjoy." He unrolled the scroll of architectural plans and David's heart sunk even lower. The footprint of the church was large, including an asphalt parking lot planned along one side. Worse still, an access road would be cut along the border of Lost Creek Farm. The amount of traffic going up and down that hill would be heartbreaking for Micah and Penny.

"Beautiful building, yes?"

That wasn't exactly how David saw it. It seemed like a large, intrusive man-made box that didn't belong there. What was wrong with meeting in homes, the way the disciples did in the book of Acts? It was a wonderful thing to bring worship into homes, right into the mundane dailiness of lives. A reminder that the ordinary, in God's eyes, was sacred.

After Zeke rolled up the plans and left the store, David was even more keenly aware of the large yawning gap between Old Order traditions and those of the Beachys. To outsiders, they all looked like Plain People. Look a little closer, and they had very little in common.

David needed some fresh air. When he told Trudy he was heading out for a bit, she held up Micah Weaver's bird log. "If you're passing by Lost Creek Farm, could you give this to Micah? He left it on the counter."

He took the log from her, sensing it as a sign from Above to go tell Micah about Wonder Lake, before he heard it elsewhere. He felt like he would be delivering a very hard blow to the quiet young man.

Over the last few years, Micah had built up a thriving guide livelihood for himself. As it developed, his confidence grew too. Watching Micah grow into manhood was like watching a flower bloom. He held himself differently—shoulders back, chin up. Even his stutter seemed to have considerably lessened. Birding had become his main source of livelihood. That eagle aerie at Wonder Lake was a year-round draw for bird-watchers who hired Micah to take them out in the field. David sighed. He dreaded telling Micah. Just dreaded it.

When David arrived at Lost Creek Farm, there was no sign of Micah. With a heavy heart, he left a note on the bird log and set it against the door of the shoe repair shop. And he went back to the store.

Tonight, on the way home, he wondered if he should stop by Lost Creek Farm one more time. The horse let out a deep and noisy exhale, tossed its head to shake its reins. Time to get moving, it seemed to be saying. Time to tell Micah and Birdy the bad news about their special place. After that, David would let Hank Lapp know and that would take care of the rest of the church finding out.

David gave a loud sigh and turned right to head toward Lost

Creek Farm. Pulling the horse to a stop in front of the guesthouse, he saw Micah off in the distance. He was coming down the hill, scope under one arm, binoculars hanging around his neck. Crossing the yard between the house and the guesthouse, he stopped short when he saw David waiting for him. He jogged over to the buggy. "What's wrong? Did something happen to P-Penny?"

David winced. He hadn't meant to create anxiety for Micah. "Nothing like that." He pointed to the shoe repair shop. "Go ahead and set your things down."

A little puzzled, Micah walked over to the shop. David followed behind, inhaling the scent of leather and stain. It was impressive how quickly Micah had mastered the art of shoe repair—a skill he had little interest in—but there was a need in the community and an opening when Ben's father, a cobbler, had passed away. David knew Micah would always, always rather be a field guide than stuck in a shed nailing old shoes together, but he stepped into that role willingly and wholeheartedly. That, David realized just now, was what set Micah apart from so many of his peers—he gave his whole heart to whatever was before him.

Micah tucked the scope under the workbench and turned to David. "H-Have I done something?"

"No. Not at all. Nothing like that. Something's come to my attention and I wanted you to know. I'm afraid it will affect you and your field guide work." When he saw Micah's eyebrows shoot up in worry, he paused. This was such distressing news to share. He fully expected Birdy to break down in tears.

He took a deep breath and explained about the farmer Hiram Lehman who had died, that he had bequeathed his land to his brother's church—the Beachy group—with one stipulation. "So they are going to honor the request of Hiram Lehman's wife and build a church."

Micah held David's eyes, as if he knew something bad was coming. "Where?"

David cleared his throat. "On the banks of Wonder Lake."

Color drained from Micah's face. "B-But how? How c-can they g-get to it?"

David winced at Micah's pronounced stutter. He felt as if he was unraveling all the growth that had been occurring in this quiet young man, like unspooling a ball of yarn. "They're going to grade a cow trail." His stomach tightened. "And pave it." He cleared his throat again. "With asphalt. To make a two-lane road up to the pond."

Micah smacked the workbench as the realization hit him. "Where? Where will the road start?"

"From the main road, along the border of Lost Creek Farm." Micah and Penny's home, a lovely hillside property that once belonged to their grandmother. *Argh*. This sounded even worse out loud. *Just say it all, David.* "The road will go all the way up to the pond. That's where the church will be built, right along the banks. I saw the plans. A big church." He just couldn't say it all. He couldn't say there was also a plan for a massive parking lot. He didn't have the heart to add that part.

A loud gasp puffed out of Micah, as if he'd had the wind knocked out of him. He was silent for a time, then he found the words, and in his eyes was a plea. "C-Can't you d-do something to s-stop it?"

David had thought of nothing else since Zeke Lehman's visit. He rubbed his face, exasperated. "The thing is, how do I stop a church from getting built? It's not an office building or a Costco. It's a church. We may have different traditions than the Beachys, but we are worshiping the same God. That spot is where they choose to worship. They own the land. They've done everything correctly. They've hired a good architect and contractor. How can I possibly object?"

"W-What about u-unity? Aren't we s-supposed to c-care about each other?"

"Yes, of course."

"D-Doesn't that include b-being g-good s-stewards of n-nature?"

David nodded.

"It's n-not right!" It came out like a roar.

David didn't think quiet Micah was even capable of a roar. He kept his voice calm and controlled. "It doesn't feel right, but it is within their rights. They went through the county's permitting process. It's all been approved."

Micah glared at David, as if he were personally responsible for this terrible thing. "Then I'm leaving Stoney Ridge." He blew out of the shoe repair shop like a storm.

David took off his hat and raked a hand through his hair.

Micah was absolutely correct in thinking they should care about each other. They were all brethren under God. Yet they held opposing views in nearly everything, and the discord was only sharpening.

Unity. If only.

The sun was sinking in the sky. Trudy was in the pasture where mares and foals were grazing. She had brought some extra hay out for the horses, as it had been a dry spring and the grass was thin. She watched the little foals as they jumped and bounced around their mothers, as if their small hooves had springs on them. Adorable. A dark brown foal nudged its mother with its nose and she pushed him away. Another mare meandered past her, two foals trailing behind. They stopped to briefly observe Trudy, then moved on. So peaceful, so calm, so content, so serene.

A twig crunched. Trudy whirled around to see Micah striding toward her. She was a little puzzled as to why he was coming so late in the day, but then she thought it might have something to do with a night bird. An owl, she hoped. She'd always been particularly fond of owls. Songbirds, she loved the most. But owls were a close second.

Most afternoons, Micah would call in to the Audubon Rare Bird Alert, and if a bird was near Stoney Ridge, he'd come looking for Trudy. Together, they'd go chase the reported rarity. Nearly always, they'd find it. Micah, mostly. He had an almost otherworldly sense of birds—as if he could think like them. As she waited for him to reach her, she tried to look natural, as if this kind of thing happened to her every day. Actually, it was happening more and more often, but she still wasn't used to it. She wondered if she'd ever get used to it.

Micah's presence tickled every part of her, from her toes to the top of her head. Something about his face took her breath away—firm features with a determined jawline, placid eyes rimmed by thick, dark brows. It was a rugged, capable face and she cherished every inch of it, including the small scar that ran through one eyebrow. Loving Micah had been such a blessing to her. He had opened her eyes to the natural world. She felt as though her heart had been awakened.

She tossed the last bundle of hay from the wheelbarrow, clapped her hands of hay dust, and turned to face Micah. As he drew close, her elation dimmed as she caught the troubled look in his brown eyes. About two yards away, he stopped short.

"What's wrong?"

"W-Wonder L-Lake." His breath was ragged.

"The eagle's nest? Did you figure out what's in it?"

"A c-c-construction s-site."

She stared at him. It took her a minute to get her head around what he was saying. "*Our* Wonder Lake? It's becoming a construction site?"

He gave a brief bob with his head. The look on his face! So angry, so upset. His hands balled into fists of frustration and her heart went out to him. He had come to let her know something important, something that had hurt him, so upsetting that he couldn't even form the words to tell her what had happened.

What to do, what to do? *Oh Lord, help!*

Beyond Micah, near the rail fence, was a large canopied tree, providing shade, a spot to sit . . . and a place to calm down. *Oh thank you, thank you, Lord.* "Let's go sit under the tree. You can tell me everything."

She didn't wait for an answer but walked straight over to the tree and sat down, leaning her back against it. She looked up at the branches above and noticed a hint of autumn starting to tinge the leaves. Micah sat down next to her, near but not too close. His legs were bent and his hands rested on his knees. She stared straight ahead, knowing Micah would be more likely to talk if they weren't facing each other. He was shy like that. She waited until he seemed more settled, his breath more even.

"D-David said the Beachys are planning to build a church on the b-banks of Wonder Lake."

"The Beachys? They're building a church at Wonder Lake? How? How could they do such a thing?"

Micah explained all that the bishop had told him. Trudy took it in, listening carefully. If she asked too many questions, he would shut down. She'd learned that through much experience with him. It meant a lot to her that he had sought her out. It was more evidence that she meant something to him. He might even love her, at least a little bit.

When he finished the story, she remained quiet for several long moments. Another thing she had learned about Micah. Don't jump in too fast. There might be more that he would say. "Well, we've just got to do something to stop it."

"No way."

"There's got to be a way."

"N-Not a chance. It's happening. David said so." He jumped to his feet. "So I'm leaving Stoney Ridge."

Her heart stopped. "You can't leave."

"I can. And I am."

"But . . . the eagle's aerie. The chick! You can't leave without knowing what it is or why it's there or what's going to happen next."

"I can t-tell you what'll happen next. The b-bulldozers will knock d-down the eagle's nest and k-kill the chicks. All of them."

"That's why you can't leave."

He plopped his straw hat on his head. "That's why I have to l-leave."

"But where? Where would you go?"

"Wherever the birds are." With that, he strode off.

She watched him for a long, long time, until he disappeared out of sight. Surely, he wouldn't just up and leave the Amish. He wasn't a fence jumper. Where would he go? He and Penny had come to Stoney Ridge from Big Valley because he wasn't permitted to be a field guide there—the ultra-conservative ministers felt it was too worldly. So he wouldn't go back.

Where would he go?

He wouldn't make such a big decision without talking to his sister. Right? And Penny wasn't the impulsive type. She and Ben had a guesthouse that Micah helped to run. It was their livelihood. They wouldn't just up and leave. Would they?

The more Trudy thought about it, the more she decided that Micah was overreacting. After all, he had enormous patience waiting for birds, sitting statue-like until they forgot he was in their midst.

But she couldn't deny that Wonder Lake was especially important to him. Something about that eagle's nest had touched him in a special way. Its wildness, she thought.

Surely he would think things over. He would calm down. He would realize how much goodness was here for him in Stoney Ridge, even without Wonder Lake (though the very thought of losing it filled her with dismay). She loved that hidden place almost as much as he did. It was where Micah had once taken her hand to tow her up a muddy trail—the touch of his rough, calloused hand against hers still sent tingles throughout her whole body. Wonder Lake was where he had given her his coat jacket when she was cold. It was where Micah would talk to her, stutter free. At Wonder Lake, he had begun to court her without even trying.

And now, with her heart sinking, she realized he'd courted her without his even knowing. He'd never asked to take her home from a youth gathering. Never invited her to anything. In all likelihood, their great romance was in her imagination.

While it was true that he had sought her out today in his distress, he had also revealed something else. No matter how much or how little he felt about her, he loved birds more.

When David arrived at the house, he found Birdy alone in the kitchen and he felt a catch in his heart at the sight of her. Sometimes he would see her and think, *How could I be so blessed?* Birdy had brought such cheer and liveliness into this home. One of the gifts of a second marriage, he'd often thought, was the acute awareness of how fragile life could be, to not waste a single moment of happiness. She glanced up from what she was doing and their eyes caught, and she smiled, as if she knew exactly what he was thinking.

"Where are the boys?" Timmy and Noah were their two spirited little boys, bursting with energy. If they'd been home, David would have known it.

"I sent them to borrow eggs from Lydie."

David's daughter Lydie lived next door, at neighboring Black Gold Farm, with her new husband, Nathan. Another blessing. It was a gift to have adult children close by, something he would never take for granted.

"And Mom is . . . ?"

Birdy frowned. "Upstairs, resting. She's been in bed all day. I tried to encourage her to come out of her room and get some fresh air. She wouldn't budge. Obsenaat." *Obstinate.*

"Ja. Glotzkopp." His mother could be a very stubborn woman. But that was another conversation that would have to wait. This was a rare opportunity to talk privately to Birdy and he knew not to waste it. He walked over to where she was working in the kitchen, leaned his back against the counter, and told her every-thing Zeke had told him.

She'd been stirring some kind of batter and just stopped, mid-stir, to stare at him, a nonplussed look on her face. "Irruption migration."

David had no idea where this was going. "Meaning . . ."

"When food sources have disappeared for migrating birds—perhaps because of a forest fire or a drought—the birds move on to find new places. They look for new sources of nourishment." She looked down into her bowl. "I think we should borrow their example."

Bewildered, he could only stare for a moment, trying to grasp her meaning. He'd expected her to cry, to be angry, but he hadn't expected *this*. "Are you saying we should move the church? Relo-cate . . . everyone?"

She picked up her spoon and started stirring the batter again, this time with a determined pace. "I think we should consider it, David. Over the last year, we've lost wonderful families because there hasn't been available farmland. Since the Beachys came in with their big black cars, we've had more buggy accidents and near-misses than ever before. There's more cars now than there used to be on these country roads. And you know as well as I do what's happening to our youth." Her stirring picked up a frenzied pace. "Our church doesn't seem able to find what it needs to grow and thrive in Stoney Ridge. I think we need to find a place of new nourishment."

He didn't know how to respond to her, so he said nothing.

"The Amish have never been afraid to move," Birdy said, mis-interpreting his silence for consent.

He was well aware of the history of Plain People's movement, and he knew it was done for a variety of reasons. One of the main reasons the Amish moved was in response to too much change happening, too quickly.

Too much change. He didn't like change either. "Birdy, I'm sorry to heap more bad news on top of the Wonder Lake news, but the Smuckers are moving away."

"So I heard." She studied him, then spun away abruptly. "Please do not volunteer me to substitute at the school while you look for a permanent teacher."

He pondered that momentarily. It hadn't occurred to him to ask Birdy, but it was a very good idea. She'd often substituted in a pinch. She was good at it. Then he remembered his mother and her broken hip and how needy she'd become. He shelved the thought of school for now.

Timmy burst into the kitchen with the container of eggs in his hands. "Dad," he said, eyes lighting up at the sight of his father, "can we go fishing soon?"

Noah appeared behind him. "Can we?" he echoed, then tripped over the threshold, bumping into Timmy, who sent the container of eggs flying. Broken shells and slimy raw eggs covered the kitchen floor. Timmy stepped right onto a bright yellow yoke. It squished and splattered under his bare foot, which set him yowling.

David picked up a rag to start cleaning the mess, but Birdy waved him off. "I'll handle this. Go see your mother. Encourage her to eat something."

On the way up the stairs, he knew he had evaded Timmy's question. All summer long, the boys had been asking and asking to go fishing. He just hadn't had any margin in his days to take off a day to fish, not even a few hours. Not after his mother's fall.

He peeked in the bedroom and saw his mother was napping, so he settled into the rocking chair in the corner. Listening to her heavy, steady breathing, he wondered why she wasn't making more progress. For the last year or so, she'd been living in the Grossdawdi Haus in the backyard, fairly contentedly, considering her discontented nature. About two months ago, she took a spill that fractured her hip. Emergency surgery had put a pin in her hip. By now, she should be starting to feel back to her old self, but she had yet to regain strength or stamina. For that matter, her interest in life.

David closed his eyes. He had a pretty good idea of how his mother, if she were well, would respond to the idea of relocating the church. She'd never been shy about sharing her opinion. As far as Tillie Stoltzfus was concerned, her son the bishop never drew a sharp enough line in the sand. She had one idea of what an Amish community looked like. David had another. She favored uniformity. David preferred unity.

David had done all he could think of to keep families from moving away from Stoney Ridge in pursuit of finding affordable farmland. He'd opened up a variety of means for a household to make a living, such as starting the farmers' market with Nathan, encouraging more home businesses like Teddy Zook's carpentry or Elsie Fisher's homemade soaps. The youth were given permission to "work out"—many at Bird-in-Hand's or Intercourse's tourist shops and restaurants.

Then he opened things up a little further by allowing more tourism into Stoney Ridge. Tour buses came through during summer months to make stops at Izzy Schrock's Stitch in Hand knit shop and Clara Glick's quilt shop. Penny and Ben Zook ran a guesthouse, Micah Weaver provided birding expeditions. Ben Zook was given permission to use his cameras to continue writing and publishing his bird books.

Others were critical that David relaxed the rules. Edith Fisher Lapp, Hank's wife, accused him of "the drift." She wasn't alone in her opinion—his own mother told him the same thing. There were plenty of others who shared their view, but those were the two who spoke their minds to him. Frequently.

Here was the rub: David didn't disagree with Edith's and his mother's reasoning for their objections. As youth worked out, off the family farm, they became exposed to worldly influences and pressed their parents for more liberties. A longing for cell phones was a steady drumbeat. There was always a looming threat of a young person leaving the fold, choosing a less restrictive church.

Recently, he'd witnessed an ominous turn. In two separate visits, anxious, teary parents came to his house because they'd found out their sons had become involved with internet pornography while "working out." Another set of parents found that their son had gotten mixed up with online gambling and owed a small fortune. These were the kinds of things that struck fear in a parent's heart. In a bishop's heart too.

He heard his mother shift in her bed and David opened his eyes, thinking she might have woken, but she was still sound asleep. He leaned back in the rocker and clasped his hands behind his head. This growing disharmony between the Beachy church and the Old Order Amish church portended something serious. Historically, when there was conflict, the Old Order Amish packed up and moved. It was a centuries-old pattern. The church avoided a head-on collision by moving on.

Irruptive migration.

Birdy might be right. She usually was. Church members were no longer finding the nourishment they needed to thrive in Stoney Ridge. Just like with a bird's migration, it all boiled down to finding the right place for the next generation to grow. But did that mean leaving Stoney Ridge?

The very thought of it made David heartsick.

Trudy Yoder, Bird-Watching Log

Name of Bird: *Eastern Bluebird*

Scientific Name: *Sialia sialias*

Status: *Low concern*

Date: *July 1*

Location: *Fern Lapp's sunflower patch*

Symbolism: *Christians see the bluebird as a symbol of hope and new beginnings.*

Description: *Brilliant royal blue on back and head, warm red-brown on the breast*

Bird Action: *Perched nonchalantly on a fence top, then made an abrupt dive downward to catch an insect midair. I watched, mesmerized, as it did it again and again. Flit, dart, swoosh . . . and catch. Astonishing!*

Notes: *The most beautiful bird, ever! Beloved by all bird-watchers. Lots of folks try to coax Eastern Bluebirds to their yards, but this dreamy bird isn't so easily bought. They don't come to feeders. They tend to be ground foragers. Males attract females by carrying nesting material in and out of the nest, but that's pretty much all the males end up doing. It's the females who build the nest and incubate the eggs, raise the clutch, and see them fledge. All the child care, start to finish. (Sooooo like certain families I know.)*

There's a good reason" the bluebird of happiness" is a common phrase. Just seeing one makes me so happy.

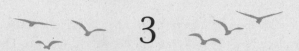

3

David woke before dawn and went downstairs so he wouldn't disturb Birdy. All kinds of thoughts were bouncing around in his mind and he wanted to capture them on paper. He sat down at his desk in the corner of the room and picked up the box of matches to light the lantern. Striking the match, he watched the head flare and settle into a flame, shedding light over his messy desktop. As he held it to the wick, he wished light could shed as easily over the burden of leading the church. He needed to untangle his thoughts, so he reached for a pad of paper and a pen to write them down. He paused, realizing there were basically two issues at stake here:

Leaving Stoney Ridge and all that would mean.

Staying put, and what would need to change.

It was true that the Amish church felt the squeeze from the arrival of the Beachy church. Zeke Lehman was a strong leader, charismatic and compelling. He had a vision of growth for his church. He hungered to bring the gospel to new listeners. He had a heart for those who did not know the love of God.

All good and worthy ambitions.

Ambitions. David leaned back in his chair. Perhaps that was what rankled him. The competition. As if the Beachys moved to Stoney Ridge to challenge the Old Order Amish to a race but forgot to tell them.

Hold it. David stopped himself. He was veering toward judging another person's intents. Once he stepped over that line, he was in dangerous territory. Self-righteousness, arrogance, pride.

Still. Stoney Ridge was not the same town that it had been before the Beachys arrived.

They had snatched up farmland before anyone knew it was up for sale, and as a result, land prices were driven up. They had gotten involved in local politics—and their positions were surprisingly liberal.

Then Zeke had made some kind of special arrangement with tour buses that visited the Amish farms. This summer, the number of tour buses running had doubled, yet they no longer stopped at Izzy's knit shop or Clara's quilt shop or Sadie's baked goods stand. Too small, the tour bus guides told David. The Old Order didn't provide enough workers. The tour buses needed shops that could manage big crowds with haste. "We have a schedule to keep," a guide said.

When David brought up some of those issues to Zeke Lehman, the Beachy bishop only smiled. "David," he said in a slightly patronizing tone, "you sound like you're in the Scarcity camp. I'm in the Abundance camp. There's plenty to go around for all of us."

But there wasn't. There really wasn't.

Zeke's suggestion had been for the Old Order Amish to *step it up*. "Market yourself. Improve your image."

David's jaw had dropped. Astounding. That was a concept completely and thoroughly opposite to Plain living.

He stopped himself. There he was again, judging as he ruminated. He had no business trying to discern the motives of the Beachys. *Forgive me, Lord God. Forgive me for putting blame on the Beachys for problems in our own church. That is a dangerous path to start down.*

He spun around in his chair and pulled out a book: *The Amish in America: Settlements That Failed* by historian David Luthy. He had read through this book last January and had dog-eared countless pages. Now he wondered why he had chosen to read the book at all. Had the Lord been giving him a sense of something on the horizon? He'd had those kinds of nudges before. Most came through Birdy. The words *irruption migration* kept nipping at his heels. Could it be true that the church was no longer finding nourishment in Stoney Ridge? Was it time to move on?

Where God guides, God blesses. David believed that with his whole heart. But the blessings came from obedience.

He opened the book and a page of notes slipped out. He'd forgotten that he'd written down points while reading the book. He held the page closer to the lantern to skim them. The main reason a settlement failed, he had learned from Luthy, was a lack of church leadership. No ministers to baptize, marry, and bury.

That much, David understood. What he wanted to figure out was why those groups had left their home in the first place. What made a group set out to start a new settlement? Because it was a risky undertaking, a dangerous thing for a church to move. It could have the opposite effect of what everyone wanted. Instead of unifying the church, it could fracture it. Churches split all the time over small conflicts.

Moving away from Stoney Ridge would require a dramatic ripping apart from generational homes. He thought about those families who had worked the land for three or four generations. Nathan Yoder's grandfather had first tilled those acres on Black Gold Farm. Amos Lapp had grown up on Windmill Farm.

On a personal note, how could he leave his sister, Dok? Her office was down the road from the Bent N' Dent. They interacted almost daily. She had left the Amish to pursue college, then medical school. They'd been estranged for decades, until the Lord brought her, miraculously, to Stoney Ridge. After moving here, she'd set up a practice and quickly became a highly respected doctor who served the Amish. Englisch and Beachys too, of course. She served the entire church community in her important role. She wouldn't move with them. She was married to a police officer. Her life was here.

How could he leave his dear sister?

He thought he might try and connect with other bishops who had considered moving, or those who had made moves. A new Amish settlement was started, on average, every few weeks. Birdy had pointed that fact out to him in the *Sugarcreek Budget* last night. But most of those settlements were one district. Zoom in a little closer, and they might even be only one or two families. Most likely, a split in their home church had precipitated the move.

If the Stoney Ridge church did consider leaving—and David really had no idea where they might go—he believed that the entire church should be in agreement. All would go. No one would be left behind. If the Lord was blessing this decision, then unity would prevail. Must prevail. Disunity, he firmly believed, meant sure failure.

But he might be asking for something near impossible. Older people would have to be willing to be uprooted, those with a long history in this town. Countless ancestors were buried in the Plain cemetery. How could he ask them to let go of that history? And for what?

David dropped the note on his desk, suddenly weary. The more he dug into this whole prickly mess—something that he had been studiously avoiding for the last few months—the heavier it grew. The messier. The more complicated. He blew out the lantern and went back to bed.

Early in the morning, Micah was out in the field guiding a group of bird-watching novices. Newbies. Typically, this was his favorite thing to do. It felt great, just great, to breathe in the crisp cold air while basking in the morning sun as it started to rise and warm the earth. He loved passing through the woods, deep and peaceful, listening for the sound of birdsong in the trees above. He understood the woods, the birds. People, not so much.

Typically, he enjoyed the wide-eyed wonder of newbies. It might sound prideful were he to say it aloud, but he felt God's pleasure as he opened their eyes to the birds that surrounded them. Common birds that had always been there, singing their songs, yet these people had been too busy to notice. On these expeditions, he would go over basic skills: Aim your binoculars on a particular tree branch, then move along the branch until you locate your bird. Easy.

But today wasn't a typical day. Today the newbies annoyed him with their repetitive questions. He felt as if he had to keep repeating the same instructions over and over and over. Stop, listen, look, identify. How many times did he need to say the same thing?

In the end, he was grateful for the distractions of the newbies because he couldn't bear to sit still with his thoughts or his emotions. Too troubled about Wonder Lake, about the eagle aerie. The eagle parents, the two eaglets, the foster-chick. What was going to happen to them once the bulldozers arrived?

As soon as he returned the newbies to their meet-up spot, Micah planned to dash up the hill to check on the nest. When one of the newbies pressed a fifty-dollar-bill tip into his hand, a wave of guilt rolled over him. He hadn't done his best work today.

"Dude," the man said, "I will never again look at a cardinal or robin in the same way."

And then Micah felt even worse. Chasing down backyard birds was pretty elementary. This guy could've opened a book on birds and learned as much as today's outing delivered. Micah didn't deserve the generous tip.

He tried to return it, but the man insisted he keep it. "You're the best, dude."

He wasn't. Especially not today.

He'd nearly crested the hill when he spotted Trudy on the large resting rock, sitting cross-legged, peering through her binoculars at the eagle's nest. He paused, watching her. The sight gave him a smile. How many times had he caught her in such a pose? Too many to count.

She must have heard him because she turned, waving him in. "It's just got to be a hawk. What else could it be?"

"Yeah, that's what I thought." He set his scope down beside her and started to unpack it.

"My guess is it's a Red-shouldered Hawk. I've seen one swirl around Windmill Farm's orchards."

"Too soon to tell." Micah wouldn't be able to identify which kind of hawk until the plumage started to appear. He figured the chick was only two to three weeks old right now. The eaglets were definitely a few weeks older.

"It pushes itself right up and under the eaglets as they eat and catches whatever they drop. Good thing they're messy eaters. That must be how it's able to survive."

He nodded. He'd observed the same behavior.

"One thing I've been wondering about." Her focus was riveted on the nest. "That hawk must think it's an eagle." She dropped her binoculars. "I can't wait to see what happens next. Will it survive as the chicks become juveniles?" She grinned. "If it does, will it spend its life thinking it's an eagle? Which species will it court?"

Interesting. Other than wondering if the hawk chick would survive another day, he hadn't given much thought as to the hawklet's development. Leave it to Trudy to think about the identity crisis of a hawk.

"When the b-bulldozers arrive to grade the trail, it's going to have to figure things out p-pretty fast."

Trudy turned to him with a solemn look on her face. "I'm not going to let that happen, Micah."

He coughed a laugh. "Yeah? How're you going to stop it?"

"Not sure yet. But I'm working on it." On that note, she shot a glance at the sky and rose. "I'm supposed to be at the Bent N' Dent soon. See you later."

Watching her head down the trail, he admired her pluckiness. He had to give her that. But her optimism was naive. He had a pretty good idea how things would play out because they'd already been happening. The Beachy church was spreading its wings wide, claiming anything or anyone in its path. Zeke Lehman believed that big was best. The bigger, the better.

As much as Micah admired David Stoltzfus, the bishop was slow to act. More and more benches went empty during Sunday services and David didn't seem to have any plan to stop it.

The church was in trouble, Wonder Lake was in trouble, and Micah sure wasn't going to stick around to watch everything he cared about fall apart.

A few days later, David asked his two ministers, Mose Miller and Vern Glick, as well as his deacon Luke Schrock, to come to the Bent N' Dent for an early morning meeting. Birdy had urged him to bring the ministers into the conversation and see what they thought about relocating the church. David agreed that the time had come to get them involved.

Mose and Vern, he expected, would strongly object to a move. Luke might be open to one. Every Amish community needed a buggy repair man and Luke was a good one.

David made coffee for the men, set three chairs in his office, and paused for a moment for a quick silent prayer. *Lord, where you guide, you bless.*

Mose walked in first and sat down, Vern right behind him. Mose was as tall as he was big, with a round belly that jiggled when he laughed. Most of the time, Mose was laughing. Not this morning. The look on his face was dead serious. He gripped his thighs with his big hands, as if bracing himself. "David, we're leaving."

David's eyes went wide. "You're what?"

"Moving. Heading out. Leaving Stoney Ridge. I can't buy a single piece of land for my eldest boy." He slapped his knee.

"There's seven boys behind him and it's only going to get worse around here." He leaned back in the chair and crossed his arms. "Yep. We're moving on."

Vern was a short man, barely five feet tall, married to an even shorter woman. "Us, too. Jeannie and me, we're thinking about a move too."

"You too?" David felt as if everything sounded warbled, like he was at the bottom of a pond. He heard the words but couldn't understand them. "You're thinking of leaving too?" He wondered how many families had been thinking about a move. He'd fully expected resistance from these two men. Maybe a relocation wouldn't be as difficult as he had expected.

"Yep," Vern said, nodding his head. "Thinking of going west."

"How far west?" David had given some thought to Indiana.

"Wyoming."

Oh. That was a lot farther west than David wanted to consider.

Mose folded his hands on his round belly. "He's going west and I'm going north. Thinking about Michigan. We both want farmland for our boys."

"And cold winters," Vern added.

That last thought came as no surprise to David. Cold-weather states held an appeal for dairy farmers like Mose and Vern. The climate was better suited to dairy farming, as well as fall butchering, with plenty of ice to harvest from frozen lakes.

Just then, Luke came through the door and sat in the remaining chair, his hat on his lap. His humorous black eyes danced with fun. "Why so serious? Somebody die?" He glanced at David and his face sobered. "What are you talking about?"

"Opportunity," Vern said.

"And it ain't here," Mose added. "Not anymore."

Luke scoffed. "Oh, I get it. This is about the Beachys."

"Yep," Mose said. "We want to move."

Luke dismissed that with a wave of his hand. "Don't jump before you're pushed. Things will settle down soon. You'll see.

Stoney Ridge is our home. It's where we all belong. Our roots are here. Tell them, David."

David couldn't bring himself to look at Luke. This whole conversation had gone in a completely different direction than he'd expected and he couldn't quite put it all together. He could feel Luke's gaze on him, Mose's and Vern's too. He forced himself to look up. "Actually, it's startling to me that Mose and Vern walked into my office to tell me they're thinking of moving"—he cleared his throat—"because I called you here this morning to discuss the possibility of relocating the church. For the very reasons Mose and Vern just mentioned. Available farmland. More opportunity." When no one responded, he kept going. "It's just something to consider, that's all. I wanted to get your input."

Mose clapped his hands. "You got mine. I think it's a fine idea."

"Me too," Vern said. "Let's go west."

Luke jumped out of his chair. "Hold it. Just slow down. Let's think this through carefully." He gave David a look as if to say, *Isn't this what you should be saying?*

Should he? David didn't think so. Slowing down and thinking it through carefully was all he'd been doing the last few days. Maybe the last few months.

"Look," Luke said, turning to the two ministers. "I know the Beachys have created some tension."

"Tension?" Mose said, his voice raised. "You call it tension when they've stolen our youth?"

Luke blew out a puff of air. "Okay, tension might be an understatement. But we shouldn't be overstating things, either. We haven't lost all our youth. A few."

Vern pointed a finger at Luke. "You just wait until your little ones are of the baptizin' age. Then you'll think differently."

What could Luke say to that? David felt for him. Still, such reluctance from Luke came as a shock. David knew, from Fern Lapp to Birdy, that his wife Izzy's knit shop sales had dropped to a fraction of what they were when the tour bus was making regular stops at Windmill Farm. "So, Luke, do you think it's wrong to consider relocating?"

"Not wrong, I guess. I just think that you should slow down. Think seriously about what we'd hope to gain in a move."

Okay, now this was turning into the kind of conversation David had hoped for. "Luke brings up an excellent point. What would you be looking for in a move?"

Silence. Mose and Vern exchanged a look with the other. "Land." Mose stroked his long beard. "Cheap land. Good land, but cheap."

"Sure," Vern said, "and we want to go someplace that's not overly settled. We want to keep our children away from the world's temptations."

"What about you, Luke?" David said. "What would you hope to gain?"

Both ministers turned to Luke for a response. He was quiet for a long, long while, then he let out a sigh of resignation. "We want to find a place where the church can thrive." He scratched his forehead. "I can't deny that we're all feeling the squeeze here. But where to go that works for everybody . . . that's a whole problem in itself too."

"Michigan," Mose said.

Luke shook his head. "Land prices are already on the rise. I know that for a fact."

Mose didn't disagree.

"Wyoming," Vern said. "Lots of open space. Hardly any Amish there."

Luke rolled his eyes to the ceiling. "That's because most Amish are farmers, not cowboys."

Vern gave that some consideration.

"What about a compromise? Ohio or Indiana?" David hoped he could rein everyone in.

"What would be different for us in those areas?" Luke said. "David, if you want to consider a move to give everyone more opportunity, then why go to an overly settled area?"

Good point. Excellent point, in fact. But David didn't want to get into a debate about specifics right now. He folded his hands together. "Please keep this quiet for now. Give this whole matter some thought and prayer. Let's meet again in a few days to talk more."

As Vern and Mose pushed off from their chairs, a loud shuffling noise came from outside the door. Vern opened the door to find Hank Lapp, holding a broomstick, with a guilty look on his face. "Just DROPPED the BROOM as I was sweeping."

A terrible realization rolled over David. When had Hank Lapp ever swept the store? When had he ever picked up a broom? Never. How long before Hank let the entire church know the ministers were considering a move? Immediately.

And to where would they move? David had no idea. But once Hank started spreading the word, he knew everyone would have an opinion on the topic.

Trudy Yoder, Bird-Watching Log

Name of Bird: Red-shouldered Hawk

Scientific Name: *Buteo lineatus*

Status: Low concern

Date: September 1

Location: Windmill Farm's orchard

Symbolism: In the Old Testament, the hawk (like other birds of prey) was considered unclean and never, ever considered to be a source of food. (Not when pretty much anything is on its menu.)

Description: The name says it all. This hawk has red shoulders, an orange-ish barring on its belly, and a gorgeous black-and-white checkerboard pattern along its wings. Longish tail too. It's smaller than its red-tailed cousin but shares its sinister look.

Bird Action: Flying over the orchards at Windmill Farm, hunting for its next meal. I watched as it swooped down to impale an unlucky field mouse with its strong talons, but somehow the brazen mouse wiggled out of its grasp and escaped. The hawk seemed downright bewildered. Made me laugh!

Notes: This bird is just about everywhere, though people often mistake its identity for Cooper's Hawk or Red-tailed Hawk. Red-shouldered

Hawks prefer to perch, especially on wires. They help farmers by ridding fields and pastures of mammal pests, like gophers and moles and voles and rats and mice. Their only flaw, in my opinion, is that they have a fondness for Mourning Doves.

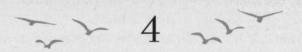

4

W hile Penny and Ben were off seeking migrating birds in Canada, Micah had been given full responsibility for Lost Creek Farm's guesthouse. Happily, he did not have to provide any meals. It had a little stocked kitchen so guests could be self-sufficient. That was probably the only reason Penny felt comfortable leaving the guesthouse in his care. She knew that if Micah had to provide breakfast for people, he'd rap impatiently on their door at 4:30 in the morning—just as he set out for birding—and hand them a box of cereal. As it was, his only duties were to check guests in and out, clean up after they left, feed Penny's animals, water the garden if it didn't rain, and keep on top of phone messages. And be available in case there were any problems. So far, so good. No problems.

Today, he noticed the mailman was trying to jam today's mail into the box, so he hurried down the driveway. He was supposed to bring the mail in each day. Mostly, he forgot about it. As soon as the mail truck drove off, he opened the mailbox and pulled out an armload of mail. Penny would be livid if she saw this backlog, even though it consisted almost entirely of junk mail. Just a few bills, and one postcard sent from Penny in Canada, saying she wished he were with them. He read it, smiling. He wished he were there too. *So why didn't they invite me along?*

He heard the phone ring in the shanty but didn't rush to answer. He preferred to just get the message and call back to confirm a guest's reservation at the guesthouse. That way, he could rehearse what he needed to say, stammer-free. He opened the door to hear the caller say goodbye and hang up. Something about the female voice struck a familiar chord. He set the mail down on the shelf and pressed the message machine to listen.

"Hi, Micah. It's me, Shelley Yoder. I'm calling because . . . I need your help." Something happened in the background. "I have to go," she said in a hushed tone, before she hung up.

Micah's heart started to pound. He couldn't breathe, couldn't think straight. He tried to get his head around this: Shelley Yoder had contacted him. *Him.* A year and a half had passed without a word from her—not to her family, not to her sister Trudy, not to him, not to anyone. He wasn't sure how he felt about hearing from Shelley like this. It wasn't as if she'd just gone vacationing to Pinecraft for a week or two. She'd *left* left. Run off.

No one even mentioned Shelley's name. It was almost like she had died. But the damage caused by her abrupt, sneaky departure, that was still very evident. Like the wake left by a motorboat. It lingered long after the boat went on its way.

Shelley's father, who'd always been on the crotchety side of crotchety, became mad at the world. In particular, he blamed Micah for Shelley's departure. There wasn't any truth in that— Shelley had pulled the wool over Micah's eyes the same way she'd duped her parents—but her father needed someone to blame. Shelley's mother had become a near recluse. She came to church with some regularity, but that was only to avoid a visit from the deacon. Trudy seemed . . . actually, Micah wasn't sure about Trudy's reaction. She never brought Shelley up and he sure didn't ask.

Micah listened and relistened to the phone message. Suddenly, Shelley needed his help? Not a single word in all this time until she needs his help? It made him so mad that he scooped up the mail and left the phone shanty, slamming the door behind him.

Five minutes later he came back and listened to the message again. Then once again. Then twice more. Man o' man, she had a pretty voice.

Later that night, David and Birdy were lying in bed, listening to the crickets through the open window. An owl hooted once, then twice. "Vermont," Birdy said.

"What about it?"

"My cousin Dana moved there. She loves it. Couldn't be happier that her church made the move north."

"I've never been to Vermont."

"I haven't either. But I think we should add Vermont to the list of possibilities for where to move the church."

David turned to face Birdy, resting his head on his elbow. "You've never been, yet you think we should uproot the church and move there?"

"I think we should consider it. Dana says it's been an ideal place for their church. Their church moved up to the Northeast Kingdom a few years ago. They've settled in well."

"Tell me more about your cousin."

"We're about the same age and she's just as tall as I am."

David had to smile at that. Birdy was over six feet tall. Taller than he was by four inches. "Isn't your cousin a . . ."

"Swartzentruber," Birdy finished.

Ah. The Swartzentrubers were one of the most conservative sects of the Old Order Amish.

David thought of the Swartzentruber homes he'd been in: big dark red barns, no indoor plumbing, old-fashioned hand pumps for water, no community telephones, no milking machines. They lived largely off the land, as self-sufficient as possible. The fact that it was Swartzentrubers who moved there provided insights to David. That remote part of Vermont was, most likely, underpopulated. Affordable land. No doubt about that, as the Swartzentrubers were extremely conscious of spending money. They held fast to farming and would frown on the small businesses that so many Old Order Amish had started in Stoney Ridge. They preferred to keep themselves to themselves. David doubted they would welcome the arrival of what they would consider a progressive church.

Ironic, as his own church considered the Beachy church to be liberal. *We're all on a spectrum of our own perceptions*, he thought.

He shifted to his back, staring up at the ceiling. "So tell me what makes Vermont such a good choice for an Amish church."

"Dana says there are a lot of dairy farms. Cows dot the hillside, she says."

"Really? That sounds like quite a sight to behold."

"And her neighbor is a dairy farmer with an on-site creamery."

"For ice cream?"

"For cheese. Vermont is known for its cheeses, you know. Apparently, Dana's neighbor has cheese-maturing caves." She lifted her arms and clasped her hands behind her head. "I would like to see those caves. I imagine wheels of delicious cheese stacked everywhere."

"The thing is, Birdy, we don't have many dairy farmers in our church. Only Mose and Vern. But we do have farmers who depend on a long growing season." David was no farmer, but he did know that much. "Cold up in Vermont, isn't it?"

"Perhaps a bit colder than Pennsylvania."

He coughed back a laugh. He remembered reading a scribe's letter from Vermont in which he had mentioned a recent hard frost. In late June! "Long winters. Short growing seasons. One thing I've learned from Nathan is that a farmer needs summer's heat."

"But the farmers need the cold too. Butchering needs the cold. Ice making needs the cold."

"Most of the farmers do like the cold, but maybe not as cold as Vermont's known to be. Not quite so dark. Those long winters are awfully hard on older folks. Say, my mother, for one. Edith and Hank Lapp."

"The cold brings good things too. There's maple syrup." She turned onto her side to face him, excited. "According to Dana, maple syrup runs like honey from the trees. She called it liquid gold. Her church has established quite a thriving business from the maple syrup. There's a market for it, apparently." She grinned. "After all, who doesn't like maple syrup?"

"I can't think of a single soul."

"The turning of autumn leaves is supposed to be breathtaking."

"I've seen pictures. Beautiful sights. But that, too, is rather short-lived." He cleared his throat. "Dana's church is in a very remote area, isn't it?" He knew it was.

"Nearly all the way to the Canadian border."

"The Bent N' Dent will need more customers than two small churches." So would other tradesmen in the church, like Teddy Zook, who did carpentry. And Luke Schrock, who did buggy repairs.

"Penny and Ben will be coming back from Canada through Vermont. I thought, perhaps, you could ask them to do a little investigation work. See if they think it might be a good place to relocate."

"Birdy . . ."

She sighed. "Dana said there is very good birding in Vermont."

Ah, see? There it was. The real reason she was campaigning for a move to Vermont. He started her favorite saying: "Birds are everywhere, as long as you have the eyes to see . . ."

"And the ears to hear."

He lifted his arm to embrace his darling, bird-loving wife and she snuggled up against him. The discussion of relocating the church could wait for now.

Trudy spent her day off from the Bent N' Dent doing errands in town, including a stop at the Stoney Ridge City Hall, tucked in a small building behind the library, shed-like. She knocked on the door once, then twice, then three times, and finally heard someone bellow, "For crying out loud, come in!"

Timidly, Trudy opened the door to a windowless room with a single desk. Behind a computer sat a rather well-endowed woman with thick blue eyeshadow, wild pink hair, and dense tattoos covering her arms and neck and who knew where else. Trudy tried not to stare at her hair, but *yowzah!* It looked just like a pink cockatoo. She forced herself to lower her eyes and fix them on the tops of her Crocs.

"What?" the tattooed woman snapped. "What do you want?"

"I was hoping to find information about the proposed building on Wonder Lake."

"There's no Wonder Lake in this town. Not in the entire county. I know that for a fact."

Trudy looked up in surprise. "But isn't this the place to go for building permits?"

"Yes." The woman let out a deep sigh. "I was just transferred to this"—she lifted her hand, palm side up, and waved it around—"grand office . . . by the county. Apparently, they think I'm difficult to work with." She rolled her eyes dramatically, as if how could anyone think such a thing? "Anyhoo, kiddo, I know this county inside and out and there's no such place."

Oh! Of course. It was Penny who had dubbed the pond as Wonder Lake and the name caught on—but only among the Amish birders. What was the name of the farmer who had owned that land? *Shoot.* Trudy couldn't remember. The longer the woman waited for her to say something, the slower her brain worked. Heat started flooding her cheeks.

Staring curiously at Trudy, the woman squinted her eyes. "Doesn't it hurt to keep your hair yanked back so tight?"

"No," Trudy said. "It's not yanked. It's bobby pinned in place." Then blurted out, "Why do you have so many tattoos?"

The woman's darkly lined eyebrows lifted, as if such a thought never occurred to her. "Because they tell my story."

"I see." But Trudy didn't. Not really.

"My turn again. Don't you ever wish you could wear clothes that weren't decided by some old male bishop?"

Trudy was suddenly caught in a game not of her choosing. "I suppose . . ." She smoothed out a wrinkle of her black apron. "I suppose I think it's quite nice to not have to think about what to wear each day." As the woman gave that some thought, the name of that farmer popped into Trudy's mind. "Lehman! Hiram Lehman. His farm has a pond on it."

The woman frowned, then started pecking at her computer keyboard. "Lehman, Hiram," she transposed aloud as she typed. After a minute, she paused and looked up to face Trudy. "Hiram Lehman is dead."

"Yes. That's true. But he gave his farm to his brother—Zeke Lehman—and his brother is a bishop and wants to build a church on that pond."

The woman went back to type on her keyboard, then stare at the computer. Type, stare, type, stare. After several long moments, she turned back to Trudy. "I see that permits have been approved for a large unimaginative building with a ridiculously huge parking lot." She tilted her head. "Why would someone like *you* want to stop a church from getting built?"

Put that way, it did seem odd. "It's not that I don't want a church built. It's just that I don't want it built *there*. At Wonder Lake. It's this beautiful piece of untouched wilderness. It'll be ruined."

"I hear ya, kiddo." And suddenly the tattooed woman lost her tough look. "The county officials don't care. They just want to fill the coffers with taxpayers' hard-earned money. They don't listen to reason." She looked at the computer again. "Whoever pulled these permits knew what they were doing. Legally, the t's are crossed and the i's are dotted." She folded her hands on her desktop, giving the distinct impression that this conversation was now over and that Trudy should stop wasting her precious time.

But her voice carried a tinge of genuine sorrow. "I wish I could help you, kiddo, but there's nothing we can do to stop it."

Sweet. Nice of the lady to say "we" when she really had nothing at stake here. The phone rang and the tattooed woman made a grab for it. Trudy backed out the door with a wave and mouthed a silent *thank you.* The woman put the phone on her shoulder, lifted her fist, and whispered, "Don't give up. Power to the people."

What did that mean? Trudy had no idea. Frankly, all of this was new to her. She felt as if she was bobbing for apples in a tub of water, hoping to catch a bite.

Outside, she lifted her face to the blue sky. A Mourning Dove caught her attention in an overhead tree, hoo-hooing its sad call.

"Don't give up," the tattooed woman had said. And she seemed to be the type who knew what she was talking about.

There had to be a way. Trudy needed to formulate a plan to protect the eagles and their nesting spot, the baby hawk that thought it was an eagle, to keep Micah from moving away. That, especially, was top on her mind.

———————

Trudy Yoder, Bird-Watching Log

Name of Bird: Mourning Dove

Scientific Name: Zenaida macroura

Status: Low concern

Date: August 1

Location: In our yard, not far from the bird feeders

Description: Grayish-brown, plump, a small brain, a long tail, stubby little legs

Symbolism: Purity, a sign of the Holy Spirit

Bird Action: A pair was foraging for seeds on the ground. A barn cat was watching and I shooed it away, just in the nick of time. Ground-feeding birds are easy pickings for predators like prowling cats, which is such a shame. Yes, cats have a purpose in this world, but I do wish they would limit their diet to mice and rats and leave songbirds alone.

Notes: Mourning Doves are just about everywhere. They have a very lament-like song, rising and dropping in pitch, followed by three fading hoots. In fact, its mournful hooting call is often mistaken for an owl's.

Sadly, these peaceful, graceful birds are the most hunted game bird in all of North America. Over 20 million are killed each year! (That is a practice that should be stopped immediately!)

Despite that chilling, grim reality, their numbers are in abundance. Last count was over 350 million. Yay!!!

On a cheery note, Mourning Doves are monogamous and often stay with one partner for life. A quality I find quite endearing. (I wonder how they know that they've met their mate?)

5

Micah lay awake long into the night, trying to puzzle out why Shelley Yoder had called him. Of all people, why him?

Guilt? Remorse? After all, she had used him as a decoy so her parents wouldn't know she was sneaking out to sing at an Englisch bar in Lancaster. She had told her mother that Micah was courting her, and her parents were so pleased that she seemed interested in an Amish boy, they never thought it was a lie. He rolled his eyes. It was a lie . . . and it was a whopper.

Maybe Shelley did feel genuinely sorry she had misled everyone.

But what about the Englisch guy? Because he was the one who had talked Shelley into running off to Nashville to pursue her dream to sing. Micah knew she wasn't bold enough to take that step on her own. Was she still with him?

Maybe not. Maybe Shelley was thinking about coming home again. Maybe she was testing the waters, seeing if she might be welcomed back.

His eyes widened. If that might be so, he figured she might try to contact him again.

The next day, Micah had two birding expeditions scheduled, back-to-back. As soon as he finished his guide work, he rushed back to Lost Creek Farm's phone shanty. Just in case. And there *was*! Another message was waiting from Shelley. He stilled when he heard her sweet, breathy voice.

"Micah, it's Shelley again. I really need your help. I'm in Tennessee at a place . . ."

He heard something in the background that made her stop midsentence. A barking dog? More like yips. Then he heard raised voices. Shelley came back on, whispering so low he could hardly hear what she said. "I have to go. I'll try to call again soon."

So. So she'd made it to Tennessee after all. He felt a zing of disappointment. He supposed a part of him had been hoping she was closer to home, maybe on her way back.

He wondered if her singing career had taken off like she'd wanted. She sang like an angel. He couldn't imagine any big-shot music producer listening to her without recognizing she was one in a million.

A spiral of delight started in his middle and worked its way up to a big, broad smile. How did he feel about Shelley reaching out to him? He felt good. Special. Really, really special. Shelley hadn't forgotten him. She was thinking about coming home—she must be, right?—and that was why she wanted his help.

The following day, he made several trips from the shoe repair shop down to the phone shanty, just to see if Shelley had called. After the fourth trip, he hung around the shanty, washing the windows, dusting corners. Waiting as long as he could before he grew hopelessly bored and went back to the shop to return to his work. He was on his way back to the shop when he heard the phone ring. He pivoted and bolted to the shanty before the call slipped to the message machine, hoping for the slim chance that it might be Shelley.

Alas. It was his sister Penny. "Hi, Micah! You must have been in the shanty."

"Yeah. Close by."

"You're out of breath."

"Ran to g-get the phone."

70

"How's everything going at Lost Creek Farm?"

"Good. All good. No problems. None. Enjoy your t-trip. Bye."

"Hold it!"

He cringed. He shouldn't have sounded so eager to get off the phone.

"The guesthouse is working out?"

"Yep. All good."

"You haven't even asked about our bird sightings."

His eyebrows lifted in interest. "Any rarities?"

"A few. We spotted a Bicknell's Thrush yesterday. And the day before, Ben spotted a Semipalmated Sandpiper."

"Nice." Micah was impressed. "Anything else?"

"We've had more dips than actual sightings."

Well, that was the story of birding. "Okay. Good luck."

A long pause followed. Penny wasn't that easily fobbed off. "Micah, what's going on?"

Should he say something? He'd actually like to hear someone's perspective. Someone he trusted implicitly. "Shelley called. Twice."

"Shelley? Shelley Yoder?"

"Yeah." Of course. What other Shelley was there? In the entire universe, what other Shelley would he be referring to?

Penny's voice flattened. "What did she want?"

"She said . . . she n-needed my help."

"And?"

"And what?"

"Are you planning to respond?"

"She d-didn't leave her phone number. She said she'll c-call again."

"Oh. I see."

"What? What d-do you see?"

"She broke your heart, Micah. Are you going to let her do it again?"

Micah's eyes went wide. As if his sister should be giving advice about unrequited love! Penny'd fallen for Ben Zook when she was just a young teenager. She waited two decades for him to return to Stoney Ridge. Two decades! He let out a snort of disgust.

"What's that snort for?"

"Worked out p-pretty well for you and Ben."

"Me and Ben? Micah, our situation was totally different."

Another snort.

"Ben and I, we both loved birds. Shelley's . . ."

He hoped Penny wasn't going to say anything disparaging about Shelley. He thought of her—aside from lying to her family, using him as a decoy, and running away from home—as near perfect.

Penny hesitated. "Well, she's not like Trudy."

Trudy? What did *that* mean? Did Penny think there was something going on between him and Trudy? Because there wasn't. Not really. Sometimes. Sort of, but not really.

"Micah, you might think you know Shelley, but have you ever had a meaningful conversation with her? Have you ever shared your dreams with her?"

He cringed. He loved his sister, but she often acted like his second mother. It annoyed him that she sounded like she knew Shelley better than he did.

Why had he thought it would've been a good idea to confide in Penny? He regretted it, but there was no undoing this. "G-Gotta g-go. Lost Creek Farm is all g-good. Bye." And he hung up before she could say another word. He went to the mailbox and flipped through the mail. Discouraged, he went back to the shoe repair shop to finish resoling a pair of boots left by Luke Schrock. Absorbed in stitching the new sole, he tried not to think about Shelley or phone calls or Penny until he finished what he was doing. The second he finished polishing the leather, he set down the rag, remembered what he'd been trying to forget, and made a dash to the phone shanty. The message light was blinking and his heart started to pound—Shelley?—but it was a woman from New Jersey who wanted to book a stay at Lost Creek Farm's guesthouse. He picked up a pencil and pad of paper, took down her information to call her back, and then saw there was a second message. He pressed the button.

"Hello, Micah. It's Shelley Yoder calling."

His whole body stilled. Her lovely, lilting, gentle voice had the same effect on him as the first time he'd heard it. His legs felt rubbery, his cheeks started heating up, his palms grew sweaty.

There was a pause. "Micah, you've always been so kind to me. I didn't know who else to call. I need your help to get out of here. Things are getting terrible." Once again, a sound in the background made her pause, then give a hurried goodbye.

Micah squeezed his eyes shut. Frustrating! How could he help her when he didn't have a clue what was going on with her?

Tonight, he decided he would sleep in the shanty, just in case Shelley called again.

Micah made a run up to the house to get a pillow and blanket and something to eat. Just as he about to head back down to the shanty, he grabbed his bird log out of his backpack. He didn't like to go anywhere without it.

When he returned, he saw the message light blinking again. He pressed the button and froze at the sound of Shelley's voice. He'd missed it! Gone less than ten minutes and he'd missed her call. He banged his fist against the wooden shelf, then blew out a puff of exasperation and listened to this new message.

"Hello, Micah. It's me again, Shelley Yoder."

As if she needed to identify herself. He would know her voice in a crowd.

"Micah, I forgot to tell you not to tell anyone that I've been in contact with you. Not anyone. Trust me, it's too dangerous." This time she hung up without saying goodbye.

Micah had to remind himself to breathe again.

What could she mean? Why would it be dangerous if anyone knew she had contacted him? What kind of trouble had she gotten herself into? Or maybe it was the guy she was with. Maybe he was bad news.

Or maybe she was worried because her dad had such a fierce temper. Maybe Shelley was only trying to protect Micah from getting pummeled.

Kind of like Penny was trying to protect him from getting a broken heart.

Well, guess what, people? he thought to himself as he tossed the blanket and pillow on the ground. *I'm a grown man. I don't need anyone's protection.* He sat down on the blanket, leaning against the back of the shanty, and took out his bird log. He thought he might try to add an entry or two about some of the birds he'd pointed out this morning. Nothing too unusual today—a Song Sparrow and several Cedar Waxwings—but the wide-eyed reaction of the newbie birders was worth noting.

Sometimes, Micah needed to remind himself of a newbie's delight in noticing overlooked birds. That was how it started for birders. One special bird. Everyone had a spark bird that ignited interest. Everyone began somewhere.

As a field guide, Micah's main objective was to open people's eyes and ears to all they were overlooking. This morning, he'd been too distracted by Shelley's calls to be at his best as a guide, but he could always count on the Lord to provide outdoor attractions. What the Englisch referred to as nature, like it was all happenstance, Jesus knew only as creation, a work of God. Even better, the Bible described the entire cosmos as a temple, full of the glory of God. An unending outdoor cathedral. That was why he loved his work. It felt like holy work.

He opened his bird log to an empty page and filled in the date but was unable to concentrate. His eyes kept returning to the phone, his mind kept willing it to ring.

All throughout the spring months, Trudy had felt so encouraged. It seemed that at long last, a spark had ignited Micah's feelings for her. Often, at the end of most days, he would come to her wherever she might be—locking up at the Bent N' Dent or feeding horses at home—and then they'd go birding together. He always knew where to find her, the same way he knew where to find birds. He seemed to just know these things, like it was a special gifting from the Almighty.

They'd had such interesting discussions. She'd read a book about birds in the Bible—birds were mentioned over 300 times—and the Christian symbolism attached to their imagery. There were the well-known ones, like Jesus pointing to a sparrow to illustrate the love of God for small, common, and insignificant things. Then there were lesser-known meanings of birds, like owls (one of her all-time favorites!) representing desolation in the book of Isaiah. Or odd things, like the last bird ever spoken of in the Gospels was the rooster crowing after Peter's three denials of Christ.

She and Micah would walk through the woods or sit on the resting rock overlooking the eagle's nest and talk and talk and talk. Well, mostly, she did the talking. He didn't seem to mind. Not one bit. She would try and make him laugh, because when he grinned, his face softened. She loved it when he smiled. He was so handsome. She had to fight the urge to put her hands on his cheeks and just soak in his handsomeness.

Then, out of the blue, Micah stopped coming. Over a week had passed since they'd gone birding. She hadn't even seen hide nor hair of him in the last few days.

This morning, Trudy decided to leave early for work so she could stop, first, at Lost Creek Farm. What if something had happened to Micah and no one knew to check on him? Maybe he'd hurt himself, or maybe he was sick.

As she pushed the scooter up the steep driveway, she noticed the door was wide open to the guesthouse, with a bag of trash out on the porch. She dropped the scooter outside the guesthouse and knocked on the open door. No answer. She heard some sounds from the bedroom, so she poked her head around the corner and found Micah changing sheets on the bed. Suddenly shy, she waited at the doorjamb. "Hey there."

He whipped around a quarter turn, caught unawares. "Hey." He bent down and tucked the sheets neatly under a corner of the mattress. Penny had taught him well.

"New guests coming in?"

He nodded. "Soon."

She took a few steps to complete a corner on the other side of the bed, to help finish making it. "Where've you been lately?"

He lifted one shoulder in a shrug, his chin tucked down. "Been busy."

"I come bearing news."

Bending over to pick up a pillow on the floor, he shot straight up like he'd seen a mouse. Blinking, he said, "News?"

She took the remaining pillow and started to push it into the pillowcase. "I went to city hall to see about Wonder Lake."

"What about it?"

Trudy stopped stuffing the pillow into the case to stare at him. "Seriously?" His face was completely blank. Strange. Barely a week ago, Micah had been ready to move away from Stoney Ridge in outrage over the issue. "Don't tell me you've forgotten that the Beachys are planning to build a church on Wonder Lake."

He dropped his chin, as if embarrassed. Tucking in the last corner, he then pulled the blanket up and over the bed, avoiding her eyes. He was acting *so* weird. "Micah. I thought Wonder Lake was important to you."

"It is."

"Then why are you acting like you've completely forgotten about it?"

He straightened the quilt before throwing the pillows at the headboard. "I have others things on my mind."

She straightened the pillows. "Like what?"

"Like . . ." He looked around the room. "Like cleaning up the g-guesthouse before the next guests arrive."

Her jaw dropped. "What's more important than stopping the utter and complete destruction of Wonder Lake?"

He rolled his eyes. "So dramatic."

"I'm not! I saw the plans. Wonder Lake will be unrecognizable. Completely paved over. The birds will leave." When he didn't respond, she added, "What's more important than that? Tell me."

An odd, conflicted look flitted through his eyes. "I just . . . I'm trying to find some . . . something that's hard to find."

Oh. Oh, now she understood. He was on a chase. "A jinx bird?"

Micah flinched, as if surprised by the term. Jinx birds were those common birds that managed to elude the experienced birder. Highly exasperating! Trudy had a very, very long list of jinx birds.

"I guess you c-could say that."

"Well, that shouldn't be hard for you."

"How so?" He stopped from picking up the small trash bin to pivot toward her. Once again, that intense look filled his eyes.

She squinted at him. "You're a twitcher. It's what you do. You find birds that don't want to be found."

Slowly, a smile started, spreading over his entire face. "You're right," he said, passing by her to go empty the trash bin. "You're absolutely right."

"Can I help?"

"Not this time." He kept going out the doorway.

"Why not? What makes this jinx bird so special?"

He stopped abruptly but didn't turn around. "This time it's . . . just s-something I need to do on my own." Then he left the guesthouse to walk over to Penny's house.

Some mood he was in! Offended by his aloofness, she smoothed out the quilt on the bed and gazed around the room, making sure everything was the way Penny would've left it. Outside, she picked up her scooter to head to work. Micah could be maddeningly distant at times, but she'd never seen him quite so standoffish. So cold. She wasn't going to hang around for more of it. Not today.

Wonder Lake needed saving, and even if Micah wasn't going to help, she was going to figure it out herself.

For a full twenty-four hours, Micah didn't get another message from Shelley. He liked hearing her voice on the phone messages she left. Liked it so much that he kept listening to them, numerous times. It was a good thing Penny and Ben weren't in town and he was the only one checking messages. They would consider his behavior to be alarming. Frankly, he considered it to be alarming. But all he could think about lately was Shelley. He was right back to where he was before she ran off, completely hung up on her. And all he knew was that she was in Tennessee somewhere and that she was thinking about him.

She was thinking about *him*. How about that for a switch?

And then one afternoon he found another message from her on the phone shanty's answering machine. This time, an urgent tremble was in her voice.

"Micah. Listen carefully. I only have a minute to talk. Please, please, please come and get me out of here. I'm staying in the yellow house somewhere in southern Tennessee. Fields of corn in every direction. That's as much information as I have. Remember, don't let anyone else know where I am. We have to be *very* careful. Please, Micah. You're the only one I can depend on."

Micah didn't know what to do, what to think. A yellow house in Tennessee. That narrowed it down to . . . a couple of million houses. "*We have to be* very *careful,*" she had said, putting special emphasis on the word *very*.

Why? What could that mean? She seemed . . . frightened. He listened to her message again and again. One more time. She did sound frightened.

If anyone laid a hand on Shelley . . . He flinched. His hands, he realized, had instinctively squeezed into fists. He took a deep breath and uncurled his fingers. Where did this come from? He had been baptized, but right now, he didn't feel much like a Plain man.

Normally, the restrictions of being Amish didn't chafe at Micah, not like they did with his friends. He had no interest in technology. He wouldn't allow any birder to use technology in the field, and they wanted to. Boy, did they ever want to. They tried to use their phones for bird calls, which he felt was an outrage to the birds. An interference with nature's ways. It was wrong to confuse a bird, to lure it close by in search of a mate, only for it to realize the mate was a tiny computer. He wouldn't let birders record sounds for identification, or even take pictures. Because bottom line, once their attention went to a phone, they were no longer in the woods. No longer paying attention to what was around them. Their bodies might be there, but their heads were gone. If they wanted to go birding with Micah Weaver, they needed to put away their electronic toys in order to remain wholly present. That was his cardinal rule.

For the first time in his life, Micah wished he had a smartphone. Most of his friends had them, carefully hidden from their parents. If he had a smartphone, Shelley's phone call would automatically have her callback number. Instead, he had to wait until she contacted him again. Wait. And wait. And wait.

He felt stymied. How do you find someone when you barely have any information to go on?

That was the question Micah asked Victoria, his favorite librarian, later that day. Victoria had come on a number of birding expeditions over the last year. She regularly set aside newly acquired birding books for him at the library. When he asked her to help him locate someone he was trying to find, she looked like he had handed her a Christmas present. "It's a snap. I can find anyone. I should have been a detective." She sat down at the computer. "Name and age?"

"Shelley Yoder. Let's see, she's, um, p-probably nineteen years old. Hold it. Her b-birthday is in June. Make that t-twenty."

The librarian typed on her keyboard, then stared at the screen, her brow slightly furrowed. "Hmm. Yoder is quite a common name. Any other specific information? A middle name?"

"Um, I don't know."

"Hmm. So far, I'm not finding anything. Any chance she'd be on Facebook?"

He hoped not. "You c-could try."

Victoria's attention turned back to the computer. "There's a lot of Shelley Yoders on Facebook. Do any of these profile pictures look like her?"

Micah watched as she scrolled through two full pages of Shelley Yoders with their tiny profile pictures. "No."

"Well, okay. Let's try another angle. Could she be a criminal?"

"Nope."

"Does she have a driver's license? And if so, what state?"

"Um, I d-don't know. She's Amish. Or rather, she was. You c-could try Tennessee."

The librarian tapped more keys. Tap, tap, tap. "Nothing. Let's try the census." Still nothing.

"What c-counties are in southern Tennessee?"

Tap, tap, tap. "Here. Look for yourself."

He looked at the screen. So many counties for such a little state. "Any farming c-counties?"

Tap, tap, tap. "Looks like central and southwest counties are predominantly farming." Victoria typed in a few things. "Interesting. I didn't know that."

"What?"

"There's Amish communities in both Hardin and McNairy counties."

He wrote down those names, but he highly doubted Shelley would be staying with the Amish. For one thing, the conservative Amish didn't paint their houses yellow. Only white.

Also, Shelley sounded frightened. She wouldn't have anything to be afraid of if she were with the Amish.

"Does she pay taxes?"

"M-Maybe?" Doubtful. At this point, he had a pretty good hunch that Shelley's singing career hadn't taken off the way she'd hoped.

Victoria tapped away. "Nothing's showing up." She looked at Micah. "Here's a thought. If she's trying to make it as a singer, could she have changed her name? Yoder isn't exactly a headliner."

Micah let out a sigh. "Maybe." Probably.

"If that's the case, I can't help you." She pushed away from the desk. "Sorry, Micah." She lifted her palms with a shrug. "Sure seems like your friend doesn't want to be found."

That. Or maybe she just didn't want to be easy to find.

———

Trudy Yoder, Bird-Watching Log

Name of Bird: Cedar Waxwing

Scientific Name: Bombycilla cedrorum

Status: Low concern

Date: December 2

Location: Penny Zook's guesthouse

Description: Pale brown with a bandit-style black eye mask, tuft on the head, and red tips on its inner wings

Symbolism: In the Christian tradition, Cedar Waxwings are believed to be messengers of peace and goodwill.

Bird Action: Foraging for berries. (What else?! Cedar Waxwings love fruit. Love, love, love it.)

Notes: It's easy to see how the Waxwing got its name. It has a small red tip on the end of its wing feathers that must have reminded ornithologists of the wax that sealed an important letter.

Cedar Waxwings are great for curious facts, so here are some: These birds are believers in community. Highly social, they're seldom seen alone except when nesting. A female Cedar Waxwing devotes 5 to 6 days to build just the right nest for her eggs. A waxwing's nest building can require more than 2,500 individual trips. (I wonder who counted?) Sometimes, the female will save herself a few trips by snitching nesting materials from other birds.

Here's a doozy: *A flock of waxwings is called an "ear-full" or a "museum." (No idea how that came about.)*

Penny and Ben Zook have a shrub with berries next to their guesthouse. One year, the berries were a bit overripe and an ear-full of waxwings, which had feasted on the berries (which they eat whole), became drunk. They flew off and crashed—all together, all at once (remember! They're social birds)—right into the large front window of the guesthouse. The terrified guest has never returned to Lost Creek Farm.

Waxwings are monogamous (at least for the breeding year). Here's something so worthy of admiration in waxwings: When a male is interested in a female, he will do a little hop. If she's interested, she'll hop back. (Wouldn't it be lovely if courting were as simple with people?)

6

D avid was well aware that life bore an emotional weight, even a spiritual one. The more he aged, the more he felt that weight. But he still couldn't believe what his mother had told him this morning.

His mother hadn't touched her meals in the last couple of days. When he'd asked her if there was anything he could bring her that sounded appetizing, she waved him off. "Nothing. I don't want to prolong things. I'm ready to die."

"What do you mean, you're ready to die?" David had known she wasn't doing well. Her broken hip seemed to have started a cascade of problems, one right after the other. Aching back, stiff neck, arthritic hands, sore feet. He could see the spark in her eyes was gone, her feisty nature had flattened. It seemed like she was giving up.

He tried to get her to talk more, but her voice was weak, and she said she just wanted to sleep. So he had left her to head to the store, feeling bothered. Helpless. Worried.

It had always been hard for him to understand how someone could get to the point where they were just done with living. The only way he could fathom that kind of deep-down fatigue was to remind himself how he felt right after Christmas or Easter services. Normally, after a few days of rest, he would feel renewal seep in. While he did have a great hope and longing for Heaven, he also loved his life. He cherished watching his children's lives unfold, to see their (hopefully) wise choices play out. And now his grand-children's. Despite all the woes and sorrows in this world, it was still a wonderful place.

That was how David normally felt. But after these last few months, he thought he might have a glimmer of understanding what his mother described when she said she was just done with living. The problems he faced felt insurmountable. The renewal he counted on from the Lord felt far off. His very soul felt weary. Yes, that was it. Mom sounded soul-weary.

He hoped his mother might regain that spark of life again, but he wasn't sure what it would take to light the match. He thought he might ask his sister, Dok, to check in on her today, though he didn't really know what to tell her. "Mom says she's ready to die." Words he'd never expected to hear from his spirited, headstrong mother. Words he never wanted to hear from her. She might be difficult, cranky, and critical, but she was still his mother.

He consoled himself with this: Mer kann net schtwerwe wammer will. *We can't die when we want to.* The time when a person passed away was God's doing and his alone.

Twenty minutes later, he arrived at the Bent N' Dent to find Billy Blank waiting on the steps. Probably waiting for Trudy to arrive at work, David guessed. Billy stopped by the store quite a bit, eager to talk to Trudy, who never seemed quite as eager. That surprised David, as Billy was considered a catch. According to his mother, anyway.

Once David had mentioned to Birdy that he thought Billy might be trying to court Trudy, but she shook her head. "It'll never work."

"Why not?" Billy was a fine young man, tall with thick muscles, very faithful and loyal. A goatherd, he raised a breed of fainting goats, which struck David as a little odd, but then again, he was no farmer. What did he know about livestock?

Birdy gave him a look that said, *You're missing something.* "It would be like trying to match a magpie and an oriole."

At that, David felt completely lost and dropped the subject.

―――――――――

As soon as Micah finished his morning field guide work, he hurried back to Lost Creek Farm to check phone messages. When he saw the light was blinking, he practically tripped himself in his haste to press the play messages button. He held his breath as soon as he heard the replay of Shelley's voice.

"Micah, when are you coming for me? I just can't stand it here any longer. I was tricked into coming. Jack said he'd booked a gig for me to sing at a big festival for brooms and now I'm locked away in this terrible place! But that's when I thought of you, Micah. I knew you could help me, and I knew you wouldn't tell anyone. You don't talk to anyone. You're a tight vault." Something or someone interrupted her and she hung up.

Whoa. A lot to process here. He listened to the message again and again.

So . . . whatever danger Shelley was in *did* have something to do with this guy she ran away with. Jack. That was new information, and it shouldn't have surprised Micah that he was a bad character.

"Locked away in this terrible place."

Did she mean that this Jack guy was holding her captive? Was he the reason she hung up so fast? His concern for Shelley ratcheted up a few notches.

"Booked a gig to sing at a festival for brooms."

What was *that* all about?

He listened again to the message. *"You don't talk to anyone. You're a tight vault."*

That rang a familiar bell. Penny was always trying to get him to open up and talk more. Early on in life, Micah had learned to keep quiet. Before Penny and Ben left on their trip, she had warned him to not turn into a hermit while they were away.

He tried not to roll his eyes at his sister. "I won't."

"You need people, Micah."

"I see p-people every day."

"Let me rephrase that. You need friends."

"I have friends."

"But you keep everyone at an arm's length."

He lifted his palms in the air. "Like who?"

"Like . . . Trudy." Penny had fixed her eyes on him. "I'm not sure you realize what a treasure Trudy is."

Nope. Micah had no interest in hearing this from his sister. He had made a quick exit.

Penny thought she knew everything, but she didn't. She didn't know what it was like to have a stutter. To not be able to talk smoothly and fluidly. How difficult it was to express yourself. And if any strong emotions—good, bad, or ugly—were involved, getting words out could be torturous.

Penny didn't consider any of that when doling out her relationship advice. She didn't know that the trouble with getting close to people was that the better they knew you, the better they could hurt you.

Micah listened one more time to Shelley's message. He needed more information. What was the last name of this Jack guy? He thought about asking Trudy, but he couldn't do that to her. He didn't even trust himself to be around Trudy lately. If he were to blurt out the news that he'd heard from Shelley, he worried it would churn up all the sadness and sorrow that she'd left behind when she ran off with that fellow. He wouldn't do that to Trudy, not until he had some answers for her. She deserved that.

Frankly, Trudy deserved a lot more from him. In a rare moment of insight, it finally dawned on him what Trudy meant to him. Sometime in the last year or so, she'd become his best friend. They were a good team. They cared about the same things. And he did share her concern over the future of Wonder Lake, he genuinely did, but everything—*everything*—had taken an abrupt back seat to his pressing concern to find Shelley.

He thought of the conversation he'd had with Trudy in the guesthouse yesterday. When Trudy framed his hunt for Shelley as a chase for a rarity—without realizing who Micah was looking for—she'd given him just what he needed: confidence. If anybody could find Shelley, he could. She was his nemesis bird, his jinx bird, the one that kept eluding him. But he was an accomplished twitcher. He would find her.

But how?

How? How was he going to narrow down the search for Shelley? The only information he had to go on was the state of Tennessee, cornfields, and a yellow house. As he closed the door to the phone shanty, he stopped in his tracks and squeezed his eyes shut, leaning his forehead against the door. *Think, Micah. Think the way you do when you're on a chase. Think like the bird thinks.*

"ARE YOU HAVING A STROKE?"

He opened his eyes and spun around. There was Hank Lapp, staring at him with his good eye. "Where'd you come from?"

Hank pointed down the road. "My mule THREW a SHOE." He held up a horseshoe. "Thought I was LUCKY to stop by a SHOE REPAIR SHOP for nails until I saw you were STROKING OUT."

"I'm not stroking out. I was thinking."

"About WHAT?"

"Hank, ever heard of a f-festival for brooms?"

"I HAVE, actually. Had a COUSIN who used to go to a Broomcorn Festival every summer."

"Where?"

Hank looked up at the sky, squinting, trying to remember. "Selmer."

"Where's that?"

Again, another long squint of remembering. "Tennessee."

Micah's heart started to pound. "What county?"

Hank took a long time with that, eyes squinted, shifting his weight from one foot to the other. "McNAIRY!"

Micah stilled.

"Are you THINKING about the MOVE?"

Micah's face scrunched up. Talking to Hank was like trying to capture wisps of steam in your hands. "What are you talking about?"

"THE CHURCH I. David's THINKING about MOVING all of us. ON to GREENER PASTURES."

What? "Where? When?"

"HE doesn't KNOW where. BUT he's OPEN to SUGGESTIONS. You KNOW DAVID. He's a CAUTIOUS man. He's NOT about to UPROOT the entire CHURCH on a WHIM. MY guess is he'll SEND TEAMS out to CHECK on a PLACE or TWO." Hank folded his arms against his chest. "I'd sure LIKE to GO on one of those SCOUTING TRIPS." He hooted. "A PAID vacation!"

Micah bolted toward the small stable to get his horse and hitch it to the buggy.

"HEY!" Hank yelled. "WHERE'S THE FIRE?"

"Gotta go!"

"WHAT about my MULE'S SHOE?"

Over his shoulder, Micah yelled, "Plenty of n-nails in the repair shop. Help yourself." He turned around, walking backward, pointing at Hank. "But leave the h-hammer on my workbench when you're done. Don't p-pocket it like you did last time." Then he turned around to slide the barn door open and grab his horse's bridle off the wall peg. He was a man on a mission. He was heading to the library to dig up everything he could about the state of Tennessee.

Three hours later, Micah walked into the Bent N' Dent and made a beeline to the bishop's open office door, barely giving a nod to Trudy at the counter—and why did she look so shocked when she saw him anyway? Was he *that* shocking a sight?

When David looked up from his desk, Micah said one word. "Tennessee." No stutter.

"Tennessee?"

"Yes. Tennessee." Micah waited for the bishop to react, which was taking a very long time.

David peered at him. "What about it?"

"That's where we should g-go. I'm all for the church to p-pick up and move"—and with that, David's eyes went wide—"s-so long as you c-consider T-Tennessee."

"Where did you hear that the church was moving?"

"Hank Lapp."

At that, David's shoulders hunched in defeat. "Of course."

"Hank's a b-blabbermouth," Micah said.

"I know." David let out a sigh. "Micah, close the door and sit down."

Micah did as he asked and sat in the chair in front of David's desk. This was working out just fine for him, because he'd rather talk to David privately. The second Hank told him that David was thinking about uprooting the church, it seemed like the timing was dropped from Above. If the church went somewhere as a whole, then he felt pretty sure that Penny and Ben would go too. Especially if that somewhere meant birds.

Micah had a folder full of notes he'd taken to make his case on moving to Tennessee. He'd even written out a script, because his stutter always came out when he was nervous. He had learned this was the best way to deliver information that needed to be said. It was a strategy that worked well on birding expeditions. He could sound smooth as molasses so long as he stuck to the script. Pretty smooth, anyway. If he got a question that was off script, he would take his time responding and answer with an economy of words. This morning a woman asked him what the most important thing was to remember as a beginning birder.

"Stop. Listen. Identify."

He was so curt that she apologized profusely, assuming she had insulted him, like he must've already explained the basics and she hadn't been listening. Nope. He just preferred to stay on script. Of course, he couldn't tell her all that and, happily, she never asked another question.

He grew antsy waiting for the bishop to start the conversation. David Stoltzfus was a slow thinker, a slow talker. Trudy said it was because he ran everything by the Lord first. She also said that if everyone did that, there'd be a lot less trouble in the world. She was probably right about that, but it did strike Micah as ironic that Trudy would think to say such a thing. She could talk the hind legs off a donkey.

"So what's this about Tennessee?"

Micah cleared his throat and opened his folder to read his prepared script. "McNairy County. Ideal place for our church. About eighty miles southwest of Nashville. Secluded but not too remote, which would be good for getting produce to the markets. Good dairy and farmland for sale. Reasonable prices. Lots of opportunity for additional income. Furniture making, for one. Lots of lumber." He paused for effect, anxious to deliver the news that he was confident would close the deal. "There's already Amish families living there. They're not just staying put, they're also growing." He closed the folder and tapped it with his hand. "All here. I did the research." Delivered without a single stutter. Not one.

David nodded in that listening way he had. Micah couldn't tell how he felt about the idea of Tennessee, but he had no doubt that the bishop was listening carefully. Another long silence, as David rolled a pencil back and forth on his desk, eyes on Micah.

"What's birding like there?" David said.

Shoot! Micah felt his face start to heat up. He hadn't prepared a script for this topic. Just the opposite. He had planned to carefully avoid any mention of birding. It so happened that Tennessee was an exceptional place for birding. Perfectly positioned to touch both the Atlantic and the Mississippi flyways, which meant a great variety and quantity of migrants. Plus, it was far enough north to harbor overwintering migrants from Canada, and far enough south to attract wandering birds typically seen in the Gulf

Coast. And then there were the autumn storms and hurricanes that pushed migrating birds from the East Coast into the Southeast. "P-Pretty g-good." Stupid stutter.

"Better than good?"

Micah swallowed. "It's, uh, a s-small s-state." Tennessee may be a small state, but serious birders described it as one of the best for birding. Not necessarily because of the number of rarities but because of the ease of spotting birds. Large quantities of them.

David waited. And waited.

Micah sighed. "Better than g-good."

A smile filled David's eyes. He reached across the desk to take the folder out of Micah's hands. "I'll take McNairy County in Tennessee into consideration."

Micah left David's office. That didn't go too badly, all things considered. He looked around for Trudy and noticed that Billy Blank had cornered her and was yakking away at her, while she was stacking bags of brown sugar. Billy had what Penny called the gift of gab. That, Micah thought, was a charitable description. No thought went unexpressed from Billy, and Micah had never felt they were particularly interesting thoughts. Dull as ditchwater.

From across the room, Micah locked eyes with Trudy. Just as he thought he might be nice and rescue her from Billy's endless droning, he heard her say in an overly loud voice, "Yes, Billy. I'd like to go home with you from next week's barbecue."

Micah stopped abruptly. Seriously? If Trudy didn't have enough sense to say no to Billy Blank, then she didn't deserve rescuing. Annoyed, he pivoted, strode down the aisle, and out the front door.

———

Trudy half listened to Billy's story about his fainting goats as she watched Micah drive off in his buggy. She had hoped he might stick around and tell her why he wanted to talk to the bishop. Could it be that he was truly considering leaving Stoney Ridge? Was that why he didn't seem the least bit troubled about Wonder

Lake? If so, she hoped that David would squelch the idea or, at the very least, slow it down. She needed time . . . to figure out how to stop the Beachy church from building at Wonder Lake. She needed time to keep Micah in Stoney Ridge.

As Micah's buggy disappeared from sight, she turned her attention back to Billy. What was he talking about now? Still on his fainting goats? Those silly goats. She had no idea why anyone wanted livestock that kept passing out. She'd always had trouble following Billy. One topic turned to another, without any pause, not even to catch his breath. There was no way to interrupt, or even say a single word. It was never a conversation with Billy. It was a monologue.

Why did she say yes to Billy's invitation to go home from the barbecue for the youth? She knew. Something ugly rose up inside her and she wanted to make Micah jealous.

For the last month, Billy had been asking to drive her home from every single youth gathering. She'd always said no, hoping he'd take the hint and stop asking. Did he? No. He just kept asking, as if he knew there'd be a time when he wore down her resistance. Like today.

Just then the bell above the door chimed and Trudy glanced over to see a customer walk through. This was her opportunity. She put her hand on Billy to stop him from talking. "I have to get back to work." The look on his face! As if he'd forgotten she worked there. As if he'd forgotten where he was. Oh, Billy.

She hurried over to the register to be available to help the customer. Billy stood there, watching her, waiting for her to finish up so he could resume his monologue. Something was a little off with him, like he didn't read people correctly. But he was sweet, sincere, and eager to help in any way. He was handsome, too, extremely good looking, though it didn't make up for being as boring as a box of rocks. On the plus side, he seemed to be devoted to Trudy. It was the way she wished Micah felt about her. Someday, maybe.

As she packed cartons of milk into a box for Izzy Schrock, it occurred to her that Billy Blank reminded her of a Downy Woodpecker, banging its head against a tree in a steady drum to attract a mate. Most woodpeckers were monogamous and mated for life. Once they found a mate, they would stop at nothing to protect their partner. Not everybody was a fan of woodpeckers. Her father considered them to be pests because they made holes in the siding of the house and he shot them, which caused great distress to Trudy. Micah, too. There were plenty of other ways, Micah said, to keep a bird from being a pest.

Trudy glanced over at Billy, who was still in the same spot in the store, waiting for her to finish up at the register.

How did you keep a boy like him from becoming a pest?

———————

Trudy Yoder, Bird-Watching Log

Name of Bird: Downy Woodpecker

Scientific Name: Dryobates pubescens

Status: Low concern

Date: June 16.

Location: At home

Description: Smallest woodpecker in North America, about 5-7 inches, with a small, thin bill like a sliver of wood. Black-and-white feathers. Males have a red patch on head.

Symbolism: A sign of God's providence. Woodpeckers find value in the most hopeless of things. (Like, finding bugs in snags! Who would consider a dead tree to be a source of nourishment?)

Bird Action: Pecking holes in the roof gutters. (Then Dad shot it.)

Notes: The Downy Woodpecker is one of the first birds that Micah teaches new bird-watchers to identify. They're common, easy to spot, and the bird-watcher is left feeling victorious.

All woodpeckers are handsome birds, but none are as cute as the little Downy Woodpecker. This skilled insect-hunter prefers to nest in cavities in dead trees. Here's what I find so especially charming about them—the male and the female take turns hammering away to create a nest. They also take turns bringing back mouthfuls of insects to their clutch. True partners. (That's the kind of marriage I'm going to have someday.)

7

It was funny how certain things kept hitting you in the face. For example, whenever David learned a new vocabulary word, it seemed he would hear it all the time. He'd wonder if more people were using that word or if, somehow, he'd just missed it until now.

That was what relocating the church seemed to be—it was on everyone's mind. Birdy's, especially. She brought up all kinds of possible places to move to, most of which he quietly dismissed. He had yet to identify a location that would benefit the entire church, not just a few. He felt strongly about that principle—if they made a move, it needed to be in the best interests of everyone.

Micah's suggestion of Tennessee was the first one that struck the right chord for him. It had many selling points—there were Amish settlements, but not progressive ones. McNairy County was distant from heavily populated areas, but not overly isolated. Farmland was available for reasonable costs, and the weather, unlike Vermont or Maine or northern Michigan, was conducive for two or three season farming.

After mulling Tennessee over for a day or so, David showed Micah's folder of notes on the state to Birdy. She read through the folder, murmuring to herself as she read. When she finished, she closed it, placed her hand on top of the folder, and announced,

"There's something meant for us here. I can just sense it, deep down."

"What do you sense? What is the something?" He'd learned, through trial and error, to trust Birdy's intuition. She was usually right.

She tipped her head in that way she had. "I don't know. There's just some . . . reason, some purpose. This is the place. I'm convinced that we should explore a relocation to Tennessee."

Well, Micah's notes *were* convincing. He'd give him that. David had no doubt there was some kind of bird angle behind Micah's reporting, but the young man was savvy enough to focus on information that would be helpful for the entire church. Like, the need for another sawmill in McNairy County. That would be right up Teddy Zook's alley. Or the lack of a well-organized farmers' market. Nathan Yoder would be just the man for that task.

"How do you think the rest of the church would respond to Tennessee?"

Birdy smiled. "Remember that old saying? 'Some people are going to be disgruntled no matter how hard you try to gruntle them.' There's just no way you can expect the entire church to be on board with this, David."

Maybe not, but that was his prayer. If there was a serious lack of unity among the church members, he would take it as a caution signal to wait. The enemy sought to divide believers; discord and separation were his strategies.

If the church of Stoney Ridge was meant to relocate, David trusted that God would bless that decision with unity. A general unity, at least.

David went through back issues of the *Sugarcreek Budget* to get a sense of the Amish communities in McNairy County. Mostly ultra-conservative Swartzentruber in the town of Stantonville. Their traditions could make the Stoney Ridge Old Order Amish church seem downright progressive.

He spent the afternoon at the public library to study the county's real estate and topography. One thing that did appeal to him was the amount of farmland up for sale in the county. Plenty of space for a church to grow, unlike Stoney Ridge.

He wondered about starting a Bent N' Dent in Stantonville. Would there be a need? He'd been a storekeeper for most of his life. His parents had run a store in Ohio, he had taken it over when his father had died, and he had started one here in Stoney Ridge. Amish-owned grocery stores blended into the community, quietly unassuming, providing essential ingredients. His people didn't have to go far to get most of the groceries and products they needed to keep family life humming along.

Reshelving the library books, he decided it might be wise to take a next step. To hire a driver and send a van of carefully selected church members to Tennessee with a checklist and see it for themselves. Maybe sooner rather than later, because if McNairy County wasn't the right place, they needed to rule it out. And if it was the right place, then they would take another step forward. One step at a time.

Later that afternoon, David closed the door to his store office and sat at his desk. First, he left a message for Andy Miller, a popular Englisch driver for the Plain People. He asked Andy to call him back at the store when he had a minute to spare. Next, he started a list of names to go on a scouting trip to Tennessee. He wanted to do the asking, rather than allow church members to volunteer. There was a clear purpose for this trip, and he wanted to avoid volunteers like Hank Lapp, who would be the first to raise his hand. Hank might be well intentioned, but he had a way of complicating the simplest things.

So then, who? Who should go on this fact-finding mission?

He thought it would be wise to have at least one of the ministers go along on the trip. Ideally, he'd like Luke to go. He wrote his name on a pad of paper and paused. The problem was, he needed people on the team who had the eyes to discern if the area would be a good place for the entire church. Luke was a buggy repair man. He could do buggy repairs anywhere, any time. He wouldn't be evaluating Tennessee the same way a farmer like his son-in-law Nathan would.

Nathan would be an ideal candidate. David wrote his name on the list. Nathan would investigate the condition of the soil and availability of water sources. Because he had managed the Stoney Ridge Farmers' Market, he'd be thinking about customers, about how difficult it might be to get a market up and going, and if there was enough traffic for farm stands. So many of the Amish women sold their jams and jellies and handcrafts at small farm stands. Maybe Lydie would go with him, but he doubted it. She was way behind in her home business of sign painting. Deeply backlogged.

Fern Lapp had excellent judgment, and it would be nice to have an older woman's point of view. He wrote down Fern's name. If she went, she would definitely need a female companion to go with her. Edith Fisher Lapp enjoyed Fern's company, but would that mean Hank would tag along? He hesitated. It actually would be nice to have some couples go together, but he doubted that would be possible. It was harvest season, a time of endless responsibilities for farming families.

Hmm, who else?

He wished he could add his own name, but it wouldn't be right for several reasons. First of all, this last Wednesday was the first day of school. Birdy had agreed to step in as the substitute teacher until he found a permanent teacher, which he had yet to do. He had waited until Tuesday night to ask her, the very last moment, and she agreed quite easily. Surprisingly so. She had two requirements: Timmy and Noah could go with her to school. And David would have to ask neighbors to stop in during the day to check on his mother.

David quickly said yes to both requests, delighted. Puzzled, too, as he'd expected it to be difficult to convince Birdy to step into the substitute teaching role, until it dawned on him that she might prefer a full classroom of pupils over caring for her invalid mother-in-law.

And that sent his thoughts to his mother. He couldn't leave her to go on a fact-finding mission, not until her health improved. At her best, his mother was dominating and demanding. Suffice it to say that with failing health, she wasn't at her best. Somehow, she'd heard of the possible church move—if David were to guess, he would say that Edith Lapp had told her—and she promptly told him that she wasn't going to move. She had some rather strong language about it.

David blew out a puff of air. He'd cross that bridge if and when he came to it. One step at a time.

He glanced at the wall clock and realized the time. He'd told the boys he'd take them fishing if he could get home well before supper today, and it looked like that wasn't going to happen. But he'd made a good start on the Tennessee project, and he could end the day with a sense of satisfaction. He set aside his pad of paper and pen and grabbed his hat off the wall peg.

Trudy said she would lock up tonight, so he started out the door, blinking against the late-afternoon sunshine. So bright. He stopped and held up the folder from Micah, as if offering it upward. *Lord, this church belongs to you,* he prayed. *Please make each next step crystal clear. Make it obvious. Give me that no-doubt-about-it kind of clarity. Amen.*

While unhitching the horse's reins from the post, he felt a strange connection to Moses and the Israelites as they crossed the Red Sea and started their journey in the desert to the Promised Land. There was the excitement of what lay ahead, venturing into the unknown. There was also the desperate need to depend entirely on the providence of the Lord to reveal each next step. He smiled. And did the Lord fail them? Just the opposite. He provided a pillar of cloud by day or a pillar of fire by night. The Lord guided their way and gave them light, one step at a time.

Nor would God fail the little church of Stoney Ridge.

Early the next morning, Micah had barely listened to Hank as he reported on David's list of names, and he bolted out the door of the Lost Creek Shoe Repair Shop.

"HEY! I'm NOT DONE!" Hank stood outside the shop, hands on his hips.

Micah was already in the buggy, slapping the reins on the horse's back. Ten minutes later, he burst into the Bent N' Dent, striding to the register where David stood. "Count me in."

David looked up. "For what?"

"For the trip to Tennessee. I want to be on your list."

David gave a sharp look around the store. No one was in hearing distance. "Where'd you hear about the list for the trip?" he said in a lowered voice.

"Hank."

David shook his head, frowning. "How does he seem to hear everything before it's even said?"

Because pretty much all Hank did was to circulate around town, gathering the latest news to share. But that was a topic for another day. "I really, really want to g-go on this trip, David."

David folded his arms across his chest. "Why?"

Shoot. Micah had practiced running through sentences on the drive over here, but he hadn't anticipated this question. He should've, though. His stomach tightened. He rummaged around his brain for valid reasons. "B-Because . . . I've moved once before. I can b-bring fresh eyes. See things c-clearly."

David watched him stammer away with that bishop-y look he had—the one where it seemed he could see right into your soul. Micah felt a bead of perspiration drip down his back. "I'm the one who t-told you about T-Tennessee in the f-first place." He had to stop talking. His stutter was only getting worse.

"Micah, if you go on this trip, birding can't be your top priority."

When Micah opened his mouth to object, David quickly added,

"I'm not saying you can't check out the birding opportunities. You can. But there's a lot more to discover in this trip than just birding. This trip is meant to evaluate McNairy County for the entire church, not just the birders."

Oh, there was so much more about Tennessee on Micah's mind than birds right now.

"Is that clear?"

"Crystal clear," Micah said. No stutter.

Slowly, David nodded. "Okay, then. Plan on going. I'll follow up with details in a few days. In the meantime, you'll want to find someone to cover your responsibilities."

Micah had already figured that out. He'd get Trudy to cover him with the guesthouse, and he'd work double-time to finish the current pile of shoe repairs, then just close up the shop in his absence.

Micah was about to ask David who else might be on the list to go to Tennessee, but an Englisch woman was approaching the counter with a basketful of spices, so he decided against it. Plus, he didn't really care about the list. He was just happy he was on it. Beyond happy. Ecstatic.

Somehow, he was going to find Shelley Yoder and bring her home where she belonged.

As Micah started to back away from the counter to let the Englischer move closer, David said in Penn Dutch, "Keep this information to yourself."

Right. Micah gave him the OK signal with his fingers as he opened the door to leave, trying hard to keep a straight face when he wanted to flat-out laugh. With Hank Lapp yammering to everyone in the church, it would be like trying to get spilled milk back into the jug. "When do we leave?"

"I don't have any dates in mind yet, so there's no hurry."

"No hurry?" It came out like a squeak.

"No hurry," David repeated. "There's plenty of time."

At the end of the day, David tidied up his desk and looked around for the store key to lock up. In the distance, he heard a horse whinny, and another answer back. Then another. He left his office to see what was going on. Through the store front windows, he saw a line of buggies driving solemnly down the lane, heading toward the store. A number of buggies had already arrived, and small clumps of men had gathered under the shade trees. A ripple of disquiet swept through him.

No one had to tell David what this was about. Hank Lapp's big mouth was like a snowball heading down a hill, gathering speed and misinformation in every roll.

David returned to his office to get the key and to take a moment to pray. For the ability to listen and understand concerns. Mostly, for patience. Again, the word "unity" came to the top of his mind. *Thank you for that reminder, Lord*. Unity was the goal.

After locking up the store, David walked down the steps to join the men. This he did as an intentional move. Rather than stand high on the porch to speak to the men, he wanted to be on the same level with them. He didn't want to turn the possibility of relocation into a decision made by the ministers. By the bishop.

Three men approached him, one of whom was Trudy's father, Dave Yoder. "What's this move all about?" Dave Yoder said. The others drifted over to them. Altogether, there were about ten men. No women, which didn't surprise David. They might've been the ones to send their men on this errand, but they wouldn't be the ones to confront the bishop.

"I'm not sure what you've heard—" David said.

Suddenly, everyone spoke at once.

"We heard you're moving the church to Tennessee."

"Hank said it was Nashville."

"I thought he said Memphis?"

"Hank told *me* it was happening right away."

"He said it was top secret."

David bit his lip. Hank Lapp should be muzzled. "I'm glad

you've all come to get the facts, because everything you just told me is incorrect."

Teddy Zook put his hands on his hips. "Then what is going on? Are you moving the church or aren't you?"

David felt a little disappointed by Teddy. He'd always thought of him as a reasonable man. Certainly not one to listen to the rumor mill. Hank's especially. "Just considering it, that's all."

A buzz of murmurs started.

"You're all well aware that land is getting scarce in Stoney Ridge. You know that some folks have chosen to move elsewhere so they can keep their families together. It seemed like it might be wise to consider a relocation. Just to check it out."

Someone from the back called out, "It's because of those Beachys."

That remark acted like a spark to dry leaves. Each man started to grumble about the Beachys moving in. David listened for a moment or two, surprised at the vehemence. It was concerning. There'd been more bad feelings brewing between the two churches than he'd realized. While he hadn't meant to add fuel to the fire, it did confirm to him that something needed to change, and soon. He doubted any of these men had even heard yet about the Beachy church's plans to build at Wonder Lake. That news would take the discord to another level.

"Let's try to stay focused," David said in a loud voice, "on the needs of our own church."

Dave Yoder swept one arm, a gesture to include all the men. "That's exactly what we're doing."

Not really, David thought. All he'd heard in the last few minutes was why the Beachy church was creating problems for everyone. "Then, let's stay focused on this fact-finding trip."

Teddy folded his big arms across his chest. "So what's the urgency?"

David shook his head. "No urgency. None."

"Hank told us," Teddy said, "that we'd better hurry and sell off our land before there's a stampede. He said land prices will drop like a rock if we all try to sell at once."

That took half a minute for David to swallow before he could respond in a calm manner. All the bearded faces stared at him, waiting to hear his response. "As I said, I'm glad you've come to me for the facts. There is no urgency to this. None." He made eye contact with each man, even those in the back. "It seemed like it might be wise to send a few people down to McNairy County in Tennessee just so we could start the process of gathering information. We'll consider other areas to relocate too. But no decision will happen without the consent of the entire church. I understand what a significant undertaking this would be. This is a decision that we will make together. Men and women both. A move needs to benefit everyone."

Dave Yoder shook his head like a wet dog. "There's no way you'll be able to benefit everyone."

"I suppose there's some truth in that. But I hope everyone will keep the church's best interests in mind. If it's good for the church, it's good for our community. And at this point, I don't know the answer to that. I only know that I feel a strong sense that we should all be willing to explore the possibility of moving. That's as far as things are right now."

That seemed to satisfy most of the men. "Who's going?" Teddy said.

"I'm still working on the list. There's room for five. If you're interested, let me know."

At that, the men started mumbling excuses as to why they were too busy to go. One by one, they slipped off to their buggies. Soon, David was left alone with Teddy. The big man had something on his mind. David waited.

"Yoder's talking about splitting the church."

"What? Which Yoder?" Yoder was one of the most common surnames among the Plain People.

"Dave Yoder. He won't move. There are others who feel like he does. He said that if you move the church, those who remain can start a new church."

"With what leadership?"

Teddy shrugged. "Don't know about that."

David looked at the row of buggies disappearing down the road. "Do others feel that strongly about not moving?"

"Some. Yoder, mostly."

"What's behind that?" Usually, doctrinal or lifestyle differences caused splits.

"You know Dave Yoder as well as I do. He doesn't talk much. But if I had to guess, I'd say it's got something to do with his daughter."

Dave Yoder was fiercely protective of his family. When Trudy was offered a job at the Bent N' Dent last year, she said she'd like to but that the bishop would need to ask her father for permission. Dave Yoder wouldn't allow any outside influence to enter his home any more than he'd let a telephone in the door. It wasn't as if Trudy was working out. It seemed a little overprotective for a mature young woman to not be able to make her own decisions about her work. "Why would he have any concerns about Trudy?"

"No. The older one. The girl who ran off. The singing girl."

Ah, now he understood. "Shelley."

Teddy nodded. "My guess is he won't leave Stoney Ridge without her. Not so long as there's a chance she'd come back." He took a step or two, then turned. "I suppose I can't blame him."

No, David thought. No, he couldn't either.

Naturally, Trudy said yes to helping Micah out while he was off to Tennessee. She'd spent so much time at Lost Creek Farm this last year that she already knew most everything Penny did to keep the guesthouse running smoothly. It didn't surprise her when Micah asked. She'd already learned of the scouting trip to Tennessee from Hank Lapp—everybody had—and she knew that Micah would want to go on that trip. Tennessee birding was legendary. Of course he'd try to get on that van.

She'd like to go, too, but she had something more important on her mind. An exciting and daunting task lay in front of her. Mostly daunting. As the Tennessee trip took shape, it fired up her determination to stop the Beachy church from ruining Wonder Lake. She had no idea how, not yet, but she knew there must be *some* way.

She wished she could talk it all over with Micah. He had come into the Bent N' Dent to ask her if she'd cover Lost Creek Farm while he was away. As soon as she'd said yes, he turned to leave the store. Why? What was the big hurry?

"Stuff to do," he said, his shoulders tense, his jaw tight. He'd hardly even looked her in the eyes.

Such a mood! To the best of her knowledge, Micah hadn't even gone back up to the eagle aerie to try and identify the hawklet. Any day now, its plumage would start sprouting. She'd been there day after day, squinting through her binoculars at the little chick. Whenever she brought it up to Micah, he seemed preoccupied, distant, like his mind was thousands of miles away. That worried her even more than the imminent destruction of Wonder Lake.

Two things she knew for sure would happen if the Beachys built on Wonder Lake: Micah would leave Stoney Ridge to seek out better birding. And if David decided to move the church, her father would not go with it. He'd already said so, many times. He would never, ever leave Stoney Ridge—not while there was a chance that Shelley might return home. Which meant that Trudy would have to stay put too. Family was everything to the Amish.

But Stoney Ridge without Micah Weaver was absolutely . . . unthinkable.

Trudy Yoder, Bird-Watching Log

Name of Bird: Canada Jay (formerly known as the Gray Jay)

Scientific Name: _Perisoreus canadensis_

Status: Low concern

Date: June 27

Location: Bent N' Dent

Description: Robin-sized, round-headed songbird with a short bill and long tail. White cheek, throat, and forehead, gray belly.

Symbolism: Some devout Christians believe that the appearance of a jay is a sign from God to persevere in what they're doing, even if it seems like a hopeless situation.

Bird Action: Stole my sandwich right off the picnic table while I was gone for barely a minute. I jumped up to help an elderly customer climb down the store steps, and when I returned to finish my lunch, it was gone. The Gray Jay had my sandwich high in a tree overhead, cackling down at me. (Micah would roll his eyes, but I do believe it was laughing at me.)

Notes: For some reason that scientists don't understand, the Canada Jay raises its brood during the late winter and not in the warm spring, like most birds do. A member of the crow family (it definitely shares a crow's trickster qualities!), the Canada Jay makes himself an unwelcome visitor. Highly curious and always on the lookout for food, it's easy to see how it earned its nickname of Camp Robber. Some say that jays prefer shiny objects to steal, but I have found them to be indiscriminate thieves. They'll take anything. More than once, I've found them poking through the garbage cans in the back of the store.

Despite its tendency toward peskiness and theft, and an obvious lack of remorse and regret, the Canada Jay is a truly beautiful songbird.

8

Micah woke in the middle of the night as if a crack of thunder shook the house. He sat straight up in bed, eyes wide open. There were some recognizable sounds in the background of Shelley's phone messages. How had he missed those? Birding was all about listening well. He jumped out of bed, jammed on his boots, and bolted to the phone shanty to listen to each message again. He'd saved them all.

There. *There* it was. The sound of a distant siren? Or was it a car alarm? He listened again, eyes squeezed shut, sharpening his focus on the sound in the background. Once more, he played all the messages.

Hard to tell. Definitely some kind of alarm. A fire engine, a police car, or maybe an ambulance. That could mean a hospital or fire station was nearby.

The next day, after finishing morning chores, he headed into town to the public library, a one-story redbrick building at the far end of Main Street. He had to wait until it opened at ten o'clock, so he paced nervously up and down the sidewalk in front, trying to calm down. He was on the brink of discovery, and waiting felt like torture.

Calm down, he told himself. *Settle*. He closed his eyes and tried to listen for a moment.

Bird chatter. He turned his head to the sound and nearly smiled when he spotted a cluster of Red Finches in an overhead tree. Trudy was crazy about all finches. Cheerful no matter what, she liked to tell him. Noisy no matter what, Micah would answer.

There were some low-lying clouds this morning, covering the sun but not thick enough or organized enough to provide rain. Just a tease. But the air felt cooler today, less humid than it had been lately. A sign of changing seasons. Fall migration would be starting soon, his favorite time of year. He looked forward to the month of October all year long, like a child anticipating Christmas. In the fall, the birds weren't in such a big hurry to return to their winter grounds, not like the rush north in springtime when they were in a race to reproduce.

Last October, he and Trudy tracked a Northern Saw-whet Owl—a real find. He would never forget the look on Trudy's upturned face when she first caught sight of that little owl on a tree branch—like she was standing on holy ground.

Thinking about birding settled his mind, helped him feel calmer, less frantic, and then he spotted Victoria in the parking lot. He bolted toward her car. "Another clue."

She had been reaching into the back seat for her purse and did a half turn, startled. "Where'd you come from?"

"B-Been waiting. I have another c-clue."

Victoria smiled. She was loving this. To her, it was a game. To Micah, it was deadly serious.

It took Victoria only two minutes to narrow the search down. A few taps on the computer and she looked up at him, beaming. "McNairy County has a fairly small population—about ten thousand people. There's only a handful of fire stations, a few urgent care clinics, one police station." She printed out the map with addresses and handed him the list.

Glancing at it, Micah was astounded at how much information could be accessed through a computer. It was like having a full library in a box. He thought about the Beachys and their use of "filtered internet" in the house. Right now, it was sounding pretty good to him. Carefully, he folded the paper and tucked it in his pocket. "Thanks."

Victoria leaned back in her chair and folded her arms across her chest. "This Shelley girl, she sounds pretty important to you."

With a shrug, he looked away.

Unlike his nosy sister Penny, Victoria didn't press him for a response. "Stop in if you think of any other clues. This is fun."

He patted his pocket. "Thanks."

On his way back to Lost Creek Farm, the sun popped out from behind the clouds, filling the world with encouraging brightness. He grinned. He had the same feeling in his gut as he did when he was closing in on a rarity. The field was narrowing on Shelley, his jinx bird.

During lunch, David had walked down the tree-lined road from the Bent N' Dent to Dok's office, hoping she had a free minute to talk. The office was locked up tight, which probably meant that Dok was out on a house call. That might be good. Maybe she'd stop by the house of her own accord to check on Mom. She often did.

He walked back to the store, feeling cheered up. A walk outside in the fresh air had that effect on him, like opening a window in his mind to let a cool breeze in, and he wondered why he didn't remember that more often. An instant mood lift.

He settled into his chair to finish the tedious task of reordering bulk spices, just as Hank Lapp burst through his open office door. "I WANT to GO! PUT ME on that LIST!"

David's heart sank. Why hadn't he closed his office door? This was just what he had wanted to avoid. "No, Hank." That was a 100 percent no.

"WHY NOT?"

"Hank, this isn't a free vacation. It's a serious undertaking."

"DON'T I KNOW it! This is BIG, David. You need EVERYONE on BOARD."

Exactly. That was why David wanted to handpick those who would go. But how to make Hank understand? "Why do you think you should go?"

"ME and EDDY, BOTH."

Oh no. Both of them? David swallowed. He had wanted a married couple to go. But not *this* couple. "Tell me why."

"WE think we have something SPECIAL to OFFER."

"And what would that be?"

Uninvited, Hank settled into the chair across from David. "YOU can't just send YOUNG ONES. What about US OLD-TIMERS? You gotta REPRESENT us. We'll be LOOKING out for the OLD FOLKS' point of view. Nobody better than Eddy and me for THAT."

"How so?"

Hank threw his arms high in the air. "Because we're old!"

Was he? Hank Lapp had an ageless quality about him. David had only known him a decade or so; in that time, he hadn't changed at all.

"I'll give the matter some consideration, Hank." David did want to include a smattering of ages.

"Of COURSE," Hank said, pushing himself up from the chair. "And then AFTER you've considered it OVER, just tell me WHAT to PACK."

As Hank left the office, David closed the door behind him, sat back down, leaned his elbows on the desk, and covered his face with his hands. He was starting to have serious concerns about this scouting trip to Tennessee. He mistakenly thought there'd be a lot of interest. So far, David had asked six people if they would go—Nathan Yoder, Luke and Izzy Schrock, Fern Lapp, Mose Miller, Vern Glick . . . and Micah Weaver. Actually, Micah had invited himself. And so far, Micah was the only solid yes. Everyone else had given David a vague, "I'll have to think about it and get back to you." He knew what that response truly meant: *Will be hunting for a reason to get out of it.*

To be fair, this time of year was especially difficult for farming families. The hayfields needed a third cutting to prepare for winter, field crops were ripening, garden produce needed canning.

But all he had asked of anyone was one week, max. One short week. Maybe even just a few days, plus the addition of two long travel days.

He hoped he didn't have to put on the bishop hat for this. "You can't say no to the bishop" was a well-known adage. He had to admit that it did come in handy at times, but for this task, he felt it would contradict the very reason the church was considering a move—unity. It couldn't be forced. It needed to come from within. Unfortunately, that meant the only ones willing and eager to go were Micah, Hank, and Edith.

A knock on his door interrupted his mulling. "Kumm uff rei." *Come in.*

The door opened and Billy Blank popped his head in. "I'll go."

"Go where?"

"On the trip. I'd like to go to Tennessee. Put me on the list."

David tried to mask what he was thinking, which was: "Not a chance." Billy was a solid, dependable young man, but he needed a lot of direction. Quite a lot. It was one of the reasons he thought Trudy might be a good match for Billy. She needed no direction. "Why do you want to go?"

Billy held up two fingers. "Two reasons. One, fainting goats."

"Fainting goats?"

"They're called the Tennessee fainting goats. That's where they were first bred."

"I see." Words failed him. Those goats of Billy's were a source of endless jokes among the graybeards who hung around the store. "And the second reason?" He braced himself.

"To help the church."

Well, that was a better answer than David had expected. In fact, it was a fine answer. The very one he'd hoped for from those he'd actually asked to go on the trip. "I'll, um, give it some thought, Billy."

Billy grinned broadly and gave him a thumbs-up, like he'd been given a ticket to go.

But he hadn't. Nor had Hank Lapp.

The phone rang and David spun around in his chair to answer. "David Stoltzfus."

"David, it's Andy Miller."

A Mennonite who spoke Penn Dutch, Andy was everyone's favorite driver, plus he had a dependable minivan that he kept spotless. David had spoken to him about driving a van load to Tennessee, but they hadn't talked dates. Only cost. With gas prices on the rise, Andy's quote had been shockingly expensive. David had deferred, telling him that he'd get back to him. But he hadn't.

"I just bumped into Hank Lapp and he said that you've got your people and you're ready to head to Tennessee."

"Oh he did, did he?" David's jaw tightened.

"Yep, and it's a good thing he did. I just found out I'm heading to Tennessee on Monday."

"What's taking you to Tennessee?"

"I'm picking up my brother. He's been hiking the Appalachian Trail. He's wants to come home for his wife's birthday, so I'm planning to meet up with him in Gatlinburg late Monday afternoon."

"Gatlinburg? That's a couple of hours east of where my team needs to go."

"It's on the way, actually. I thought I'd pick him up and head west to drop off your people, then head back north."

"It sounds good, Andy, but I wasn't quite ready to send the team off by Monday."

"Well, if you change your mind, we can split the cost of gas."

Split it? David's interest level rose. "When do I need to let you know?"

"I need an answer by tonight. If you're not interested, there's a couple who wants to go to Nashville. I just thought I'd ask you first, since we'd had that talk about Tennessee."

"Okay. I'll let you know by tonight." As David hung up, his stomach started churning. He shouldn't have had that second cup of coffee this morning. Or was it his third? He knew better. His sensitive stomach was always there to remind him how vulnerable he was. Especially to stress.

David was well aware that he was considered to be an overly cautious man, reluctant to move too quickly, but this sudden urgency unsettled him. This scouting trip felt like it was getting out of hand, like he'd lost control of it.

Birdy. She'd know what to do. She was the one he needed to talk to. He jumped up and bolted through the store, waving to Trudy—who looked startled as he dashed to the door—shouting a quick reassurance that he'd be back as soon as he could.

Trudy didn't know what had happened that had caused the bishop to fly out of the store like his pants were on fire. Normally, David moved at a steady pace; he was a deliberate man, calm and thoughtful. She'd never seen him angry, never heard even a spike of irritation in his voice. Customers could be frustrating, demanding, especially the Englisch ones, yet David treated each one with great respect.

It was something she'd always appreciated about the bishop because it was so opposite of her own father. She never knew what kind of mood he'd be in when she got home from work. She never knew what might set him off. Lately, he'd been grumbling nonstop about the bishop's proposal to relocate. After supper last evening, her dad left to go talk to some like-minded farmers—he didn't say who they were but Trudy could guess—to discuss splitting off from the church to start a new one. She could see what was going to happen, as clearly as if written on the wall. If David moved the church, her dad would campaign to keep members here.

The chimes on the door rang and she looked up to see the mailman, holding a bundle of mail in one hand. She took the mail from him to set on David's desk. Midair, her hand froze.

David had scribbled down notes on a pad of paper left right on top of his desk: *Andy Miller, Tennessee, depart early Monday morning.*

Trudy hadn't set out to go snooping, but there it was, plain as day. So this must be how Hank Lapp did it. How he found things out before anyone else. Hank's talent for eavesdropping was legendary, but she hadn't realized he also went nosing around David's desk. Shamed at stooping to Hank Lapp's level, she hurried back to the counter in the main part of the store.

Slowly, it dawned on Trudy that David meant *this* Monday. A mild panic started. Too fast! Everything was happening too fast. If Micah returned with a good report about Tennessee, he would be the first to leave Stoney Ridge. She knew he would. When Micah made a decision, he stuck with it. No turning back. He could be stubborn like that.

She wasn't sure how long the team would be gone on the Tennessee trip, but she knew she had to stop the annihilation of Wonder Lake before they returned to Stoney Ridge. She had her work cut out for her. Because if David tried to relocate everyone to Tennessee, her dad would see to it that the church would be cut in half.

The wrong half for Trudy.

Trudy Yoder, Bird-Watching Log

Name of Bird: Common Grackle

Scientific Name: Quiscalus quiscula

Status: In steep decline (Worrisome!)

Date: August 5

Location: Right in front of the Sweet Tooth
Bakery Shop, undeterred by the presence of a
large, boisterous group of Englisch teenagers
standing nearby.

Description: A Grackle looks like a blackbird that's
been slightly pulled like taffy, beak to tail.
A very long tail. Robin-sized, colored entirely
bronzy-black, though males have the dramatic
flair of an iridescent turquoise head cap.

Symbolism: Sadly, blackbirds (Grackles are in the
Icteridae family of blackbirds) do not have
a positive connotation in Christian tradition.
They're associated with Satan and sin.

Bird Action: Foraging for food in the garbage can
out in front of the bakery. Grackles will eat
anything. ANYTHING.

Notes: Grackles can be difficult to ignore, even
if you are trying. This exceptionally chatty
songbird seems to enjoy the sound of its own
voice. Some consider Grackles to be a nuisance
bird (farmers, in particular, because Grackles
have a fondness for corn sprouts). I can't

help but admire its audacious attitude toward life. It is fearless. But do keep an eye on your lunch if you're picnicking on a summer day (like I was). This bird is a bold scavenger.

An interesting tidbit: *Females pick the nest site and males help to construct it. After building has begun on a nest, females will often change their mind and choose another site. The males don't object. They just follow along and do what they're told. (If only that could be true of some human males I know!)*

9

As the horse slowed to pull the buggy up the steep driveway that led to the Stoltzfus house, David spotted Birdy over by the clothesline. As soon as it crested the hill, the horse went right to the sprawling shade tree and stopped. David jumped out, not even bothering to hitch the horse's reins to the post. He strode over the lawn—noticing that the grass needed cutting—to where Birdy gathered sheets off the line. "Where are the boys?"

"Lydie took them to the library this afternoon." She handed him one end of a dry sheet to help fold. "Are you home early to take the boys fishing? They should be back soon. They'll be so excited."

Fishing? "No. Soon, though," he said quickly as he caught the look of disappointment on her face. "I just stopped by for a moment." He glanced up at the second-story window where his mother was recuperating. "Did Mom eat something today?"

"Nothing." Birdy shook her head. "I tried. Offered her everything I could think of that might tempt her. But she had no interest." She shook the sheet to remind him that they were trying to fold it.

He spread the two corners of the sheet as far apart as his arms would allow, while Birdy matched the corners. "This trip to Tennessee. It's getting complicated."

One eyebrow arched. "Hank Lapp?"

"Partly. Mostly, actually." He followed her lead to fold the sheet into a tidy package. "How did you know?"

"He stopped by here just a short bit ago. Said he needed to borrow some sleeping bags for Monday's trip."

David sighed. "Did he tell you that he already talked to Andy Miller?"

"He did. He said that Andy needed to leave Monday to get his brother off the Appalachian Trail."

"How does Hank Lapp seem to know everything?"

"Ears like a hawk," Birdy said with a grin. She unclipped another sheet. "So what's bothering you? Hank? Or that the trip is poised to start on Monday?"

"Both. Hank invited not only himself, but Edith. And now Billy Blank wants to go."

"So how many is that?"

"Four." The only one he had any confidence in was Micah, albeit rough-hewn, still unfinished, on the cusp of adulthood. This would be a good test for a man still waiting to happen. "Suddenly, Micah Weaver is the leader. Yet he has no experience with this kind of thing."

"No, but then again, neither do you."

He couldn't argue that. While he had dealt with some difficult things in the church, he had never tried to relocate a church. "So you think I should let those four go?"

Birdy turned back to the clothesline and unpinned another sheet. "Would you feel better if you went with them?" Her voice sounded a little flat, vague and far away.

"I've thought of it. I would definitely have greater peace of mind if I could be the one spearheading this. I mean . . . who knows what trouble Hank could stir up? Edith will complain about everything. I doubt Billy will have much to offer. So it all rests on Micah." He let out a deep sigh. "I want to go, but that would mean asking an awful lot of Trudy Yoder. She's certainly dependable, but she's young. Easily intimidated by others. And then . . . there's Mom.

It doesn't seem right to leave. Not with the condition she's in. Not fair to you. Especially with you teaching all day long."

Birdy spun around, a look of abject relief on her face.

Ah. I see, David thought. Maybe he should have led off with that last thought.

She walked up to him and put her hands on his face. "It's not like you to underestimate people so severely."

"But, Birdy," he whispered, looking right into her eyes, "this is Hank."

She smiled. "I think you've got a van of four people who truly want to go on this trip. All you're asking them to do is to bring back their observations. That's all. No decisions need to be made."

Right. She had a good point.

"Edith might complain, but she'll make sure that you get the answers you want about McNairy County."

He nodded.

"She'll keep Hank in line. And Billy is a good soldier. He might need guidance, but he's very sincere. Very earnest."

Calm was returning to David. He knew Birdy would have the right perspective. A smile tugged at his lips. "And Micah will check out the bird scene."

Her eyes lit up at that. "But don't put Micah Weaver in a box. He's always struck me as a trustworthy young man."

"He is."

She turned and resumed her task, but he could tell there was something else she wanted to say. "What? Go ahead and say it."

She unpinned a towel and folded it, before dropping it in the large wicker basket. "I can't altogether explain it, but suddenly—I just sense a powerful urge that you should say yes to this. Send the team to Tennessee as soon as possible."

He took that in, as well as the solemn look on her face. Birdy believed that those urges she felt were sent from the Lord. Skeptical at first, over the years, David had come to agree with her. If Birdy had a sense that there was a reason to send the van now rather than later, he trusted her. He smiled, thanking the Lord for providing this wonderful helpmate. "All right, then. On my way back to the store, I'll stop and let those four know the plan is in place to leave early Monday morning."

"Good. Just think of how your faith will grow through this."

He lifted his eyebrows. "My faith?"

"If you were to go, or if the other ministers were going, you'd rely on them. But this way, you're going to need to depend completely on the Lord." She gave him a quick kiss on the lips. "Because this is Hank Lapp you're sending on that trip. Sei Hank waar gut, awwer er ist net ganz gscheit." *Hank has good intentions, but he's not at all wise.*

With that reminder, David's fragile calm shattered.

———

As soon as Trudy's shift at the store ended, she scootered over to Lost Creek Farm on a hunt for Micah but saw no sign of him. The shoe repair shop was locked. She found the key in its hidden spot, opened the door, grabbed one of Micah's Sibley bird books, and hurried up the trail that led to Wonder Lake. She couldn't stop thinking about that little chick. She was obsessed with it! It seemed vitally important to try and figure out the hawklet's story, of how it got in the eagle aerie in the first place. She was determined to figure out the identity of this chick. It probably didn't even matter, but she was desperate to know. Even as she hiked up the trail, she fought a wave of discouragement. She knew she didn't have the birding skills to identify the hawklet, not at this stage of development. She needed Micah for that and he was no help. None. He barely even spoke to her anymore.

Hiking up there without him, realizing this might be the way her future rolled out if he left Stoney Ridge, was the loudest quiet she'd ever heard.

———

Micah had done something today that he would've never, ever thought he'd do. In his possession was a cell phone. For a month's time, anyway.

After David stopped by Lost Creek Farm this afternoon to tell him to start packing because he was leaving Monday morning for Tennessee, he knew he had to get his hands on a cell phone. Right now. If Shelley were to call Lost Creek Farm while he was away, he wanted to provide a number on the message machine so she could reach him. Better still, he could pick up her calls and talk to her, rather than piece her messages together like puzzles with missing parts. He hoped he'd correctly narrowed her location down to McNairy County, but even that felt like a needle in a haystack. The only solid clues he had were these: a yellow house, cornfields, an alarm, and a broomcorn festival in Selmer, a town in McNairy County. And the source of that last clue came from Hank Lapp. Highly suspect.

At the farmers' market a while ago, Micah remembered overhearing a Beachy boy brag about his cell phone. He had recognized the boy from the shoe repair shop. Months ago, the boy had dropped off a red cowboy boot with a broken heel to repair. He'd never bothered to pick it up.

Briefly, Micah considered running the borrow-the-cell-phone idea past David. Not the since-Shelley-might-call-me part, but the since-we'll-be-on-the-road part. The more he thought about it, the more he figured it would only backfire.

Micah would say, "This could help us report back on everything."

And David would say, "We can just plan on connecting each night. I'll be in the shanty at a certain time, waiting for your call."

And Micah would try to explain that the cell phone was for the team's safety.

And David would fix his gaze on him in that way he had. "Why would you put your security in a man-made device? Why not trust the Lord for your safety?"

That was where Micah's defense fell apart. He lost the argument in his mind.

Yeah. Bad idea.

Micah found the Beachy boy's repaired red cowboy boot on the shelf in the shop, dusted it off, and drove the horse and buggy over to his house. As he pulled into the driveway, he saw the boy walk across the yard toward the garden. Micah parked the buggy and followed his path to the hose bib. When the boy saw Micah approach, he stopped filling a bucket with water. Micah held up the boot. "All fixed. B-Been waiting for you to p-pick it up for two months now."

The boy grimaced. "Well, see, I don't have the money right now." His eyes darted to the house. "My mom . . . she doesn't exactly know about those boots."

"No charge."

"Nothing? Cool." He reached out for it.

Micah pulled the boot out of his reach. "But I d-do need a favor."

"A favor?" The boy's eyes narrowed in suspicion. "Like what?"

"I n-need to b-borrow your cell ph-phone for a week or so. A m-month, t-tops." Stupid stutter.

Slowly, a smile spread over the boy's face. "Your church doesn't allow cell phones, does it?"

Micah didn't answer.

"It'll cost you."

"I fixed your b-boot for free."

"My phone's worth a lot more than those old boots." He was getting cocky. "What do you need it for?"

"That's my b-business." But Micah did have a question. "Can it t-track a call?"

"Oh yeah. And once you've got that number, you can trace it right to the source."

"How?"

"Google it, dude." From the blank look on Micah's face, the

boy could tell he didn't know what that meant. "I can show you how." He turned his phone toward Micah for proof.

Twenty minutes of negotiation later, Micah had the cell phone in hand. He ended up paying a dear, dear price. His conscience did too. It pricked him all the way back to Lost Creek Farm and he couldn't stop wondering if he had just crossed a line. He kept reminding himself that borrowing the cell phone was temporary and meant for a very good cause. But he knew it could land him a stint on the sinner's bench. Humiliating.

For Shelley's sake, it was worth it.

———

Trudy Yoder, Bird-Watching Log

Name of Bird: *Common Loon*

Scientific Name: *Gavia immer*

Status: *Low concern*

Symbolism: *Its mournful call is thought to represent a yearning, an unfulfilled longing. (It does for me!)*

Date: *March 13*

Location: *A farmer's pond in Strasburg Borough*

Description: *A male, black and large, with that striking black-and-white tuxedo. Its eye color turns from gray in the winter to crimson red in the spring and summer.*

Bird Action: *A late-in-the-season snowstorm must have sent this Common Loon off course. The farmer thought it had crash-landed in his pond. Micah and I rushed over to see it. It was trying to take off and fly but couldn't get going. The pond was only one acre—too small. Loons are like airplanes and need a looooong runway.*

Notes: *Loons are one of the best reasons to go out bird-watching whenever you can. Once you hear its call, you'll know why. Micah said it's the loudest bird call in the world. An eerie, piercing, wailing cry that echoes off the water. It'll put shivers down your spine.*

    Loons may look like ducks and act like ducks,

but they're more closely related to penguins or albatrosses. Most birds have hollow bones, but loon bones are solid. They're incredible divers and can hold their breath under water for eight minutes. They need clear water because they hunt by sight. Despite being fairly heavyset, they're terrific fliers. They can reach speeds up to 70 miles per hour, but getting airborne is no small task. I wonder if they feel embarrassed around other birds with their slow, clumsy takeoffs.

Loons tend to be solitary birds. No wonder their eerie call sounds so sad.

10

Trudy knew that Andy Miller was picking the travelers up in front of the Bent N' Dent at five o'clock in the morning, and she planned to be there. She'd even arrived early, just to be sure. She was cold, frustrated, and now she was mad at Micah. Furious. She'd come to see him off and wish him a good trip, but less than a minute after she'd arrived, she was sorry she'd made the effort. She shouldn't have bothered. Everything about Micah—his eyes, his tone, his body language—had taken on a stony quality. One syllable responses—more like grunts—to her many questions. They stood near the store's porch, waiting for Billy Blank, Hank, and Edith to arrive. David and Andy Miller were over by the minivan, studying a map.

Keep trying, Trudy reminded herself. *Don't give up.* She handed Micah a plastic container. "I made cookies for the trip."

"Thanks."

"While you're gone, I'll keep working on a plan for Wonder Lake."

He lifted his eyebrows, as if Wonder Lake was the furthest thing from his mind. *Why is that?* she wanted to ask. *What's wrong with you that you suddenly stopped caring about the hawk chick in the eagle's nest? Stopped caring about me? What's happened to make you so cold and uncaring?*

130

But instead of saying anything more, she waited for him to say something. Hoped he would tell her what had been preoccupying him lately.

"Don't forget the g-guesthouse," he said, breaking a long silence.

Don't forget the guesthouse? Was he kidding? Her heart stung.

"Remember—you don't need to b-bother with the phone shanty. I'll call in t-to get messages. Just leave it t-to me."

Yes, he had told her that three times. "Micah, you're acting weird."

His mouth jammed shut, his dark eyes went flinty. "I'm not."

"You are. You're acting really weird and I want to know why."

Frowning, he considered the charge. "I'm not acting weird."

She put her hands on her hips. "You're hiding something."

"I'm . . . it's . . . um . . ." His face took on a frustrated look from trying to find words to defend himself.

Guilt.

That was what she saw flit through his eyes. In the red flame up his cheeks. No doubt. She knew him well. He was guilty. But she couldn't imagine what he felt guilty about, and before she could ask, Billy Blank, Edith, and Hank arrived, driven to the store by Billy's dad.

Billy hopped out of the buggy before it came to a full stop. "Trudy! You came to see me off." He sounded delighted.

"HOLD it, ROMEO," Hank said. "LET'S GET this SHOW on the ROAD."

Billy took a couple of steps toward Trudy, but Micah grabbed him by the shoulders and turned him around. "Yeah. We g-gotta go." Micah steered Billy toward the minivan and right into the back seat.

Trudy picked up her scooter. Billy knocked on the back window and frantically waved to her. She gave him a smile, though it probably came out all wrong. Forced and frozen. Her eyes met Micah's. He lifted a hand in a wave, but she didn't return it. She turned, instead, and scooted down the road. She'd barely made it to the end when she realized with a kind of horrible, seeping awareness that maybe Micah felt guilty because there was some other girl in his life.

———————

As Andy Miller's minivan crossed the state border into Maryland, Micah felt a stirring of excitement. He'd never been out of the state of Pennsylvania, not until this very moment. He'd been so focused on finding Shelley that it hadn't occurred to him to consider all that awaited him on the road. Granted, most of it was Interstate 81, but the route took them through some of the prettiest country he'd ever seen—lush green rolling hills, thick stands of trees, tall conifers and leafy deciduous. Against the gray sky, some leaves on the trees were just turning a faint yellow. *Imagine what this interstate will look like in mid-October*, he thought, wishing he could see it. Oranges and reds and yellows. A stunning display of autumn's coming.

Colors seemed more vibrant here, more vivid. Was it like this in Stoney Ridge? Or had he stopped noticing?

And then there was the perception of distance. It changed when you were in a minivan humming along an interstate highway. At a trot, a horse and buggy rolled along at eight to ten miles per hour. A mile took some time, five miles was a long way, fifteen miles was at the limits of most travel. But in a minivan speeding down the road at sixty-five miles per hour (seventy-to-eighty when Andy knew Edith was sound asleep), the world seemed much smaller.

And so they drove over rolling hills and through thick walls of oak, ash, chinquapin, and pine that lined the highway. The farther south they went, the more sullen the skies grew, until a drizzling rain started. Andy planned to take breaks at rest stops every four hours. When they stopped in Harrisonburg, Virginia, to fill the van with gas, Micah got out of the van to stretch. He walked to the edge of the gas station, facing west, thinking about the Mononga-

hela National Forest in the distance. It almost hurt to be this close to where Golden-winged Warblers might be found, a bird Trudy wanted to add to her lifer list. She was crazy over songbirds, as devoted as he felt about raptors. Migratory songbirds, in general, were in decline—a troubling reality that frustrated Trudy to no end. But the Golden-winged Warbler was in a steep, rapid decline, although it hadn't been put on the endangered species list. Not yet. These particular warblers needed mature forests to survive, which were disappearing. The warblers had retreated to protected land. National forests, mostly.

He squinted, peering out at the forest, wishing he had time to set up his spotting scope. Wouldn't Trudy be pleased to hear he'd seen a Golden-winged Warbler? Maybe it would make up for the awkward goodbye at the Bent N' Dent. He knew she was upset with him, exasperated with how distant he'd been lately. He knew, but he just couldn't tell her why. Not yet.

Speaking of exasperation, Hank had quickly annoyed Andy by sitting up front and steadily offering his terrible navigational skills to tell him where to drive. Laughable, as Hank was forever getting lost even in Stoney Ridge. After Andy filled up the gas tank and they all got back in the minivan, he announced he had decided on a new plan for the rest of the trip. "New plan. Micah sits up front. Hank sits in the far back of the van."

Hank frowned. "Do you have any OTHER plan in mind?"

"Yes," Andy said. "Duct tape." Turned out, Andy Miller liked quiet in his car.

Trudy had been miserable ever since Micah left for Tennessee. She'd felt distracted, irritable, and kept making mistakes as she rang customers up at the store. She'd overcharged six people! Around three o'clock, the bishop suggested that she could go home early. He'd been patient with all her mistakes—each time, she'd had to get him from his office and ask him to sign off on a refund—

but getting sent home early only made her feel worse. Time was ticking and she still had no plan for Wonder Lake. And without a plan, there'd be no way to expect Micah to stay put.

She scootered over to Lost Creek Farm to check on the guests in the guesthouse, but no one was there. She fed Penny's chickens and filled Junco's water bucket. She tossed some hay in his stall and went to get the horse from the pasture to turn him in for the night. The horse came right to her, pushing his big head against her. His way of exchanging hellos. "I know, I know," she said, stroking his velvety nose. "You miss him like I do."

She glanced over Junco's head to the ridge behind the farm. Since she'd left the store early, her mother wouldn't be expecting her for a while. If she hurried, she'd have time to check on the eagle aerie. Maybe an idea might strike her once she was there. She let out a puff of air. She sure hoped so.

As Trudy reached the trail that led up the hill to Wonder Lake, she realized someone had been here today. Small red flags were planted in the ground along the cow trail. Each one was marked with numbers. Red ribbons circled specific trees. She studied the narrow trail, looking up and down the hill. The *road*. That must be what the flags had marked out. Survey stakes. She took a guess that those rising numbers scribbled on the flags were elevation heights. Those trees with the red ribbons—they must be the ones slated to be cut down.

Shivering as if a cold wind blew through, she closed her eyes, unable to swallow the lump of fear that suddenly clotted her throat. This was just what she'd been afraid of. Time was running out.

No! Her eyes flew open. No, she wasn't going to let this happen.

Anger flooded her, pushing away any fears. She was so mad, she pulled up the flags. It was the first time in her life she had broken the law and she hoped she wouldn't be caught and thrown in jail for it. But even the worry of a life sentence didn't stop her from yanking every single little red flag out of the ground, all the way up the hill. She had to figure out how to stop this. The best she could

do was to do, well, the best she could do. Unlike Micah Weaver, at least she'd be doing *something*.

At first, Hank Lapp was hurt that he'd been relocated to the back of the minivan, but then he discovered a rapt audience in Billy. Incredible. Micah wished he'd had a dollar for each time Hank would end a long and rambling story and Billy would say, "Ah, tell it again." Bless that Billy. He could be annoying, but Hank was worse. All day long, he never slept. He just talked.

Edith Lapp was a champion sleeper, except for brief unexpected spurts of life when she would awaken to correct Hank's many inaccuracies. Those were always slightly terrifying moments to Micah, like accidentally flushing Ptarmigans from a bush while in the field. A startling explosion as the Ptarmigans shot into the sky, followed by fussy complaints. That was Edith.

They brought their own food to eat along the way, though Micah didn't have much of an appetite. His mind was stuck on finding Shelley. Late in the day they crossed into Tennessee. In the heavy rain and dying light, Micah couldn't make out much. He glanced at Andy. "Know m-much about Tennessee?"

"Some."

"T-Tell me what you know about M-McNairy C-County." *In particular, do you know where the fire stations are? Police stations? Does the county have an ambulance?* And was there someone in town who knew everybody's business, like Hank did? That was what he wanted to say, but Edith would have wondered why he seemed so interested in disasters and who the local busybody was, and he had no idea how to answer her.

"Never been there."

"I KNOW all KINDS of things about the COUNTY, Micah. ASK me ANYTHING."

Micah rolled his eyes.

Few people had less helpful information in the brainbox than

Hank Lapp. His inventive explanations were legendary. As Hank provided his wildly imaginative descriptions of McNairy County, Micah stopped listening, which was standard for him whenever Hank got rolling on a topic. He started to wonder how quickly he could get the answers on David's long list—his first priority—so that he could spend time hunting for Shelley. The quicker, the better.

Picking up Andy's brother off the Appalachian Trail proved to be a boon. Unlike Andy, his brother was a natural talker, plus he had pent-up words after a month on the AT with little companionship. In a stroke of good fortune, he had spent time in McNairy County and was delighted to share his firsthand knowledge—things you wouldn't learn from a book. "It's a pretty county. Not overly populated—nothing like Memphis and nowhere close to Nashville. Has a bit of interesting history too. Davy Crockett had a law office in McNairy. I believe he also ran a sawmill in town."

"THE FRONTIERSMAN?"

Startled by Hank's volume, the brother turned around to see who belonged to that loud voice. "The very one. There's even a museum about him that's worth going to. More of a log cabin, but worth a visit."

"EDDY! We're GOING!"

Edith half opened her eyes, raptor-like, then closed them, but Micah took note. This was his opening. His opportunity. That field trip might allow him some free time to go exploring on his own.

"Who's Davy Crockett?" Billy asked.

Micah rolled his eyes. He would need to make sure Billy went on that field trip with Hank and Edith.

"And the first of your people came to the county in 1944," Andy's brother continued. "Three families from Mississippi. They'd heard that the First National Bank was selling some land and bought it, sight unseen. Took one look and thought they'd made a big mistake."

"WHY was THAT?"

"The land they'd bought was poorly nourished. But you people, you sure know what to do with poor land. It's in your DNA. Those first Amish, they stuck with the land, fertilized it, rotated crops. Turned it into lush farmland. You'll see for yourself."

Excellent. That piece of information checked off a couple of things on David's list. The land was good, and if not good, it could be made good. That was David's top concern, as most of the Stoney Ridge church were farming families.

Close to midnight, they arrived in Stantonville. David had arranged for them to stay with an Amish family, a distant cousin of someone in the church. The men were to sleep in the barn in sleeping bags laid out on beds of straw, and Edith was provided with a bed in the house. Andy and his brother planned to leave at daybreak to return to Pennsylvania. The men settled in quickly and were soon fast asleep, snoring like buzz saws. All but Micah. He couldn't sleep. So much had happened in such a brief time. His mind was spinning. He felt almost dizzy just thinking about it. Was he really in Tennessee, closing in on Shelley's whereabouts? It was a lot to take in.

Quiet as a mouse, he checked his rented cell phone for messages from Shelley—none, though there were plenty of text party invitations for the Beachy boy. He settled into his sleeping bag but lay awake for a long time, thinking about what tomorrow might hold. Praying it would lead him to Shelley.

Trudy Yoder, Bird-Watching Log

Name of Bird: Pine Siskin

Scientific Name: Spinus pinus

Status: In steep decline

Symbolism: All finches (which includes Pine Siskins) are associated with the passion of Christ, probably because of the European Goldfinch, which has a bright crimson patch on its head. Legend has it that the European Goldfinch tried to remove the crown of thorns from Jesus's head. In doing so, the bird was stained with Christ's blood. (Sooooo touching.)

Date: August 1

Location: Suet feeder at Bent N' Dent

Description: Small bird, brown on top, pale underneath. Tails are short, bills are long and slender. Often mistaken for a sparrow.

Bird Action: Hanging upside down to peck at the suet feeder.

Notes: Clever, intelligent birds. They are quite the nomads. Unlike most other birds, they migrate by day. Their migration stretches to a vast swath of North America. An interesting fact about finches is that they can be trained. That's probably why some people put finches in cages. (Don't even get me started on how I feel about a caged bird!)

The mere sound of a singing Pine Siskin is sure to boost anyone's mood. What's not to love?

11

Micah finally fell asleep so heavily that he missed the departure of Andy Miller and his brother, and would've slept right through breakfast were it not for Billy Blank's pushy rousing. They'd met the farmer last night after arriving. Titus Gingerich was a bespectacled man with a droopy face. Kindly, in a no-nonsense way. He looked like a man who'd spent his life outside, his skin permanently freckled. His coarse, wiry gray beard was untrimmed, reaching to his belly. He told them to come to the back door of the farmhouse for breakfast. He said he wouldn't be there, but his wife would make sure they were well fed.

In the light of day, walking from the barn to the house, Micah realized they were at a Swartzentruber farm. No colored reflectors on the back of the buggy parked in the dirt driveway. No slow-moving vehicle sign. No headlights, no rearview mirror. No turn signals. Not even a front windshield in the buggy. These were people who had truly steered clear of anything that smacked of worldliness—even if there might be some wisdom in it. Yep, Micah thought, looking around the farm, these people clearly refrained from just about everything cheerful or colorful. No flower beds lined the house foundation like they did in Lancaster County homes, no flowers even in pots or window boxes.

But the front door was blue, as pretty as an Eastern Bluebird.

Micah tried to remember why the Swartzentrubers had blue doors. Some said the color blue warded off evil. Others said it meant they had a daughter of marrying age. Most likely, the blue doors were just an old custom. "It's always been that way" was the answer for the majority of Amish traditions.

Inside the house, dark curtains on the windows, pulled to one side, were held up only with a string. A few kerosene lanterns sat on the top of a bureau—no propane gas was permitted inside these homes. A dry sink lined one wall in the kitchen, right under a window. No running water to the sink, of course, because there was no indoor plumbing. Another wall had a board full of nails that held pots and pans and utensils. A wood-burning stove in the center of the room provided heat. A treadle sewing machine sat under the window. The kitchen had a long table, big enough to seat ten people, with stiff wooden chairs on both sides. Most Amish homes Micah had been in had a couch in the kitchen. Not the Swartzentrubers. The most comfortable chair in the entire house was a hickory rocking chair. Black bonnets and black hats hung on wall pegs. Despite the lack of comfort, the house was spotless, and cozy in its own austere way. Well cared for.

Titus Gingerich and his wife, Alice, fit the role. Alice regarded the visitors with the crinkled squint of someone who couldn't see very well. She was a graying woman, small and plump, with an ample bosom, and dark eyes that crinkled at the corners when she smiled. Seemed like she'd had a lot of teeth pulled, which might be one of the reasons she hardly said a word to them. On the other hand, her quiet demeanor reminded Micah of the ultra-conservative Amish church he'd been raised in, over in Big Valley. When around strangers, women and children deferred to men. They acted nearly invisible.

Thankfully, food was not an area of restraint for the Swartzentrubers. Man o' man, could Alice cook. On the large farm table sat a bowl of steaming scrambled eggs, a mountain of crisp bacon slices, a platter of fried scrapple with a bottle of ketchup next to it, a casserole dish of baked oatmeal, a stack of toast from what looked like homemade bread, and strawberry jam that was sweet enough to make your eyeballs roll up into your head. Bottomless cups of coffee too.

Not ten minutes in, Hank said, "THIS has to be the WORLD'S BEST BREAKFAST."

Alice's jack-o'-lantern grin turned into a kind of beam. Edith shot him an aggrieved look.

Hank plowed on, oblivious. "The BEST breakfast I've ever had in my ENTIRE life."

Micah paused, a forkful of scrambled eggs halfway to his mouth, as he realized Hank's plate was already empty and he was going in for seconds. Edith kept a steady gaze on Hank. Micah had to hand it to Edith. She didn't really gripe at Hank in front of others. She just gave him a lot of beady-eyed looks, and yet he didn't seem to catch on to any of them.

"Andy and his brother," Billy said between bites, "better hurry in or there won't be anything left."

"They've been gone for hours," Edith said. "Halfway to Pennsylvania by now."

"But . . . then . . . ," Billy said, his mouth full of scrambled eggs, "how are we gonna get back home?"

Micah tried not to roll his eyes. David had gone over all this information with them. It was then that he realized what it was that bugged him most about Billy Blank. Bugged him even more than his endless chatter about his ridiculous fainting goats, or his persistent attempts to court Trudy despite how many times she said no to him. Billy Blank seemed chronically confused. Permanently muddle-headed.

Edith stepped in to answer Billy, in a slow voice as if she were speaking to a small, dimwitted child. "Since we don't know how long this scouting trip might take, David thought it best to not tie Andy Miller down. Instead, when we're ready to go, we'll let David know and he'll find a way to get us back home."

142

Billy chewed slowly, trying to absorb this alarming discovery. "But"—he swallowed—"I might not be back in time to take Trudy Yoder home from the barbecue this week."

"Definitely not," Edith said.

"I should let her know."

Edith snorted. "You don't think she's already figured that out?"

"No." Billy seemed genuinely concerned.

"T-Trust me," Micah said. "She has."

"Maybe I should call her." He looked to Alice, who gave a sharp shake of her head, like *Not on this farm*. Of course not. These were Swartzentrubers. No community phone.

"Eat up," Micah said. "L-Lots to d-do t-today." Argh. His stutter was worse than ever, especially after only a few hours of sleep. It was always worse when he was tired. Billy went quiet, troubled about missing the barbecue. Micah wondered if there really was something between Billy and Trudy. If so, he questioned Trudy's judgment.

Since the bishop didn't need Trudy at the store until after lunch, she scootered into town. She had to talk to the tattooed woman who worked in the tiny city hall office behind the library. Last night, it had occurred to her that she'd asked the woman all kinds of specific questions but neglected the most important one: "What would it take to stop the construction on Hiram Lehman's hillside?" That was the question she wanted an answer to this morning.

The tattooed woman blinked a few times at the sight of Trudy poking her head into her office. "What would it take? Kiddo, those permits are cut-and-dried. I went through them myself. The contractor who filed them knows the ins and outs of city regulations. I know him. He's a contractor with no imagination whatsoever. His work looks like Josef Stalin's cakeboxes in Moscow."

Cakeboxes in Moscow? Interesting image, but now wasn't the

time to get distracted. "But what would it take? Surely, there have been other times when a project gets stopped."

The woman peered up at the ceiling, as if the answer might be written up there. "Once, there was an endangered bat in an area that was supposed to be a housing development. Construction stopped until the bat could be relocated. Any chance you've got bats up there?"

"Bats?"

"Bats are in big trouble. The white-nose syndrome is wiping them out."

"White nose?"

"Yes. It's a fungus. Devastating the bat population. Already killed millions of them. We need bats, you know."

The phone rang and the woman stopped to answer the call, giving Trudy a few minutes to ponder the plight of bats. She'd never felt particularly empathetic to bats. In fact, they terrified her when they swooped and swirled around in the sky. She'd always thought of them as rats with wings.

The woman hung up the phone and looked at Trudy. "So any endangered bats up at the cow pond?"

"I don't think so."

"So what's the big deal that's got your knickers in a twist?"

"Well, there's an eagle's nest with chicks."

"Couldn't be." The woman waved a hand in the air, dismissing the thought. "Wrong time of year."

"Yes, true. Mostly true. But not always. Nature is full of surprises."

The woman stilled. Without moving an inch, her eyeballs lifted in interest. "Go on."

"There's a hawk chick in this eagle's nest, right along with two eaglets. The hawk thinks it's an eagle."

"Not possible."

"It's true. It's not an eaglet. It's a hawk chick."

"A hawk chick is surviving in an eagle's nest?" She shook her head in disbelief. "If there is something in that nest, then it was probably just brought in for a midnight snack."

"The parents keep feeding it. I've been watching the nest every day now for over two weeks. Every single day."

The woman leaned back in her chair, arms folded against her chest, clearly considering the validity of the story. Or maybe . . . the credibility of the storyteller.

Progress! Trudy was pleased. This conversation had taken a sudden uplift. "Do you like to go birding?"

That question evoked a loud snort. "Kiddo, you're looking at the president of the local Audubon Society."

Trudy's eyes slid down the woman's sleeve tattoos. Birds! They were *all* bird tattoos. How'd she miss *that*?! "Maybe . . . you've heard of Ben Zook."

Everything was silent for three seconds while the woman fixed her eyes on Trudy. "You know Ben Zook? The guy who writes about rare birds?"

"I do. I know him well."

"Has he seen your hawklet?"

"Well, no. He's in Canada right now. But Micah Weaver has seen it." She saw a little zap of shock in the woman's eyes the very second the recognition hit her. A little thrill of satisfaction swirled through Trudy.

"The Amish birder?"

Trudy confirmed with a nod. "That's him. Micah Weaver the field guide." *The most amazing twitcher in all of Pennsylvania.*

"You know him? The guy who makes me wait two long days for the mail to deliver his Christmas Bird Count results while the rest of the county emails them in a split second?"

"That's him."

The woman's eyes narrowed. "How well do you know him?"

"He's . . . my friend." *More than a friend. He's my future husband.* She took in a deep breath. *I hope.*

Her eyes flickered to her desktop. "So . . . is he as good as his rep?"

"Better."

The woman's sharp gaze brushed Trudy, up and down, side to side. "You're *sure* there's a hawklet in the eagle's nest? Absolutely, positively sure? It's a highly improbable story."

"I know. But it's true."

"And Micah Weaver has confirmed this sighting?"

Trudy nearly didn't want to dignify that with a response. Why wasn't her claim enough to satisfy this woman? "Yes. Of course." She gave her a cool nod. "He's the one who showed me."

She leaned back in her chair and clasped her hands behind her neck, and it was then Trudy noticed a row of quail tattoos lining the inside of her arms, starting with two adults and ending with five tiny babies. "Maybe we can talk it up to the newspaper. See if they'll get a photographer out there. This would make a great human-interest story."

Again, she used the *we* pronoun. Super sweet. Trudy appreciated the suggestion, but it wasn't enough. "Actually, I'm looking for a way to stop the construction altogether." Some more effective way than just pulling up the survey stakes.

The woman raised her fist in the air like she was punching it. "Civil disobedience! It's the only way to bring about change. Protests and marches. We could have a sit-in at city hall." Her gaze swept the small windowless room. "Well, maybe not that."

Definitely not that. Trudy would end up on the sinner's bench if she were to do something so bold and controversial as that. The church discouraged its members from getting involved in worldly affairs.

But this lady was on a roll. Her eyes lit up with fire and her whole body seemed poised for action. "We'll call it the 'Save Wander Lake!' campaign."

"Wonder. We call it Wonder Lake."

The woman slapped her palms on her desk. "We have to get the local people riled up!"

"Most of the local people who live near Wonder Lake are Amish."

"So?"

"So we don't get riled up."

The woman frowned. "I suppose not. But if we got enough push-back from the newspaper article, it might put the construction project on ice."

"On ice . . . as in . . . for good?"

"Well, no. Probably only until the chicks fledge the nest. But it could buy us some time."

Time was good, Trudy thought, but she needed more than just time.

The woman sat forward intently, her small eyes zeroing in on Trudy. "So what kind of hawk is it?"

Trudy lifted her palms in the air. "The chick is still too small to identify."

The woman whirled around and grabbed a pair of binoculars hanging off the back of her chair. "Not too small if you happen to be the leading expert on raptors for Lancaster County."

"Yes, but Micah is out of town right now. I'm not sure when he'll be back."

She narrowed her eyes. "I was talking about *me*." She turned off her computer, jumped to her feet, and snapped off the overhead light. As she marched out the door, she said, "Come on, kiddo. What are you waiting for? Let's go check out this eagle's nest."

"Now?"

"No time like the present." Her footsteps pounded down the path to the parking lot.

At last! Trudy had someone interested in the plight of Wonder Lake. Someone was finally willing to help.

A car drove up the driveway and Micah was pretty sure to whom it belonged. David had scheduled time for the team to drive around with a real estate agent, Rodney Hertzler. Micah excused himself to go meet him out front. As Rodney emerged from the car, Micah was struck first by his height—he must've been half past six feet tall. Long and lean, even his face was all points—sharp chin, long nose. "Welcome to Paradise," he said, as he shook Micah's hand.

Before Micah could respond, Hank, Edith, and Billy joined them. Rodney repeated his "Welcome to Paradise" phrase to each one, pumping hands with a vigor. "We have the makings of another flawless day in Stantonville. Abundant sunshine. Invigorating, minty-clean air."

Hank howled at that. Titus and Alice Gingerich were pig farmers. When the wind blew from the direction where the pigs were kept, the sour smell brought tears to your eyes.

Rodney opened the car doors to usher them in. "Let's be off." Business was on his mind. "An ideal piece of property just went up on the market this last weekend." Rodney's car bumped and jiggled down the dirt driveway. "Huge farm. You could subdivide it and still have plenty of land for everyone."

Edith sat in the front seat and peppered Rodney with questions that were important to her, most of which Micah thought were very low on the priority list of questions. Things like, "Where's the closest fabric store?" and "Is there a donut shop in Stantonville?" But at least she didn't talk nonstop like Hank would've. She asked questions, and Micah was able to get an idea of what Stantonville was made up of. Not much, he quickly realized.

"What about chiropractors?" Edith asked.

Micah leaned forward in the car, eager to hear the answer.

"There's a clinic with a chiropractor," Rodney said.

"That's GREAT news! Isn't it, EDDY? Eddy has a DREADFUL pain in her backside. TROUBLES her to no end."

Edith turned around to glare at Hank, with a look that said, *You're the pain in my backside.* Micah had no doubt.

Rodney didn't pay Hank any mind. "For more serious medical procedures, you'd have to go to Hardin Medical."

Edith looked at him. "How far is that?"

"You came through Adamsville. Only eight miles or so from there."

"What do people do in Stantonville?"

"Amish folk? Titus farms pigs. Alice makes baskets. Over in Ethridge, there's the Amish Welcome Center and Museum. They offer wagon tours."

Hank guffawed. "SOUNDS like EVERY DAY for us. Right, Eddy?"

Rodney ignored him. "The Center has a gift shop full of locally made products. All Amish."

"Like w-what?" Micah said from the back of the car.

"Furniture, candles, soaps. I bought my wife a real nice bird-house there."

"So," Micah said, "there's g-good b-birding here?"

Billy gave him that confounded expression. "I'm pretty sure that birds are everywhere. Aren't they?"

Micah cringed.

"But is there room for newcomers?" Edith said. "Are there enough tourists coming through to support more Amish crafts? Or would a new Amish church in the area create too much competition?"

Way to go, Edith. Way to go. *These* were the kinds of questions that David needed answers to. The last thing David wanted to do was to arrive and put the squeeze on a church, the way the Beachy church did to Stoney Ridge. He told them to look carefully for signs of growth and expansion. Room to thrive, he called it.

"This part of Tennessee is booming. Booming, I tell you!" Rodney's long arm stretched wide, all the way out the window, to make his point.

"According to the *Sugarcreek Budget*," Edith said, peering at him over her spectacles, "the town of Stantonville declined in population from the 2000 census to the 2010 census."

Rodney held a finger in the air. "I meant to say, we're poised for a boom. Like Ethridge was, a while back. Ethridge is running out of room. It's gotten harder and harder to find land. The tourist market is flooded over there. That's why people should be heading out here. I'd put my money on Stantonville."

"No wonder, then," Edith said. "The *Sugarcreek Budget* reports that Ethridge is the largest Amish settlement in the south. Top twentieth in the nation."

Micah glanced at Rodney to see if he was annoyed by Edith's constant input. Her sole news source was the *Sugarcreek Budget*. She quoted it with great reverence, as if it came in a close second to the Holy Book.

But Rodney hardly paid her any mind. "Did I tell you about the Plowboy Produce Auctions over in Ethridge? People come from more than three hundred miles for these auctions."

"What's getting sold?"

"Produce, three times a week, April through October. Straight from the field to the auction."

Edith turned in the car. "Micah, are you taking this down? Nathan will want to know about this."

He was. He held up a pad of paper and pencil for her to see.

"In the spring and fall," Rodney continued, "they hold consignment auctions. Furniture, farm equipment, buggies, horses, you name it." He lifted a hand in the air and nearly hit Edith. "And 90 percent of what gets sold is from the Amish."

"But is there room for more Amish?" Edith said.

"Maybe not in Ethridge, but there sure is room for you in Stantonville. We're on our way to become the Lancaster of Tennessee. Just a day trip out of Nashville, you know. Your church is welcomed and wanted." Rodney turned into a long, winding gravel driveway. When it came to an end, he stopped the car and hopped out. Everyone followed his lead. "Wonderful, isn't it?" Rodney said, waving his arms as if he had just conjured everything up.

In every direction were fields of waist-high weeds. A sea of weeds.

"WHAT are we supposed to be LOOKING AT?" Hank said.

Rodney turned, a surprised look on his face, as if he couldn't believe they didn't see what he saw. "This! It's over two thousand acres of farmland, just waiting to be developed." He looked at Micah. "It's going to be snatched up soon, so you need to call that bishop of yours and put in an offer. Stat."

"WHAT does STAT mean?"

Rodney frowned at Hank. "Immediately."

"Sounds good to me," Billy clapped his hands, pleased.

"ME TOO! We did what we CAME here to do."

"Two thousand acres could be divided up by the whole church," Billy said. "It would be about . . . let's see . . . if you want seventy acres per family . . ." Confusion covered his face.

"I LIKE the way your MIND works, son. But NOT every family in our church FARMS. Me and EDDY, for example. WE only want FIVE ACRES."

Now Billy was completely baffled. He gave up trying to divide the land. "Seems like there's plenty to go around."

"IT SURE DOES." Hank couldn't be more satisfied. "TIME to give DAVID a call."

Rodney beamed. "Excellent."

"N-Not so fast," Micah said.

"Micah's absolutely right." Edith nodded. "We need to see a whole lot more of this area than just one farm. This is a big decision for our church. We want to see every nook and cranny of this county before we call David with our findings."

Rodney's sharp eyebrows shot up. "The whole county?"

She nodded. "The whole kit and caboodle. Every square inch."

Rodney let out a long sigh of disappointment. "Fine. Get in the car."

Trudy Yoder, Bird-Watching Log

Name of Bird: Gray Catbird

Scientific Name: <u>Dumetella carolinensis</u>

Symbolism: Gray Catbirds (part of the Mockingbird family) aren't mentioned specifically in the Bible, but many Christians consider them a symbol of God's mercy and compassion.

Status: Low concern

Date: July 28

Location: Dok Stoltzfus's office

Description: Small gray bird with a black cap, rusty red feathers.

Bird Action: Calling out its scratchy meow sound from under a huge hydrangea bush. I only noticed because it sounded just like a cat.

Notes: Unlike their bolder mockingbird cousins, which sing on perches out in the open, catbirds stay under cover. Generally harmless, they are fiercely protective of their nests and defend them aggressively. Because catbirds frequently imitate so many other vocalizations (like the meowing of a cat!), they aren't considered to have a true voice. To me, any bird that can imitate the sound of its number one predator should not be underestimated.

12

Micah was starting to have a new appreciation for Edith Lapp. Unlike her husband Hank, she stayed focused. She didn't let Real Estate Rodney push them around, and he would've if he could've. He was a salesman hungry to seal the deal.

Micah was just about to follow behind Billy to get in the back seat of Rodney's car when he heard a siren. One foot in the car, he spun to face Rodney. "Fire or hospital?" No stutter. *Nice.*

Squinting, Rodney lifted his chin, as if straining to listen for the sound. "That siren is from our fire truck. We have an impressive fire station. Best in the state."

Hank poked his head out of the car window. "BEST in the ENTIRE STATE?"

Rodney frowned. "Well, best in this part of the state, anyway." He turned to Micah. "Why does he shout?"

Micah lifted his shoulders in a shrug. Who knew why Hank shouted all the time?

"My mother's a little hard of hearing too," Rodney said.

"I can hear JUST FINE," Hank said, half leaning out the window.

Micah listened to the siren as it grew louder, then as it faded.

It wasn't the same sound that he had heard in the background of Shelley's phone messages. "Hospitals?"

"Not in Stantonville. Closest hospital would be Hardin Medical. Best in the state. Serves the whole county."

Micah settled into the car and wrote that information down in the notebook David had given to him.

The town of Stantonville, Micah soon learned, had a long way to go before it would be the Lancaster of Tennessee. It was made up of State Route 224 linking Adamsville to Stantonville. Far from anywhere, a blink-and-you-miss-it kind of town. Nothing fancy but curiously likable.

Commercially, there wasn't much, but that wouldn't be a problem for David, as the church members were fairly self-sufficient. Plus, there was a Walmart Supercenter in Adamsville, Rodney said with great pride, to fill in the gaps.

The more Micah saw of Stantonville, the more he thought this town might just check all of David's boxes. Fairly flat farmland, with evidence of good soil. Micah saw field after field of Amish farmers leading a team of horses to bring down corn. The soil had a slight orange tinge to it. Minerals? Micah wasn't sure which ones. Nathan would know. Micah wrote it all down on his note pad, everything he could think of that David might find of interest.

Even the weather seemed conducive for farming—four seasons, Rodney said, but fairly mild ones. That would mean a long growing season.

And tourism, Rodney assured them, would be welcomed. That, Micah knew, was of concern to David because these Amish were on the conservative side of conservative. The Schwartzentrubers sold goods to outsiders but only through small kiosks on their farms. Driving through the county roads, he saw countless handwritten signs of items to sell that indicated an Amish household, each one adding that telltale *No Sunday Sales*. Furniture, cookies, breads, jams, honey, even Queen Bees. Many in the church of Stoney Ridge relied on those kinds of cottage industries to bring in extra cash, including Micah with his field guiding business.

The Plowboy Produce Auction in nearby Ethridge would be a boon. As Rodney said, Stantonville was only a few hours' drive from both Nashville and Memphis. The cities were just starting to tap into the produce of central Tennessee. "Opportunities await!" Rodney said, waving his long arms in the air again. Micah could practically hear Nathan Yoder's enthusiasm for supplying that kind of ready market with his fine organic produce.

Only one thing doused Micah's enthusiasm for Stantonville. Shelley clearly wasn't here. The distant alarm sounds he heard in the background of her phone calls were not to be found in McNairy County.

Trudy trotted behind the tattooed woman to her car—a rusted Volkswagen bus—and climbed into the back seat because the passenger seat next to the driver was missing. Completely gone. The interior of the car was as bad as the exterior. Not only messy, with seat cushions so torn in places that you could see the wire springs underneath, but it had an odd smell, a combination of rotten fish and old socks. The Volkswagen bus shuddered and coughed before roaring to life. It lurched forward . . . and suddenly they were zooming through the streets of Stoney Ridge and out toward the countryside like two women on a mission, which they were.

Exciting! Trudy's stomach, though, felt as if she were on a roller coaster. She wasn't used to moving at such a fast speed. Buggies plodded. This woman drove like she talked—speeding fast, two-wheeled corners, abrupt stops, unrepeatable words shouted at slow-moving cars. The Volkswagen bus turned the final corner that led to Lost Creek Farm and nearly rammed right up against the back of a bulldozer as it moved slowly up the road. "Oh no," Trudy said. "No, no, no! They're already starting."

The tattooed woman gunned the engine and passed the bulldozer.

Trudy hung on to the tattered seat cushion for dear life. She yelled, "Shortcut!" and lifted a hand to point out the driveway to Lost Creek Farm, then quickly grasped the seat again as the woman made a sharp right turn.

At the top of the driveway, near the guesthouse, she slammed on the brakes and turned off the engine, which took a few shuddering gasps before it died. "Let's make tracks before the machines of doom arrive." She hopped out of the car and Trudy followed. "Where to?"

Oh, right. Of course! While the tattooed woman seemed to act as if she knew just about everything there was to know, she had no idea of Wonder Lake's whereabouts. Trudy went ahead of her to start up the path to the trail, hoping it wasn't too steep a climb for the woman. She needn't have worried. They'd gone only halfway up when the woman overtook her and Trudy had to hurry to keep up. It wasn't long before they stood on the resting rock overlooking the pond.

The woman huffed, casting a disapproving glance at Trudy. "Wonder Lake, indeed."

True. Definitely true. From the disappointed look on her face, Trudy knew the pond didn't seem like much to crow about. Certainly nothing to raise up the hackles of city hall. Suddenly nervous, Trudy started chattering. "We call it Wonder Lake because of the birds. All kinds have made it a nesting site."

"Rarities?"

"I don't think Micah's ever spotted any rarities up here. I know I haven't. But still, it's a . . . wonder to us. We just love this place. Penny, Ben, Micah, Birdy, me. We come up here all the time."

The woman ignored her. She was peering through her binoculars at the eagle aerie, silently watching the nest's activities. The father eagle was absent, but the mother eagle was in the nest, her head tucked. There was no sign of the chicks. Not eaglets, not hawklets. Trudy squinted, hoping the hawk was still there. Hoping the woman believed her, hoping she could see the beauty

156

of Wonder Lake. After all, there was life everywhere—buzzing insects, twittering birds, scampering chipmunks. And today's weather was ideal.

Trudy knew this could be a long wait, but she wasn't sure if the tattooed woman knew just how long it could be. Birding required patience. "I don't think I ever introduced myself. My name is Trudy Yoder."

"Shhh."

"I don't know your name."

No answer.

"Wonder Lake might not seem like much—"

"Hush. Birders should be silent."

Well, Trudy knew *that*. She was no novice. She was starting to understand why this woman had been transferred from the county office. She barked at Trudy as if she were three-quarters stupid. All Trudy had been trying to tell her was that you had to squint pretty hard to get any notion of the tranquil beauty that existed at Wonder Lake during springtime.

It wasn't at its best right now. In late summer, especially this year with the drought they'd been experiencing, the creek that rolled lazily through the narrow valley to feed the pond had been reduced to half its normal size. If rain didn't come soon, the pond would become stagnant. Trudy could already see algae growing along some of the pond's edges. The velvet-green hills that notched the small valley like a V were now brown. No, Wonder Lake wasn't much to look at right now.

But in the spring, it looked magical. During spring migration, when birds were in such a hurry to find mates and make nests, they could enjoy respite and nourishment here before continuing their long journey north. It was part of the miracle of this forgotten cow pond. That was all she was trying to say.

"Aha," the woman said.

Trudy turned and saw the father eagle soaring toward the nest with an unlucky rat in its talons. The mother eagle hopped up to sit on the edge of the nest, and that action seemed to signal to the chicks that a meal was arriving. Two little heads popped up.

Where was the hawk chick?

A minute passed, then another. And another.

Trudy glanced nervously at the tattooed woman, whose attention remained riveted on the nest. "Sometimes, I've noticed the hawk chick sits right underneath the eaglets, like it's waiting for leftovers."

The woman ignored her.

Trudy turned back to watch the nest, wishing she'd thought to bring her own binoculars, or had stopped by Micah's repair shop to borrow his spotting scope. She squinted, but there wasn't much she could make out with the naked eye. *Oh hawk chick, where are you?* It was there last night. *Please, please be there.* If that chick was gone, then Wonder Lake's fate would be sealed. Trudy felt panic creeping up in her stomach. Her breathing felt wrong. Her heart was going to explode. *Please, chick, please be there.*

A high-pitched little gasp escaped from the woman's throat. "I see it."

Trudy's eyes went wide. "Really?" It came out in a squeak.

"Clear as day. Right between the two eaglets. The mother is tearing the rat apart and feeding it to each one. Including the imposter." Then she stilled. "Extraordinary."

"I know! It's pretty amazing." Trudy let out a happy sigh, colossally relieved. "Wouldn't it be wonderful if birds could talk? I'd love to know how the chick got there in the first place."

No response.

"Can you identify the chick? I just couldn't find anything distinctive about it other than gray fuzz, which is pretty much what all hawk chicks look like."

A sharp "Shhh."

Not fair! So the woman could talk . . . but Trudy couldn't? So not fair. Yet she didn't say another word. There was something slightly terrifying about the tattooed woman. She stared at the

158

aerie through her binoculars until the rat was completely disposed of and the father eagle flew off, in search of more provisions. The nest quieted down and the heads of the chicks disappeared. Only then did the woman drop her bins. She turned to Trudy. "No rarities, huh?"

"None."

"So this renowned Micah Weaver couldn't identify this hawk chick?"

"No."

A smile filled the woman's face—but not a happy smile. A sly smile. It looked odd. A little crooked. "Do you have any idea what this means?"

Was she serious? Trudy had spent every possible minute here since Micah had first shown it to her. "Um, I do. It's kind of a miracle that a hawk is being raised by eagle parents. Even you said it was an incredible human-interest story."

The woman looked at her. "Didn't you notice the color of its eyes?"

"Eyes?"

"Kiddo, you have no idea what you're doing, do you?" With that, she started down the hill, striding like a general off to the battlefield.

What did *that* mean? Baffled, Trudy watched the tattooed woman march off. Snapping into action, she hurried down the path to catch up. What? What had she missed?

When the tattooed woman arrived down on the road where the bulldozer had parked, she marched right over to the two construction workers standing in front of the big yellow machine, studying building plans. "Turn that dozer around and take it home, boys."

One worker ignored her, the other barely glanced at her.

The woman didn't like being ignored. She grabbed their plans. "Hey!" one said. The other said, "Lady, we've got the permits."

"That was before an endangered species was found on the site."

The construction workers exchanged a long look. "You've *got* to be kidding."

"Nope. There's a Northern Goshawk chick in an eagle's nest up there."

Trudy's eyes went wide. Seriously? A Northern Goshawk? A super secretive bird, found usually in mature forests. And . . . recently declared an endangered species in Pennsylvania! A wave of jitters flooded her at the thought of telling Micah. She couldn't wait to tell him.

"A Northern *what*?" The workers said it in unison, as if they'd rehearsed the line.

The woman shook her head, as if she could barely tolerate such ignorance. "All you need to know is that all permits are revoked until further notice."

One worker pushed the tip of his hard hat back to scowl at her. "Says who?"

"Says the current head of the Stoney Ridge city planning department." She gave another one of her sly smiles. "And the future mayor of Stoney Ridge." Under her breath, she whispered to Trudy, "I knew there was a reason I was transferred to this backwater, squat village. This town needs me. Desperately."

Real Estate Rodney gave the team thirty minutes in a Dollar Tree store to wander to their hearts' content, which probably meant Edith had asked him for time to shop. Rodney stayed in the car to check his phone messages, which reminded Micah to check messages on his borrowed cell phone. He'd kept it off so the battery wouldn't wear down and hadn't had a chance to turn it back on, not with Billy as his constant shadow. As soon as Billy and Hank went off to find the men's room, and Edith got absorbed in the greeting cards aisle, he backtracked out of the store and went around back. As soon as he turned on the cell, it started bombarding him with texts and voicemails, all intended for the

160

Beachy boy. He scrolled through recent calls to see if any were from Tennessee. Nothing. But then he saw one that had an unknown caller. He pressed on the voice mail and listened: "Micah, is this your number? It's me. Shelley. Things are getting worse, Micah. I'm terrified. I've got to get out of here. I need your help NOW. I don't know how much longer I can stand this."

Micah's heart started pounding. He had to get to Shelley. He pressed the callback number and held his breath as it rang. And rang. Finally, someone answered. "Yellow House Project."

Micah cleared his throat. "Sh-Shelley Yoder. I'm l-looking for Sh-Shelley Yoder."

There was a long silence. "I'm sorry. There's no one here by that name. You must have the wrong number." Click.

He went back to the car and asked Rodney if he knew of a place called The Yellow House Project. Rodney gave him a strange, upraising look. "Why are you asking?"

"Just w-wondered," Micah said.

Rodney hesitated, then looked away. "Never heard of it."

A jolt went through Micah. On her voice message, Shelley had said *the* yellow house. Not *a* yellow house. How'd he miss *that*?

Trudy Yoder, Bird-Watching Log

Name of Bird: Northern Goshawk

Scientific Name: Accipiter gentilis

Symbolism: Hawks are mentioned several times in Scripture. They're considered to be a symbol of wisdom.

Status: Endangered in Pennsylvania (which is good news, actually, because now they are protected. Very, very good news!)

Date: September 12

Location: Wonder Lake

Description: Adorable gray fuzzy chick (which will soon grow into a terror-striking raptor with talons as big and sharp as a bear's claws).

Bird Action: Gulping down the leftovers of a rodent or fish as morsels dropped from its adopted eaglet siblings' beaks.

Notes: The largest of the hawk species, this powerful raptor has few predators. They have reddish-orange eyes with a white stripe above them. (Eerie!) Hooked beak and sharp talons make this hawk perfectly designed to kill small animals.

It can reach a speed of 61 miles per hour. (That is FAST.)

Solitary birds except during breeding season, when pairs will often mate long term.

SUZANNE WOODS FISHER

Goshawks can become very aggressive and territorial, especially of its brood. Females are not afraid of clashing with anything that draws close to the nest, including people. They will attack. Seriously. Stay far, far away.

163

13

Micah rolled out his sleeping bag in the barn to prepare for bed. Fatigue had finally caught up with him and he had trouble keeping his eyes open during Alice's substantial supper. He felt his cell phone buzzing in his pocket and spun around to check the caller ID without Hank or Billy noticing. The phone had been vibrating all day long with calls and texts for the Beachy boy. This time, he recognized it as the number Shelley had called from. He bolted outside, running around the edge of the barn, swiping the screen desperately to answer before she hung up. "Shelley?"

"Micah? Have you come for me?"

He melted. The sound of Shelley's breathy voice had always gotten to him. "Sh-Shelley, w-where are you?" He winced. *Stupid stutter!*

"Where are *you?*"

"I'm here. In T-Tennessee. I'm t-trying t-to f-find you."

"I've been waiting for you! You've got to get me out of here. Micah. I can't stand it anymore!"

"What's h-happened?"

"Jack Spencer, that's what happened. He's the one who promised to help me launch my singing career. He's the one who talked me into leaving my family to run away to Nashville. And next thing I know, he's got me locked away in an insane asylum!"

"Y-Yellow House P-Project?"

"Yes! That's the one! Micah, you've got to get me out. Please, come as quickly as you can!" Some commotion occurred in the background—the sound of a dog barking frantically—and she hung up.

Micah stared at the phone, trying to make sense of everything.

Jack Spencer. The day Shelley had run away from home, Trudy had told him about this guy. No details, no name, only that they'd been seeing each other on the sly, Trudy had said. He had gotten Shelley some singing gigs in bars in Lancaster. Micah wished he could talk to Trudy, to let her know that he was getting so close to finding Shelley. But he couldn't tell her. Not for Shelley's sake, not for Trudy's sake. Not for his sake. He didn't want to involve anyone in this. Not yet.

"Micah?" Billy Blank had come looking for him. "You okay?"

"Yeah, yeah," Micah said, jamming the cell phone in his pocket.

"I came out to find a bush to water and thought I heard you talking to someone."

Micah pointed to a stand of trees that lined the road. "Owls."

"Owls?"

One hooted, and another answered back, as if they knew to corroborate Micah's story.

"See?" Billy said, giving him a thump on the shoulder. "Did I not tell you? Birds are everywhere." He laughed, like he had made a great joke. "I'm sure glad I came on this trip with you. Hasn't it been an adventure? Couldn't be better."

Was he for real? "Billy, does it ever occur to you that it's not normal to always be so happy?" Micah regretted the words even as he spoke them. Too harsh.

Billy studied him for a long moment. "I'm not always happy, Micah." He let out a long-suffering sigh. "I called Trudy today. I found a pay phone outside the Dollar Tree and called her at the

Bent N' Dent. I told her I didn't think I'd be back in time to take her home from the barbecue. You know what she said?"

"What?"

"She said, 'What barbecue?'" He let out another deep sigh. "She didn't even remember. Then she said that while I'm very nice, she's not interested in me. Not interested at all. She repeated it twice."

Good for Trudy. Good for her for being straight with Billy Blank. Because the more Micah got to know him, the more he'd been wondering what was wrong with Trudy that she would find this guy appealing.

"So I'm not always happy." But then a smile broke through, like the sun coming out from behind a cloud. "This trip sure came at a good time. Lots to keep my brain distracted."

Billy went off to find a bush. Micah watched him, thinking that he must have a very small brain if a change of scenery was all it took to forget someone.

Micah turned to head back to the barn. His fatigue had vanished, he felt ready for anything. He couldn't believe the suddenness with which everything had changed. He'd found her! He had actually found Shelley Yoder.

Tomorrow, somehow, some way, he would get Shelley out of that terrible place.

The next day, after a full morning with Rodney of touring farms for sale, Edith announced she wasn't feeling well and needed to return to Alice and Titus's farm, pronto.

"She's feeling LAID LOW by some BAD CLAMS," Hank volunteered. Edith elbowed him and he yelped in pain.

"Clams?" Billy said. "We didn't have any clams, did we?"

Edith let out a long-suffering sigh. Micah wasn't going to touch that one.

Rodney turned the car around and drove them back to the Gingeriches'. He didn't offer to show any more properties to Micah and Billy, probably thinking they were too young for decision-making. Not worth his time.

Not true. But, for now, that suited Micah just fine.

Billy and Hank followed Edith into the farmhouse, hoping for lunch, but Micah passed, saying he wanted to go birding. Walking along the road, binoculars hanging around his neck, he was feeling pretty good about slipping away without telling a lie. As valuable as the cell phone was to him, he didn't like that feeling of crossing the line. Too hard on the conscience.

He heard the sound of a car and turned to see a cloud of dust come his way—an old pickup truck, moving down the road at great speed. As it approached, he put his thumb out, and to his surprise, it lurched to a hard stop. A man with a cowboy hat on stuck his head out the window. "Where to?"

"Y-Yellow House P-Project."

"The nuthouse?" He gave Micah a serious head-to-toe onceover. "In that case, hop in the back."

As Micah scrambled into the bed of the pickup truck, he saw Billy Blank running toward the truck at full speed. "Hold it! I'm coming too!" and he dove into the bed of the truck.

There was no time to get Billy out of the truck and send him back to the barn. The cowboy stepped on the gas pedal and the truck shot out on the bounciest, most terrifying ride Micah had ever been on. He and Billy held on for dear life in the open back, leaning first this way, then that. The cowboy sped down the country roads with reckless zest, bouncing over potholes with such force that Micah and Billy were thrown inches into the air. The ride brought up a memory of a roller coaster Micah had once ridden on at the state fair. When the ride had finally ended, he had thrown up. That was exactly how Micah felt now. The cowboy screeched to a stop and pointed an arm down a long one-lane road. "Nuthouse is that way. Good luck, boys."

They climbed out as quickly as they could, with unsteady legs. Brushing themselves off, Billy looked at Micah in his usual muddledheaded way. He rubbed his nose with a knuckle. "All this way just to buy nuts?"

The two of them stared at the pickup truck zooming off down the road, a cloud of dust in its wake. "That was quite a ride," Billy said. "Reminded me of sledding down Dead Man's Hill."

"Billy, g-go back to Alice's."

"I'd rather go birding with you."

"I g-got something I got to d-do."

"I figured that's why you left. That's why I came. David wants me to look for ways to help. To be watching and looking, he said. Find opportunities to be helpful to Micah. Listen to Micah. He told me that very thing. Many, many times." He patted his pants. "He even made me write it on an index card to keep in my pocket."

"It's s-something I n-need to do alone."

"Not a good idea," Billy said, shaking his head woefully. "We're a team. The bishop said so. We have to work together. What's best for the church is best for us."

As annoying as Billy was—and he really, really was—this kind of blind devotion was beyond Micah. The way he talked about Trudy, for instance. Like he regarded her in a special tone of awe. It bugged Micah. Billy bugged him.

And right now, Micah would like to shake him but couldn't figure out how to do it. Billy had Velcroed himself to Micah. How was he going to scope out The Yellow House Project with Billy talking nonstop, asking pointless questions? He took off his hat and raked a hand through his hair, trying to think of a way out of this conundrum.

Just then a small car drove by and slowed down. A young woman sat behind the wheel and did a double take when she caught a glimpse of Billy waving to her. She stopped the car and unrolled the window. A tiny white dog was on her lap. "Are you lost?"

"We're looking for the nuthouse," Billy said. "My friend here wants to buy nuts."

Micah winced, the young woman giggled, and Billy didn't even crack a smile. She mistook Billy's literalness for a joke. "I'm the receptionist for the nuthouse. It's just down the road." The way she smiled at Billy, Micah could tell she thought he was schee. *Handsome.*

"Can I give you a lift?" She hadn't stopped smiling at Billy, who kept smiling back at her. She probably thought he was flirting, but Micah knew better. Billy acted the same way toward everyone, like it just made his day to see you. Like seeing you was even better than Alice Gingerich's blueberry pancakes . . . and that was saying a lot. Grudgingly, Micah had to admit that was a quality to admire. He preferred the company of birds to most people.

"Sure, we'd love a lift," Billy said, forgetting to ask Micah. What happened to being a team? What happened to David's orders to listen to Micah? Billy hopped in the passenger seat, leaving the back seat to Micah and the small dog, which had jumped over the console and was now in Micah's lap. It stared at him with beady little eyes. Ugly, ugly, ugly dog. And it had terrible breath.

"I'm Billy Blank. My friend in the back seat, his name is Micah Weaver."

But the young woman didn't care who sat in the back seat. She only had eyes for Billy. Big, blinking eyes. "My name is Julianne. Friends call me Jules."

"Well, we hope you'll consider us your friends, Jules." Billy smiled, revealing those two big, irresistible dimples, and Julianne giggled, and Micah felt as if he'd just been handed a gift from Above. *This* was how he was going to get into The Yellow House Project. Billy Blank wasn't good for much, but from a girl's point of view, Micah supposed being schee was coming in as an asset.

On Wednesday, Trudy wasn't needed at the store until midafternoon, so she spent a good part of her day at Lost Creek Farm. She checked out the guests, cleaned up after them, and got the guesthouse ready for the next booking. Then she fed the chickens, refilled the bird feeders, and made sure Junco had water in his bucket in the pasture. After all that, she knew she needed a shower before she went to work.

As she scootered toward home, her mind kept sifting through yesterday's surprising turn of events with the tattooed woman. There were two ways, she concluded, to look at this situation. One was that Trudy had used entirely legal means to stop the construction of the Beachy church, and she had used it in an indirect method. The indirect method was acceptable for the Plain People, if not downright common. People misunderstood the Plain People, assuming they were passive. Not so. You just had to find a way *around* things.

Hadn't David Stoltzfus done something similar when he encouraged the town of Stoney Ridge to start a local farmers' market? And then he did it again when he strongly advocated Nathan Yoder to be the market manager. Trudy's father, among others, had been critical of David for getting too involved in town politics. He had overstepped, her father had said, but the Stoney Ridge Farmers' Market ended up benefiting everyone. Even Trudy's father had come around. This last summer, he rented a booth at the market to sell excess garden produce.

But there was a second way to look at the situation. This one—which, in Trudy's head, eerily resembled her father's voice—was that she had gone too far. Way, way, way too far. By visiting city hall, by taking the tattooed woman out to Wonder Lake, she had put something in motion that the Plain People tried to avoid. And she couldn't exactly disagree with that, because she was involved. Heavily involved.

As she scootered up the driveway, she saw that her dad's buggy was gone. She set her scooter against the house, then went up the porch steps and reached for the door handle, pausing. This moment was always a sad one for her. A reminder that her family was not like other families in their church. Not the kind of family she wished they were.

"Mom?" Trudy looked around the downstairs for her mother,

hoping she might be engaged in a task. But she knew better. Her mother would be sitting on a rocking chair in Shelley's darkened bedroom. Her mother did this whenever her dad was away from the farm.

Trudy went upstairs and leaned against the doorjamb. The room looked exactly like it did on the morning Shelley ran away. Even the bed was left unmade. Her mother wouldn't let Trudy or her dad touch a single thing in it. "She'll be back," her mother would say, if Trudy ever said something about it, even something small like offering to wash the sheets. "I want everything left as it is for when she comes back."

Trudy hoped her mother was right about Shelley, but she doubted it. Her sister hadn't contacted them since she left—not to let them know she was all right, nor where she was living. Or that she missed them. Nothing. But that was Shelley.

The two sisters were not even three years apart, but they'd never been close. Not the way most sisters seemed to be. It was like Shelley was always lost in her own world. "She's very special," her mother would say.

Trudy knew there were probably other terms to describe Shelley, but such things weren't talked about in the Yoder home.

What was talked about were her mother's memories of Shelley. What she was like as a baby, a toddler. Sie is en grosser Saenger. *She has such a fine singing voice.* Sie hat's Garaiss. *She's very much sought after by the boys.* On and on and on.

Trudy knew it was her mother's way of keeping Shelley present in their lives. Not forgetting her, the way Dad seemed to. Or pretended to.

The funny thing was that Trudy knew her dad suffered from Shelley's absence even more than her mother did. Not mentioning Shelley's name, not letting anyone else bring her up—that was his way of ascribing to the church's policy of shunning. Trudy sensed it was his way of coping. It was his way of holding everything together, because if he acknowledged how much it hurt to have his beloved, vulnerable daughter run away from home, he would shatter into a million pieces.

Neither of them ever asked Trudy how she felt about Shelley's absence. Nobody ever asked, not even the bishop. Maybe it was just as well. She wouldn't know how to answer. It had never been easy to be Shelley's sister, and her leaving made it even more difficult. Trudy felt the burden of responsibility for her parents' well-being. They relied on her heavily, yet she was nearly invisible to them, just as she'd always been to Shelley.

So Trudy would sit on the floor with her back against the door and listen to her mother ramble on with memories of Shelley, and she would wonder what was going to become of her parents. They seemed frozen with their loss, each in a different way. Shelley might have left home, but home hadn't left her.

Trudy Yoder, Bird-Watching Log

Name of Bird: *Bobolink*

Scientific Name: *Dolichonyx oryzivorus*

Status: *Declining, and scientists have no idea why (which is so very troubling).*

Date: *June 10*

Location: *Jimmy Fisher's hayfield*

Description: *Small velvety black-and-white songbird. Pale yellow patch on the top of its head.*

Symbolism: *A member of the blackbird family, which is a bit unfortunate. (Blackbirds are often used to symbolize Satan and sin in the Bible, due to their black color and enticing songs.)*

Bird Action: *Helping itself to seed-bearing weeds in an overgrown pasture next to Lost Creek Farm.*

Notes: *The sight of a male Bobolink is breathtaking. It takes my breath away. There's just no other word for it than dazzling. The only bird in North America to have a white back and black underparts. Males have a velvety yellow head patch. Bobolinks aren't just known for their sparkling beauty. They're a farmer's best friend! They consume copious amounts of insects, helping to rid pastures of pests. Even more remarkable, these small birds migrate an impressive 12,500 miles in a year. That's more* than just about any other songbird! During a Bobolink's lifetime, it will fly as much as 4-5 times around the world. (Micah did the math, so that figure is credible.) Not what you'd expect from a bird the size of a tennis ball. The song of a Bobolink sounds like a bubbly laugh, which is probably how they got their name. Charming!

14

The Yellow House Project was, indeed, a yellow house. A drab two-story house at the end of a drab little one-lane road. Micah couldn't imagine why Shelley would be here, of all places. But there were a lot of things he didn't understand about Shelley, or the situation she was in. From the parking lot, he and Billy followed Julianne into the house. Right before entering it, Micah pulled Billy's arm to hold him back. "K-Keep her busy. Flirt. Talk. Just k-keep her attention on you." Billy's jaw hung open, like he was trying to absorb this, so Micah quickly added, "I'll explain everything l-later. J-Just d-do it."

They went through the front door to the reception desk, where Julianne was engaged in a conversation with a stern-looking older woman. Listening to them, Micah realized Julianne must have arrived for a work shift and was getting updated by the older woman, who looked like she was preparing to leave. Scolded more than updated. Sounded like the woman didn't think that ugly little dog belonged at work.

"I've told you before," the woman said, "that you must not bring that dog to work."

"It's just this one time," Julianne said.

"That's what you said last time. And the time before!"

175

"I won't let her wander the house this time. I'll keep her right by my desk."

As Micah listened to the back-and-forthing of the two, he realized this was his moment. He started to inch past them, unnoticed, but then the older woman spun on her heels.

"Where do you think you're going?"

"B-B-Bathroom," Micah said. This woman unnerved him. Her face had a chiseled-in-stone appearance, the skin stretched thin over sharp bones, her beady eyes like those of an eagle.

"This isn't a public place," the woman huffed.

"They're with me, Mrs. Beamer," Julianne said, handing Micah a key with a long handle on it. "First door on the right."

"And that's another thing," Mrs. Beamer said, attention back on Julianne. "How many times have I told you that you must not bring friends to work?"

Right before Micah turned the corner, he looked back at Billy, who stood watching him almost cross-eyed in confusion. Micah made a talk-talk gesture with his hand and pointed to Julianne. Then he hurried down the hall, trying to figure out where Shelley might be. Room after room was locked tight, until he found one unlocked door. Slowly, he opened it and poked his head in. Empty, thank goodness. The room had a narrow bed, a desk, and a chair in it. And a window! He hurried to it and saw small clumps of women standing together in a fenced backyard.

And then he sucked in a gasp of air.

Far on the other side of the yard, there was a girl sitting alone on a bench. Her chin was tucked on her chest and her arms were folded tight, her blond hair was cut short. He couldn't see her face, but something about her seemed to suggest Shelley. *Look up*, he wanted to shout. *Look up!*

"Just what do you think you're doing?"

He whirled around to face Mrs. Beamer from the receptionist desk. He held up the bathroom key. "Got a l-little l-lost."

176

She narrowed her eyes suspiciously. "The restroom is across the hall. The door with the large sign on it that says restroom."

"Ah." He walked past her, trying to smile, but it probably came out looking all wrong. His insides were shaking. His palms were sweaty.

Reality was setting in. He had found Shelley. But also . . . he had found Shelley.

———————

Trudy Yoder, Bird-Watching Log

Name of Bird: *Eastern Screech Owl*

Scientific Name: <u>*Megascops asio*</u>

Status: *Low concern (but thought to be declining in some areas, which is of great concern to me).*

Date: *May 12*

Location: *On a moonlit birding walk with Micah*

Description: *It took a while for us to spot it, as these little robin-sized owls are rarely seen but often heard. Short and stocky, with no neck. (Micah said it reminded him of Vern Glick, one of our ministers.)*

Symbolism: *Throughout the Bible, the mention of an owl is connected to loneliness, solitude, longing, and mourning.*

Bird Action: *Perched on a snag's branch, then suddenly seemed to know it was being watched and it was off in a flash.*

Notes: *Despite its adorably cute size and its lovely, magical trill, this little bird is one tough cookie! It hunts by watching its prey and then swoops down on it for the kill. It's such a shame they are so hard to spot because their cuteness should be widely appreciated.*

Sadly, they are known to feed on songbirds. (Sooooooo disappointing.)

15

On the walk back to the main road, Billy pressed Micah for answers. "I don't know why we were there in the first place. There were no nuts there. And I don't know why you wanted me to talk to Jules while you went to the bathroom. What took you so long, anyhow?"

Micah didn't answer, didn't even listen to Billy. His mind was spinning. Shelley said she was in danger. But she didn't look like she was in any danger. Just sad. Abandoned. She looked so small out there in the courtyard, so frail, like a little bird abandoned by its flock.

A feeling of protection rose up in Micah. She had asked him for his help. She'd told him he was the only one who could help her.

He had to get her out of there. But how? He was a novice at this hostage rescue business.

A car drove past them close enough that they had to move on to the grassy shoulder of the road. The driver, Mrs. Beamer from the reception desk, slowed to glare at Micah as if she was onto him. Onto what? He had no idea.

A wave of panic washed over him. What was he doing? He wondered if the time had come when he should call David and let him know he had located the whereabouts of Shelley Yoder.

But had he? Was that girl really Shelley? He was pretty sure that

179

girl was Shelley. Like, 90 percent sure the girl was Shelley. Maybe 80 percent. His confidence was starting to evaporate.

He shook his head. He couldn't overthink this. Shelley needed him. He had to figure out a way to get back to the clinic and get Shelley out of there . . . assuming that girl was, indeed, Shelley Yoder.

And Billy Blank was his partner in this risky endeavor. He rolled his eyes.

They were halfway down the lane when the ugly little dog came tearing after them, yipping and barking. Behind the dog came Julianne, waving her arms and yelling for the dog to return to her. It didn't. It barreled straight toward Micah and as he crouched down to catch the dog, it jumped into his arms, licking his face with its disgusting fishy breath.

Julianne reached them, panting for breath, eyes fixed on Billy. "I'm sorry! Cece seems to be taken with your friend."

Stiff armed, Micah held the dog out to her. The dog's legs spun in the air like a whirligig, then it started to whimper a lovesick, mournful wail. *Pathetic.* Any real dog would be embarrassed by this behavior.

And then it dawned on Micah that this pathetic little dog might be the answer to get back into The Yellow Project House.

By the end of the day on Wednesday, as David was getting ready to close up the shop, Trudy asked him if he'd heard from the Tennessee team. "Nothing yet," he said. "I did hear from Andy Miller. He's already back home. He said they arrived safely in Stantonville late Monday night. I was hoping I might get an update this afternoon. I suppose they're busy, though. I gave Micah quite a long list."

Standing behind the cash register, Trudy's hands stilled at the mention of Micah's name. David noticed. "You haven't heard anything, have you?"

"No," she said, a sad tinge to her voice. "Not a word."

David wondered if she sounded sad because she hadn't heard from Micah . . . or from Billy? He didn't know and didn't want to ask. Matters of the heart weren't his specialty.

He walked toward the cash register. "Trudy, what do you think about the church relocating?"

She looked up. "Me?"

"Yes. I'd like to know your thoughts."

She had such a shocked look on her face that David wondered if Trudy's thoughts didn't count for much at home. Trudy took her time before answering his question. "My father, he isn't in favor of a move."

There weren't many people whom David tried to avoid unless absolutely necessary, but Dave Yoder was one of them. After Shelley ran off, he had gone to speak to the Yoders, to provide comfort and encouragement. He hadn't known Shelley well, couldn't even remember ever having a conversation with her. All that he knew about her was that boys went wide-eyed and slack-jawed whenever she walked by, and that she had a lovely singing voice. But Dave Yoder shocked him by shutting down the conversation. He told David not to mention her name.

"But Shelley hasn't been baptized," David had told him. "She doesn't fall under the Bann. Keep your hearts open to her return. Be ready to welcome her back."

Nothing David said, even as a bishop, could change that man's mind. What troubled David the most was that he thought pride was the root of the problem. It was easier to put all the blame on others, even on Micah Weaver—who had nothing to do with Shelley's leaving but Dave Yoder still blamed him for it—than to accept the truth that Dave Yoder might have to shoulder some responsibility because of shortcomings as a father. What father did not have his share of flaws and failings? He certainly did. Too many to count.

"But, Trudy, what about you? What do you think about moving the church?"

She seemed extremely reluctant to share her thoughts. That was unusual for Trudy. Normally, she was chatty, easy to talk to. Something was wrong here. Something needed to be brought to light that wasn't getting said. He was just about to ask when he heard the phone ring in his office. "I'd better get that. It might be Micah." He hurried to his office and grabbed the phone. "Hello?" He listened for Micah's voice, but all that he heard was a recording about a car warranty running out. He hung up. When he left his office to go back into the store, Trudy had left for the day.

Saved by the bell. Trudy skipped out of the Bent N' Dent as soon as David answered the telephone—not even waiting to hear if Micah was the one who had called. Imagine that . . . the bishop asking for her opinion about relocating the church. No one ever asked for her opinion! Meals were so quiet at home that you could hear everyone chew. It wasn't like that in most Amish homes, but that really didn't matter to her father. Viel geschwetzt, awwer wennich gsaat. *Whoever talks much, says little.* That was her dad's favorite saying.

Imagine that . . . the bishop asked *her* what she thought. Amazing!

Still, she didn't want to get into a conversation with David about the church's potential move. There was something about the bishop that made it hard to not reveal more than she wanted to. It was the compassion in his eyes, maybe. The sense that he understood more than he let on. If she started to talk, she would've said too much. She would've told him that her father and mother were waiting for Shelley to return, and while Trudy didn't think her sister would ever come home again, she couldn't leave her parents. When you're Amish, family was everything.

But she also couldn't imagine life without Micah in it. So her mission had to be to find a way to stop Micah from leaving. And with the help of the tattooed woman, she'd done it. She'd actually done it! Temporarily.

After telling the bulldozer men to leave the site or face dire consequences, the tattooed woman had driven Trudy back to city hall where she'd left her scooter. She told Trudy to come in and watch the magic. Trudy had listened, wide-eyed, as the woman called the contractor and notified him that the building permits had been yanked, effective immediately, and to get those bulldozers off the property. As in today, she said, or face fines. Then she called the Beachy bishop, to tell him that the land was now protected under the Endangered Species Act.

Trudy could hear Zeke Lehman's loud sputtering on the phone. "But it's private land!"

"The Goshawk chick holds the property rights for now," the tattooed woman said, her voice oozing with self-congratulations. "The bulldozers can't touch an inch of dirt until that chick fledges. And by 'fledge,' I mean making it to a stage of total independence from the parents, not just departing now and then from the nest." She hung up and smiled. "Not on my watch."

Wonder Lake was safe, at least for another few weeks or so. Trudy would have to do the math, something for which she had little ability. *Let's see*, she thought, ticking off her fingers. Goshawk chicks left the nest around day thirty-four or thirty-five. Then again, this chick thought it was an eagle. Eaglets stayed in the nest for ten to twelve weeks, then the fledglings tended to stick close by to hone their flying and feeding skills. Eagle parents would dump a fish into the nest and the fledglings would rush in to finish it off.

So maybe . . . Wonder Lake could count on a bit of a reprieve before the bulldozers returned. But one thing she knew to be certain: Sand was slipping down the hourglass.

On the long walk back to the Gingeriches' farm, Micah made an impulsive decision which he hoped he wouldn't regret. He told Billy everything. All of it. Hearing from Shelley, tracking her down, seeing her just now in the fenced-in backyard of The Yellow House Project.

Naturally, Billy was confused. "Shelley Yoder?"

"Trudy's s-sister."

Billy slapped a hand against his chest. "My Trudy?"

No, not your *Trudy.* Micah felt like smacking him. "Shelley l-left a while b-back."

"I don't remember her."

Micah stopped to stare at him. "You d-don't r-remember Shelley Yoder?" How could anyone not remember her?

Billy shrugged. "No one ever talks about her. Mostly, Trudy just talks about birds."

Of course. "She loves b-birds." Everybody should. Micah started walking again. "She's a sharp b-birder."

"Yeah. She's real smart. Sometimes . . . I think she might even be too smart for me."

Micah did not say a word to that. Not a word.

"Birds are okay, I guess."

Micah faced him. "Okay? B-Birds are j-just okay?"

Billy waited for him. "I mean, they're nice."

"What *do* you like?"

Billy scratched his forehead, as if such a thought had never occurred to him. "People. I like everybody."

Really? Yeah, Micah had to admit, Billy did seem remarkably accepting of people. Hank Lapp, for one. Edith, for another.

"Do you like people?"

"S-Some." He gave Billy half a grin. "I like every b-bird."

"After spending the last couple of days with you, I have to say . . . once you start noticing birds, you can't unsee them." Billy's gaze drifted to a treetop of cawing crows. "They're all over the place."

Micah's grin spread.

Billy's gaze swung back to Micah. "But I think people are more important than birds. And church is more important than people."

Well, sure. You couldn't grow up Plain without knowing that.

"Maybe we should call Trudy and let her know we found her sister."

Micah shook his head, hard. "No."

"I think she'd want to know. Maybe we should call the bishop?"

"D-Definitely not."

"Why not?" Billy scrunched his face. "My dad always says, 'If in doubt, call it out.' Seems like this is one of those situations that the bishop should handle." He scrunched up his face. "Seems like we could get in trouble for this."

The same thought had occurred to Micah, many times. But he had concluded that he would deal with those consequences later. And if Shelley returned home, maybe there wouldn't be a need for any consequences. Her dad might even start to like Micah. "No t-time." He explained that Shelley thought she was in danger. And then he detailed out his rescue plan, which included Billy and the dog. It was a brilliant plan, he thought at first. Less so as he described it. In fact, out loud, it sounded pretty lame. But it was the best he could come up with.

While retrieving the dog from Micah, Julianne had mentioned that she was working the early shift tomorrow and that she was glad, because she had to bring her dog to work again and didn't want to face Mrs. Beamer's dog-at-work disapproval. She said she had kept the door propped open with a brick, just enough to keep from triggering the alarm, so that the dog could go in and out, and that made Mrs. Beamer very angry. "Violating security issues," she said, rolling her eyes. Julianne was a talker. Big-time.

"You," Micah said, "n-need to k-keep J-Julianne busy. F-flash your d-dimples."

"That's it? Just smile at her?"

"T-Talk about her d-dog." Julianne seemed obsessed with that hideous dog.

"Got it," Billy said earnestly. "Even if it means time on the sinner's bench"—he shuddered as he said it—"but I'll help you, Micah. You can depend on me."

For all that was wrong with Billy Blank—and there was so much—Micah couldn't deny that his loyalty was endearing. But there wasn't an original thought in his head. Not one. To top that off, he thought birds were just "okay." If Trudy heard him say that, she would've reacted with horror. But loyal, yes. Billy Blank was devoted.

Twenty minutes later, Micah reversed his opinion about Billy Blank and concluded he was an idiot. As soon as they returned to Gingeriches' barn, Hank Lapp asked what they'd been up to and Billy told him everything.

"COUNT ME IN!" Hank said, rubbing his hands together.

Micah whacked Billy on the shoulder, giving him a look of utter disbelief.

"What?" Billy lifted his palms in the air. "He asked me. I can't lie. If I have to sit on the sinner's bench, it's not gonna be for a lie."

Grinning like a Cheshire cat, Hank said, "Let's GO."

Micah squinted. "Now?"

"Yes, NOW. NO TIME like the PRESENT. Let's RESCUE our damsel in DISTRESS before Eddy feels BETTER. She doesn't AP-PROVE of subterfuge and espionage." He picked up his hat and plopped it on his head. "MICAH, I am IMPRESSED. And I am a man not easily IMPRESSED." He tapped Micah on the shoulder. "You have a GIFT. You can TRACK down ANY rare BIRD."

Billy blinked rapidly and Micah knew exactly what was coming next. He could've written the script.

"Hank," Billy said in that annoying you-should-know-this tone, "Shelley Yoder is no bird."

———

Earlier today, David had promised his mother that he'd come home for lunch, hoping some relaxed time together would encourage her to eat. To get out of bed and start on her prescribed exercises. That was his intention.

But just before lunchtime, two van loads of Englisch tourists came into the store. Each one filled up a grocery cart to the brim, enthusing over the low prices of bulk items, and David was needed to help weigh and price each thing so Trudy could keep the line at the register moving. Sitting at his desk for the first time in hours, he realized how late it was. Nearly closing time. He let out a puff of frustration. He'd neglected his promise to his mother. He glanced at the phone and puffed another sigh of frustration. Micah Weaver had neglected his promise to call David to fill him in on what the team was discovering about McNairy County, Tennessee. Considering Micah hadn't bothered to call, it probably meant there was nothing to report.

Ten cars drove past Micah, Billy, and Hank's attempts at hitch-hiking before the same white pickup truck from earlier this afternoon swooped past and slammed to a stop. The driver popped his head out to shout at Micah. "Back to the nuthouse?"

Micah nodded and jumped in the truck's bed, not even bothering to wait to be told. Billy leaped over the edge and turned back to help Hank scramble over, head over tail. "Hang on tight," Billy said, not a second too soon. The driver stepped on the gas pedal and the truck went flying down the road. Hank's eyes went wide, then a big smile came over him and he crawled toward the cab, then stood up, hanging on to the top of it, shouting out whoops of delight. His hat flew off and Billy made a lunge for it, catching it with one hand, then looking pleased with himself.

Even Micah had to smile. Hank Lapp was one of a kind.

Ten minutes later, the pickup truck dropped them off on the road. The driver shot his hand in the air to wave goodbye as he zoomed off. Hank giggled like a schoolboy. Slapping his hat on his knee, he said, "Haven't had THAT much FUN in years." He plopped his hat on his head and sobered up. "Now, point me in the DIRECTION of Shelley's LOCATION."

"Hold it, Hank," Micah said. "We have t-to s-stick t-to the plan."

"Right-O. So WHAT's the PLAN?"

Micah tried, without much success, to hide his exasperation. He explained the plan as they walked down the road, but he had very little confidence in Hank Lapp's ability to follow directions. The man didn't listen. Talked and talked and talked, but never listened.

On second thought, Hank's nonstop talking might prove useful. "Hank, you n-need to k-keep the r-receptionist d-distracted." Argh. Micah's stutter was worse than ever. He knew why—he was nervous about what they were about to do. Trying to do.

Trudy popped into his mind. She prayed a ton, even about the birds she was hoping to spot in the field. As much as Micah admired Trudy's faith—to be honest, he was a little envious of it—he just didn't think the Lord of all creation should be bothered with a request to find a bird.

He knew how Trudy would respond to such a thought, because she'd told him, many times. "Jesus noticed the sparrows. And the widow's mite. And the lilies in the fields. He welcomed little children that the disciples shooed away. Nothing was too insignificant for Jesus. So why shouldn't we take every concern to him?"

Okay, Micah thought, silencing Trudy's voice in his head. *Okay, here goes. Lord, I'm doing something that isn't exactly right. But I'm doing it for a good reason. I'm trying to bring Shelley Yoder home to her family and I need a little help here. So many things could go wrong. So many.* He glanced at Hank and Billy. *Lord, I don't want to make this situation worse for Shelley. So I'm asking for your help. Smooth out this path, and help us to bring Shelley home, Lord. Amen.*

Five seconds later, Julianne's horrible dog was bounding toward him at full speed, yapping away. It jumped up into Micah's arms and started licking his face with its scratchy tongue, smothering him in its fishy breath.

"Cece! Cece, come back here." Julianne hurried toward them, arms outstretched to retrieve her ugly little dog, her eyes glued on Billy.

Julianne, Micah saw, had left the front door to the clinic propped wide open without the alarm going off.

To Micah's surprise and delight, Hank Lapp caught on quickly that Julianne was the receptionist whom he was supposed to distract, and he did so with a thespian's flair. He snatched the dog out of Micah's hands and held it close to him. "There's SOMETHING not quite RIGHT with this DOG'S gait. A THORN in its FOOT, maybe?"

As Julianne dove in for an inspection of Cece's paws, Micah slipped away, unnoticed, and right into the clinic through the open door. He stopped abruptly when he realized a security guard was in a chair by the window, until he realized the big man was sound asleep. Had he been here earlier today? Micah didn't think so. He tiptoed past him and started down the same hall that he had walked down earlier today. No more than a few steps down the hall, his phone vibrated. He grabbed it from his pocket, looked at the caller ID, and whispered, "I'm h-here."

"You're here? Where?"

"N-near the front d-door. No one is at the d-desk."

"I'll be right there." She hung up.

A door opened and out slipped Shelley. She scurried up the hall, swerving past him to shoot out the front door.

He took her lead and followed behind her, holding his breath as he went past the security guard, then letting it out as he went through the front door into the sunshine. Shelley was moving so fast that he broke into a run to grab her arm, stopping her before she came face-to-face with Hank and Billy and Julianne and the horrible dog. "N-Not that way." He grabbed her hand and pulled her in the opposite direction, into the parking lot to weave through a few cars until they came to the edge. From there, they ducked down behind a truck. He motioned to her to keep out of sight, and he peeked over the truck's hood to see if Billy and Hank had kept Julianne occupied. They were still in a tight huddle, focused on the dog's paw.

Suddenly, an alarm went off. That sound! *That* was the siren-sound Micah had heard on Shelley's phone messages. The security guard came through the front door, looked around, saw Julianne and yelled her name in a frustrated tone. She grabbed her dog out of Hank's arms and started toward the clinic, just as another worker ran outside, yelling, "We've got a runner!"

The security guard pointed at Hank and Billy, then ordered them toward The Yellow House Project. Billy followed obediently, but Hank protested, sputtering objections. "WHAT? WHY? THIS is ALL a BIG MISUNDERSTANDING!" The security guard herded them through the front door, first Hank, then Billy, then closed it behind them.

Oh no, Micah thought. *No, no, no, no, no.*

———————

Trudy Yoder, Bird-Watching Log

Name of Bird: Song Sparrow

Scientific Name: Melospiza melodia

Status: Low concern

Date: April 8

Location: Bent N' Dent

Symbolism: Despite being small and plain, Song Sparrows are noted for their productivity and diligence.

Description: Small, predominately brown streaked. Males have a white "shield" on their chest.

Bird Action: Attacking its reflection in the front window of the store (thinking its reflection was an intruder).

Notes: Song Sparrows might not be fancy birds, but they do have a wonderful characteristic. They sing almost constantly through the spring and summer. People assume that sparrows sing to celebrate springtime, which is a lovely thought despite it being rather naïve. It's all about breeding season. In most cases, when you hear a bird singing, it's probably a male. Through singing, males are marking their territory while seeking a special lady. They do not give up until they have attracted their chosen mate. Do. Not. Give. Up.

16

First things first, Micah decided. Shelley was in such a state of anxiety, such a bundle of raw nerves, that he thought it best to get her to the farm as quickly as he could. There, she'd be safe and sound and he could go back and try to free Hank and Billy from . . . whatever might be happening to them at The Yellow House Project.

Just beyond the small parking lot was a field of thick, tall cornstalks. Micah motioned to Shelley to follow him and they went into the cornfield, moving at a quick pace, not talking at all. He was able to gauge directions by the sun's angle, and knew which way to head to get to the Gingeriches'. He felt a keen appreciation for all the time he'd spent birding in densely wooded areas where there were no trails.

The first cornfield led them to another, though this one was a field of stubble. The corn had been harvested. An autumn haze drifted across the field and far in the distance, Micah could see a farmer, pitchfork in his hand, burning a pile of leaves. They moved on, passing fields and patches of woods, and then an apple orchard with the scent of fruit warming in the sun. Shelley lagged behind, and he would turn now and then to see her squinting at the sky. When he felt confident no one was following them, he stopped to let Shelley rest under an apple tree in the orchard. She sunk to the ground, hugging her knees. He picked an apple off the tree and checked it for worms, then handed it to her. He picked one for himself, and bit into it, chewing slowly, swatting away at a bee that buzzed near his head. He wasn't at all hungry, but the apple gave him an excuse to not talk, to soak up the moment, to steal glances at Shelley. He couldn't believe she was right here, just a few feet away from him. And yet he felt like he was staring into one of those circus mirrors, where everything was slightly off.

In the last few weeks, he had imagined Shelley's face at least a hundred times, yet now that he was actually with her, she wasn't exactly what he'd remembered. He used to think the distant look in her eyes made her a little mysterious. He could never tell what she was thinking. Now, studying her discreetly, she reminded him of a child who was afraid of the dark. Her eyes, huge and shiny, darted back and forth. She startled at the slightest noise—a squirrel racing through a tree's branches, a bird's call. Then she would stare off at nothing in particular. Once or twice, she would flash him a brief, nervous smile, as if she'd just remembered that he was there, and he wondered if her insides were tumbling around like his.

He sat down next to her. "T- Tell me what h-happened."

Her eyes widened. "This is all Jack Spencer's fault. First, he promised that he'd get me a singing gig at the Blueberry Café in Nashville. It never panned out. So then he booked me in these little gigs in tiny little farm towns. RV festivals and gun festivals and pumpkin festivals. I sang at all of them, just like he told me to. They were awful, Micah. No one even listened to me. But the final straw was the Broomcorn Festival—where people watched a man make brooms. Brooms! Nothing ever turned out like he said it would. Nothing. I told him that he had to do something to fix this and he said it was all my fault." She pointed to herself. "Me! He said my voice needed work. Next thing I knew, he took me to this yellow house and told me it was a place to help me improve my singing. But then he drove off. He left me there. Just left me high and dry!" Her blue eyes grew shiny. "It's not a place for singers. It's a place for crazy people." She cupped her cheeks with her hands. "They were awful to me in there, Micah. They badgered me with endless questions. They tried to listen in to my phone calls. It was just . . . terrifying." She turned to him, wiping tears that had begun to trickle down her cheeks. "I'm pretty sure the staff does experiments on the patients. Everyone in there, they're all . . . narrisch." *Insane.*

They'd locked her in? A shiver went down his spine. He couldn't imagine being locked indoors. "S-Sounds t-terrible."

"Schlofschtermich," she said, leaning against him with a sob. *Nightmarish.*

Micah put his arms around her, letting her weep, and his heart nearly broke for her. Right on the heels of sympathy came another emotion—a thrill that shot straight through his vitals at the feel of her body in his arms. He'd never held a woman in his arms before. He'd always wondered what a woman's skin might feel like—and now he knew. Soft and smooth and warm.

He'd never dreamed he'd be this close to Shelley Yoder, so near he could smell her sweet scent, a woman-smell. A rose-warmed-by-the-sun kind of smell.

She was so near that he could touch her cheek by merely lifting a finger. Touch those lips . . . He slammed his eyes closed. *Pull it together, Weaver!* he told himself, reining in his wandering and carnal thoughts. *What's wrong with you?*

When Shelley had finished her cry, she wiped her face and tucked her short hair behind her ears. She looked up at him, blinking those big blue eyes, her thick lashes spiked with tears. "I knew you'd come for me. I knew I could count on you. Everyone knows that. Du kannscht dich uff Micah verlosse." *You can always depend on Micah.* She leaned against him again and he felt pleasure spiral through him.

Encouraging. To hear Shelley use a Penn Dutch phrase seemed like a very good sign. Maybe she was returning to her roots. As they sat there, sunlight broke through leaden clouds. Another good sign, Micah thought. It felt like a door had opened, spilling light onto them.

A Black-capped Chickadee flew from an apple tree branch down to the ground, not far from them, and Shelley twitched, frightened by the small songbird. She pulled away from Micah and her face became guarded. She put her fingers to her lips and whispered, "They're looking for me. We'd better keep going."

She was probably right, though Micah was a little sorry for this intimate moment to end. He rose and held out a hand to help her up. Delicate as bird bones, her small hand. "L-Let's go."

She cocked her head in confusion, a bit concerned. "Micah, where are you taking me?"

"Home. T-To Stoney Ridge."

She nodded, then smiled a real honest-to-goodness smile. He was glad she was ready to finally come home again. That made everything about this Tennessee trip good, and right, and purposeful. Shelley had been locked in a crazy house, but now she was freed. Safe and sound, ready to go home.

Only one nagging thought kept poking at Micah, disturbing his happy relief. Hank and Billy were now locked up in the crazy house. Mostly, he worried they would buckle quickly under questioning and point everyone straight to the Gingeriches' farm.

———————————

David happened to be near the front of the store when he looked out the window and saw his sister Dok's car pull into her office parking lot, not far down the road. He bolted out the store and down the steps to catch her before she disappeared. "Ruth!"

She turned at the sound of his voice and walked over to meet him halfway. "You look exhausted."

He frowned. That wasn't why he'd stopped her. "I'm fine. Have you seen Mom?"

"I'll stop by on my way home from work today. Any change? Is she up? Practicing her exercises?"

"No. She doesn't leave the bedroom. She just seems so defeated. She's hardly eating."

"Think she's in pain?"

"I've asked, but she says no."

Dok looked over at the horses under the trees. "Hip surgeries can be hard to recover from. The loss of independence, mostly."

"But that's just temporary. She'll be able to live in the Grossdaadi Haus again, won't she?"

"It's possible. But the fall she took, that must have scared her."

Shame filled David. His mother's fall had taken place on one of those rare days when the entire family had been gone for most of the day, off to a wedding. His mother had been getting over a cold and decided, at the last minute, that she didn't feel up to attending the wedding. They were long, all-day events, and the day was cold. Birdy and David didn't think twice about it. In fact, they thought she had made the right decision to stay home. Birdy had even remarked, "Colds take a lot out of older people. It's good she'll have a quiet day to rest."

Looking back, David should have found someone to stop by and check on Mom. Why hadn't he thought to do so? In a hurry, he supposed. They were running late because Timmy and Noah had gotten into a scuffle and one of them—he couldn't remember which one—had a bloody nose.

So off they went to the wedding, oblivious to what was going on back at home during their absence. Mom, who had spent the morning in a chair, reading, didn't realize her foot had fallen asleep. When she rose to leave the chair, she miscalculated a step with her numb foot and tripped, falling, causing her hip to fracture. When David and Birdy and the boys returned that evening and found his mother on the floor in the Dawdihaus, her voice had grown hoarse from calling out for help. Just thinking about it still made him shudder. He would never forgive himself for that day.

"At her age," Dok said, "living alone can be frightening."

David had thought about that very thing. Maybe that was why

she seemed reluctant to work on her exercises. "She could always stay with us in the big house." Which wasn't terribly big, not by Amish standards.

Dok shot him a questioning look, like *Think so? With your two wild boys?*

"It's not like Mom to be . . . unnergedrickt." *Depressed.*

"No. It's not. She's lost her feistiness. She's always needed to be needed. A broken hip has changed everything for her. I think she's afraid of the future."

"She says she wants to die. But that's just a temporary feeling, isn't it? I mean, she'll be back to herself once she starts feeling better. There's no other reason for her to be ailing. It's just that hip."

Dok kept her eyes on the horses. "Sie is schtarrkeppich." *She's stubborn.* The door to her office opened and her receptionist called to her. She gave her a wave and started toward the office. "I'll check in on her later today."

"You didn't answer my question. Mom will be all right, won't she? I know thoughts can be powerful. I know depression is real. Debilitating. But it can't kill you, can it?"

Dok stopped and pivoted, a serious look on her face. "Sie kann schtwerwe un gsund waerre." *She will get better or she will die.*

He watched her go, mystified. What did *that* mean? David walked slowly back to the store, left with an unsettled feeling.

Shelley wrinkled her nose. "What is that awful smell?"

"P-Pigs." Micah had led Shelley on a long and wandering walk, but when he came to a clearing and got a whiff of the pungent pig farm smell, he let out a sigh of relief. Few things in this world smelled worse than the sour stink of hogs, but today he was thankful for it. He'd made a decision to stay off the roads and find a back way to the Gingeriches' farm. He doubted anyone could track them, but he wasn't taking any chances.

He paused at the fence that bordered one pasture, scanning the farm to see if there were any unfamiliar cars. Nothing. The farm looked as it always did, tranquil, like time stood still. He exhaled, finally breathing easy. They'd made it. He had found Shelley and there was no way the bishop or anyone else could object to the rescue. Right? She'd been in a terrible situation, and he was bringing her home. His chest puffed with happiness. He turned to Shelley with a smile. "We've b-been s-staying here."

She didn't budge. She was staring off in the distance again. He looked to see what had caught her attention.

"Micah, do they have a lot of those back at home?" She said it in a whisper so soft he had to lean in to understand what she was saying.

"What?"

She pointed to a hawk soaring overhead.

"It's a R-Red-tailed Hawk. Yeah. Lots of those b-birds are back home."

Fear flashed through her eyes. "Micah," she whispered. "They aren't really birds."

He looked up just as the hawk made a dive. It was on a hunt. "They're b-big, b-but they're s-still b-birds. Hawks d-don't f-flap their wings m-much, to c-conserve energy. They'd r-rather s-soar." Stupid stutter.

"That's what they want you to think." She stared at the hawk as it circled above her.

"Who?"

She turned her head to the side. "They look like birds. They sound like birds. But they aren't really birds."

"N-Not really a b-b . . ." He stammered to a stop.

"They're listening to everything we say."

"The b-birds?"

"Shhh! I keep trying to tell you." There was a faint note of hysteria in her voice. "They're *not* really birds."

His head started to spin. "Then . . . w-what?"

She looked at him as if it was the most obvious thing in the

198

world. "They're listening devices." She touched her finger to her lips. "No one can know anything about this."

"About w-what?"

She gestured around the sky, like *All of it.*

Micah looked at Shelley, then at the hawk soaring in the sky, back at Shelley, and it felt like a red flare went off in his head. A terrible realization trickled over him, starting slowly, blooming wide and large. Everything started to unravel, right before his eyes.

Oh man. Oh man oh man oh man.

He was in over his head. Way, way, way over his head.

———

Trudy Yoder, Bird-Watching Log

Name of Bird: Red-tailed Hawk

Scientific Name: Buteo jamaicensis

Status: Low concern

Date: July 25

Location: Not far from the Bent N' Dent

Description: Large with a red tail, streaked wings that look amazing when they're soaring in the sky, spread out in flight.

Symbolism: Hawks are birds of passage in the Bible. They're praised in the book of Job for their ability to tell time, seasons, to know when to migrate and where to go. The Israelites of the Old Testament were forbidden to eat hawks or other birds of prey.

Bird Action: Chanced upon it while scootering down the road. It was picking away at an unlucky squirrel that had been hit by a car. (Disgusting. But I do appreciate that a carrion's peculiar taste for dead food plays a vital role. They help stop the spread of disease.)

Notes: A lady came into the store the other day and noticed my field guide book by the cash register. She asked if I knew that the scream of a Red-tailed Hawk was used in old TV westerns for eagles. I didn't know that, but I wasn't terribly surprised because eagles don't have much of a screech. But a Red-tailed Hawk—its call is alarming, similar to a buzzard's scream. Micah says hawks scream to defend their territory or warn off intruders. They have an eerie, raspy scream that puts a shiver down my spine.

There's much to admire about Red-tailed Hawks. Here are a few fun facts: These hawks can adapt to just about any environment, even city life. They are in abundant numbers across the entire country (yay!). Their keen eyesight is eight times better than mine. They mate for life. They reuse nests (and they keep their nests clean).

But here's the best fact of all: They co-parent. They really do! They build their nest together with sticks and leafy branches, often in a tree, but sometimes on a cliff ledge or building. The pair shares duties incubating their eggs for 28 to 35 days—though the female is usually the one sitting on the nest, while the male hunts. Once chicks are born, this division of labor continues. The male hawk catches prey and delivers it to the female, who feeds it to the young in small pieces. Yes, hawks have a sinister look and a spooky call, but I think there's much that people can learn from this wonderful partnership of hawk parents.

As they sail high in the sky, these speedy birds do seem majestic.

The only thing I don't admire about Red-tailed Hawks is that they will hunt songbirds. Setting that character flaw aside, they are still very cool birds.

17

Just like clockwork, the mailman arrived at the store at four o'clock to deliver the day's mail. As Trudy set the mail on David's desk, the office phone rang. She picked it up to answer. "Bent N' Dent."

"Trudy? Is that you?"

Her heart stilled when she heard Micah's voice, then jump-started, pounding with happiness. "Micah! I'm so glad you called. So glad! You'll never believe what's happened with Wonder Lake. It's a miracle. Just a miracle!"

"Is David there?"

She frowned. No *Hi, how are you?* No *What's going on with you?* No *I've missed you.* "He's at the store, but he's out front with Zeke Lehman."

"Go get him."

"Well, you see, Zeke Lehman had just heard the news about Wonder Lake"—*All about the miracle, which you would know about if you'd only ask*—"and he was pretty upset. Outraged, I would say. In fact, he got so loud that David took him outside to finish the conversation."

"T-Trudy," he said, sounding frustrated now. "Get David."

She let out a huff. "Aren't you at all interested in Wonder Lake?" So much was happening and she had so many questions for him.

203

Could the Northern Goshawk chick survive on an eagle's diet of fish, fish, and more fish? Goshawks relied on a more varied diet. As it grew, would its calls sound like an eagle's (a bit pathetic for a raptor) or would it automatically be that screechy, piercing hawk scream? Songbirds, she knew, learned their songs from their parents. Would it be the same for the Goshawk?

"G-Get David," he said, in a tight voice. "It's an emergency."

Oh. Oh! "Why didn't you say so in the first place? Hold on. I'll go get him now." She supposed she should forgive Micah for being indifferent and cold, considering there was an emergency. Hurrying out the door, she waved to the bishop to come. "Micah's on the phone. He says there's an emergency."

David had been deep in conversation with Zeke, standing outside by the Beachy bishop's van, and he didn't completely register what Trudy was saying. Not at first. Then he sprinted toward the store and straight back to his office. Trudy followed behind him to listen. "Micah? What's going on?"

Trudy watched as David's brow furrowed. He listened for several long moments, as if he couldn't quite make sense of what Micah was saying. "Micah, slow down. Hank and Billy are . . . where?" His eyes darted in Trudy's direction with an odd look on his face. He grabbed a pad of paper and a pen. "Micah, tell me your phone number. I'm writing it down. I'm going to talk to Dave Yoder and get back to you within the hour." He covered the mouthpiece. "Trudy, go home and get your father. Tell him to come to the store immediately."

At that, Trudy flew out the door, racing down the steps to get to her scooter, leaning against the tree right next to Zeke Lehman's van. Zeke looked at her as she grabbed her scooter, but she didn't stop to explain. On the way home she prayed she could find her dad easily on the farm. It was a large farm, fields fanning out from the house in every direction. If her dad were harvesting corn, she would have trouble seeing him beyond the thick cornstalks. If she couldn't find him quickly, she thought she might ring the dinner bell long and hard, until he heard its summons. But as she turned into the driveway, she saw him leading a horse out to the pasture. *Thank you, thank you, thank you, Lord.* "Dad!" She waved to him, and he waved back, but he kept walking. "Dad, halt ei! Halt ei!" *Stop! Stop!* She scooted over to him and explained that David needed him at the store. Right now.

Her dad shook his head. "He'll have to wait. I have chores to do."

"Dad, it's about Shelley." She had seen David write down Shelley's name on the pad of paper, right below Micah's phone number.

A blanched look covered his face. "What about her?"

"I don't know. I really don't know anything other than David wants you at the store immediately."

He seemed in a daze, as if he wasn't quite sure what to do.

"Dad." Trudy grabbed the horse's lead rope from him. "Go to the store. Now."

Her dad gave a slight nod of his head and started walking slowly toward the buggy, then it was like something clicked in his head and he picked up his pace, breaking into a run.

When Zeke Lehman came into the Bent N' Dent to find out what emergency had pulled David away from their tense conversation over building permits, he listened to him explain the situation and offered a ride.

"All the way to Tennessee?" David said. "Why would you offer such a thing?" After all, ten minutes ago, Zeke had been yelling at him.

"Because," Zeke said, his face softening. "Because this is what the family of God should do for each other."

Touching. Touching and true. "Still, I can't ask that of you." But David was in a bind. There was a tremor in Micah's voice that worried him. He sounded overwhelmed, needing help. Frightened. He kept repeating that he was in way over his head.

Zeke was insistent. "It's an off Sunday week. I can take you all the way to Tennessee. You pay the gas, of course."

"Of course." David was indebted to Zeke for such a generous offer of time.

"We can finish our conversation on the drive."

That took the shine off such a generous offer.

Just an hour earlier, Zeke had marched into the Bent N' Dent to confront David. His contractor had informed him that the permits to build the church were temporarily revoked. And his contractor said that someone in David's church was behind that action.

David was puzzled. "What makes you say such a thing?"

Just at that moment, Trudy dropped a jar of spaghetti sauce in the store. It created a commotion—splattering a wide path of broken glass and red tomato sauce, as gruesome as a crime scene. David saw a customer stop to help Trudy clean it up, so he decided to take Zeke outside to finish their talk. From there, the conversation took a rapid downhill descent. Zeke had a litany of complaints about the Old Order church. When Trudy interrupted to tell David that Micah was on the phone, his first thought was sheer relief. He had no idea what Zeke was talking about, and after hearing Micah's news, he didn't care.

But now, he was glad that Zeke had come by the store when he did. And he was truly thankful for the offer to drive him to Tennessee tonight. Surprised, a little skeptical, but thankful.

———

People could surprise you. Micah would not have expected the reaction Edith Lapp gave to Shelley Yoder when he knocked on the farmhouse door. Edith opened the door and started to question Micah about where Hank had gone to. Then she saw Shelley, standing timidly behind him. Edith stopped midsentence, eyes widening with recognition. Her permanent scowl softened into a near-smile. "The lost lamb has been found," she said, opening her arms wide and scooping her into a tight embrace. "Shelley Yoder. Poor baby. Poor, poor little lamb."

Edith led Shelley into the farmhouse and Micah wasn't sure if he should follow or not. He decided *not*. Instead, he went to the barn to wait for David's return call. He definitely didn't want Edith to see the cell phone in his pocket, and he'd rather not have to answer her question about Hank's whereabouts.

Man o' man, he hoped Hank and Billy were okay. Shelley had made The Yellow House Project sound terrible, but then again, was Shelley to be believed? She had warned him that if he tried to go back and get Hank and Billy, then he'd be locked up too. Could she be right? He didn't know. Frankly, he didn't know what was up and what was down anymore.

It would be best to let the bishop handle the situation.

Inside the barn, he sat on a bale of hay and leaned his back against a stall. He should feel relieved, but he was too tight, too frozen to feel any release of emotions. He took off his hat and rubbed his face. His mind was having trouble making sense of everything. Shelley Yoder . . . the beautiful songbird girl . . . she wasn't quite right in the head.

After seeing the look of pity on Edith's face, he had an odd feeling that she'd known that Shelley wasn't quite right. Did others? Hank didn't seem to, but then again, he missed most things.

Did Trudy know? She must. How could she not? They were sisters, after all, though different in every way.

Memories started flooding his mind. He thought of a time when he and Trudy had gone to Blue Lake Pond to spot a Pink-footed Goose. Shelley happened to be there, dressed in Englisch clothing, surrounded by a bunch of less-than-desirable friends. Micah had left Blue Lake Pond feeling disappointed. In Shelley's friends. In Shelley's duplicity.

Afterward, Trudy had warned Micah that he couldn't ask Shelley to be someone she wasn't. Was that her way of hinting that Shelley wasn't normal?

Another time, Shelley had invited Micah to a youth barbecue at the Yoder house, encouraged him to come, pleaded with
him until he finally agreed. Normally, Micah didn't go to youth
gatherings. He didn't have anything in common with most of
the young people. This time, he went, only because Shelley had
asked. And then she ignored him the entire time. Like he wasn't
even there.

He thought of one spring morning at church, when he sat directly across from Shelley so that he could watch her on the sly.
She kept gazing at the barn rafters with a worried expression. Her
mother, sitting beside her, would pat her hand as if to remind her
to pay attention. Micah assumed Shelley was distracted by the barn
swallows. They were distracting to him too. He wondered where
their nests were, and how many eggs were in the nest, and if any
in the clutch had hatched yet. Now he wondered if her mother
was patting her hand to settle her mixed-up mind.

He raked his hands through his hair, shocked by his ignorance.

He'd been thoroughly dazzled by Shelley—her looks, her singing voice—without ever really knowing her at all.

Why do people cherish the rare and disdain the common? It was
an insight about birds that he'd woven into a poem about LBJs,
during a time when he thought he might like to write poetry. It
was his only poem. He thought he'd been pretty clever with it—
he never dreamed that insight described himself. He squeezed his
eyes shut. *Idiot. I'm a complete idiot.*

The phone vibrated and he bolted off the hay bale, nearly dropping it in his haste. "David?"

"Micah, what's going on now? Have Hank and Billy shown
up yet?"

"N-No."

A beat of silence. "What about Shelley? How's she doing?
Where is she now?"

"In the f-farmhouse with Edith."

"Glad to hear that. Edith will take good care of her."

In other words, Shelley was out of Micah's hands. David didn't even need to voice his relief aloud. Micah felt it for both of them.

"Here's the plan. Dave Yoder and I are getting into Zeke Lehman's van soon. He's going to drive us down to Stantonville. We should arrive sometime near dawn."

Micah drew a shaky breath. "Good." Really good. The bishop couldn't get here soon enough.

"I want to hear more about how you happened upon Shelley, but there will be time for that later."

Micah rubbed his forehead. He wasn't looking forward to telling the bishop the whole story. "B-Billy and H-Hank? What sh-should I d-do?" He winced. His speech felt slow and clumsy.

"Nothing. After all, they're grown men."

Sort of.

There was such a long pause that Micah wondered if David might be thinking the same thought. "Well, anyway . . . don't do anything. I'll handle the situation when I arrive in Stantonville."

After David said a hurried goodbye, Micah slumped back against the hay bale. He felt spent. So tired that the barn swam. So relieved he felt almost dizzy. He couldn't handle much more of this. He closed his eyes and found himself muttering, *Thank you, thank you, thank you, God.* And then, *Please watch over Hank and Billy.*

Suddenly a vision of Trudy filled Micah's tired mind. He knew he'd been short with her on the phone and that she was probably mad at him. He wondered how she'd react to the news that her sister had been found.

He must have drifted off, because the next thing he knew, the barn door squeaked open and in walked Hank and Billy. Micah jumped off the hay bale to greet them, elated. They didn't look too worse for the wear.

Billy wore his normal expression—confused. "Micah! Where'd you go?"

Hank plopped down on the hay bale that Micah had just vacated. "THAT," he said, "was an ORDEAL."

"T-Tell me," Micah said. *Tell me everything you saw and heard.*

Billy leaned against the barn wall. "Well," he said, slowly, as if he was replaying the experience in his mind. "Well, you see, when the front door gets left open, it triggers an alarm. That seems to get everybody in a tizzy."

"I'LL say!"

"Big tizzy." Billy nodded.

"THEY assumed WE were talking to that girl with the LITTLE DOG because we wanted to CHECK IN. Asked if we were on DRUGS. Said we looked like we were HOMELESS."

"They said we seemed disoriented." Billy's eyebrows rose. He pointed to his chest. "Us."

"Said we seemed CONFUSED. Can you imagine that?"

Actually, yes. Micah could definitely imagine it.

"I told them that was RIDICULOUS. A confused person is too ADDLED to recognize that he's confused. So if you THINK you're confused, then YOU can't BE confused."

That in itself, Micah thought, could've gotten them checked in.

"Julianne got fired," Billy said in a mournful tone. "She keeps leaving the door open. Cuz of her dog Cece." He shrugged. "Turns out she was going to quit anyway, so she didn't mind so much."

"D-Did they f-figure out S-Shelley had gone?"

Hank lifted his head. "She wasn't THERE! They said they never had a SHELLEY YODER."

Micah turned to Billy, then back to Hank, then to Billy. "What?"

"Hank's right," Billy said. "You must've been mistaken, Micah."

Hold it. Something was off. "So they d-didn't l-lose a p-patient?"

"Oh, they definitely had a runner. A girl, about the same age as Shelley. She's supposed to have a . . ." He circled his finger around his ear. "Hmm . . . they had a term for it. What was it, Hank?"

"PSYCHOTIC DISORDER."

"That's right. Sounds terrible. Sure hope they find her."

Hank pointed a long, bony finger at Micah. "YOU took us on a FOOL'S ERRAND for nothing."

"Hank's got it right this time, Micah," Billy said, nodding. "This girl's name is Jane Doe."

Trying not to audibly groan, Micah dropped his head in his hands.

Things were happening fast.

Dave Yoder stood at the bottom of the steps of the Bent N' Dent, hands on his hips, face grave, eyes fixed on David. Even Zeke Lehman sensed the seriousness of the moment. He patted David on the back and said he was driving home to tell his wife he was heading out on a road trip, that he'd be back in an hour with a packed bag.

"What's this all about?" From the somber look on Dave Yoder's face, he seemed to be bracing himself for a death message.

"Let's sit down," David said, pointing to the picnic table under a tree. As they settled onto the benches, he shot a silent prayer upward. *Lord*, he prayed, *give me the right words for this sensitive situation.* "I heard from Micah Weaver this afternoon." David caught the frown on Dave Yoder's face. "Apparently, he has found Shelley."

Dave Yoder made a slight curl forward, as if he'd just been hit in the gut. He cleared his throat. "Is she all right?" He leaned farther forward, tightly gripping his hands as if they were holding him together.

"She's fine. She's with Edith Lapp now. They're staying with a Plain family."

"Where did he find her?"

"Tennessee. Somehow Micah was able to narrow down her location. Apparently, Shelley's been in touch with him."

That fierce look fired back up in Dave Yoder's eyes. "And that boy didn't think to tell anyone?" He practically spat the words. "Not her mother? Not her father?"

"I don't know the whole story. I only know that Micah said Shelley's been staying in a facility."

211

"What do you mean? What kind of facility?"

"From what Micah described, it's a place for patients who have some needs." David cleared his throat. "Mental health needs." From the flat look in Dave Yoder's eyes, it was clear he wasn't entirely shocked by that information. Not the way David thought he would've been. "Were you aware that Shelley might have some mental health concerns?"

Dave Yoder's mouth worked from side to side, as if he was trying to figure out what to say. "Over the years, there's been some . . . episodes. Spells."

"What do you mean? What kinds of spells?"

"Times when she seemed to . . . not be thinking quite right." Leaning on his elbows, he cupped his face in his hands. When he lifted his head, his eyes were shiny. "My mother had these spells. Things would get bad for a while, then she'd snap out of it and be herself again. I thought that's how it would be for Shelley . . . she just needed more faith to get better. We told her to get baptized and she'd feel a whole lot better. So that was the plan. Shelley was going to get baptized. Everything was going along just fine." He sucked in a deep breath, let it go. "Until Micah Weaver got involved with her, and it wasn't much later that she up and left."

That wasn't at all true. David had a pretty good hunch that Dave Yoder knew it wasn't true as well. It was just easier to blame Micah than face what had happened with Shelley.

What really bothered him was that Dave Yoder and his wife hadn't helped their daughter at all—not by pressuring her to become baptized, not by hiding her condition. David never wanted youth to get baptized under pressure, not for any reason. He didn't want anyone to be "half-Amish." God wanted a whole heart.

And then there was Dave Yoder's false claim that getting baptized would cure Shelley, that she only needed more faith to be healed. That kind of thinking did far more harm than good.

But Dave Yoder's errant thinking had to be set aside for another time. Right now, they needed to get on the road to Tennessee.

"Zeke Lehman has offered to drive us all the way to Stantonville tonight. I'm going. I want you to come. Shelley needs you."

Dave Yoder nodded. "I'll take my rig home and let my wife know. Trudy will drive me back."

David rose from the picnic bench. "We'll leave in an hour." He started toward the store steps, then stopped and pivoted. "This is good news, Dave. Your daughter has been found and is returning to the fold. Sie geht do rum wie'n verlore Schof." *Like a lost sheep.*

Softly, Dave Yoder said, "Ja, meine Schofli." *Yes, my little lamb.*

Alice Gingerich had loaned Shelley a somber-looking brown dress to wear. Edith added a Lancaster-style prayer cap, shaped with a heart, and pinned up her short hair. When Micah saw Shelley come down the stairs and to the kitchen for supper, he thought she looked pretty much like the Shelley he remembered. He had to remind himself that he had never really known her at all. Nothing, he was learning, was as it seemed.

Micah decided not to even bother to try and prepare Hank and Billy for the sight of Shelley Yoder in Alice's kitchen. The whole situation was way too complicated for their jumbled brains to handle. He was almost amused by the flabbergasted look on their faces, the popped eyes, the slacked jaws, the "But how in the world? Where did *you* come from?" questions.

Micah left the explaining to Edith and she did a fine job. "Close your mouths," she snapped, "and sit down at the table so the food doesn't get cold. Leave this poor child in peace. She's been through enough."

Amazing. To think that Edith Lapp had a sympathetic bone or two in her body. It was a wonder. She'd even come close to giving Micah a compliment for his tracking skills. "So I guess it's true," she said, "that you can find any bird. Folks said it but I didn't believe it." She arched a thin eyebrow. "Fix shoes, chase birds, find a lost girl. Is there anything you can't do?"

Plenty, Micah thought.

Billy, even more than Hank, was thoroughly bewildered. "But what happened to Jane Doe?"

Edith silenced him with a protracted glare. "Did I not tell you to let this poor girl eat her supper without peppering her with questions?"

At that, Billy kept flashing puzzled looks at Shelley, but he didn't say another word.

Hank said enough for both of them. Something about this modest farm reminded him of his childhood home. "I grew up on a DAIRY farm," he explained, as if anyone had asked. "One of the BEST REASONS to GROW up on a DAIRY FARM is CREAM. On summer's HOTTEST DAYS, our MEM would save the CREAM off the top of the milk jugs so that she could make us a batch of HAND-CHURNED ICE CREAM. Mem would add in FRESH BERRIES. PEACHES or CHERRIES. My brother and me would take turns CHURNING until our poor little arms ached. When the cream got too FROZEN to churn another round, the WHOLE FAMILY knew it was time to GATHER ROUND. Mem would PRY OFF the top and PULL OUT the PADDLE." Hank rubbed his hands together in delight. "My brother and I would TAKE TURNS licking the DASHER." He closed his eyes, as if transported to another time.

Throughout Hank's long, rambling walk down memory lane, Micah kept glancing at Shelley. She was being awfully quiet, not even laughing at times when Hank was genuinely funny. She picked at her food and kept looking out the windows, frowning, especially when thunder growled. Her eyes darted around the room, sweeping it like a flashlight.

When Alice rose to get dessert, Shelley excused herself, saying she was tired, and she did look pretty tuckered out. Hank's storytelling had that kind of effect on people. "You go right ahead, dear," Edith said. Even Hank seemed astonished by his wife's tender words.

Micah watched Shelley go up the stairs, wondering what was running through her troubled mind. He turned his eyes back to the table and realized Billy had been watching Shelley too. Only he looked at her the way Micah used to . . . like she was an angel. Sort of dumbstruck. Sort of a struck-by-Cupid look.

Great. Just great. Now Billy Blank had succumbed to the Shelley Yoder effect. To the Shelley Yoder illusion.

Micah's thoughts wandered to Trudy. Whatever spark Billy had for her had just been doused. He felt a little sorry about that. Not too sorry, because he thought Trudy deserved someone with more brain wattage than Billy Blank's. But he did feel sad to see how quickly Trudy became overshadowed by her older sister. Shelley drew attention wherever she went.

Yet Trudy was the one to count on. She was the faithful, steadfast one. Micah thought of her as a little brown sparrow, an LBJ. He hoped bringing her sister home again would make up for what a lousy friend he'd been to her lately. He regretted how abrupt he'd been on the phone this afternoon, but he just couldn't tell her more. He wanted to, but he couldn't get the words out. He could sense that he'd offended her by the hurt tone in her voice. He seemed to be doing that a lot lately.

It was strange how he became less of the man he wanted to be whenever he'd found himself sucked into the Shelley Yoder effect. Even now, even though he knew more. An image of the African Jacana bird bounced into his brain. Dazzled by the female's size and appearance, the male jacana ended up tending the nest and feeding the chicks while its spouse was out with other male birds. *I'm no different.*

Shelley had never cared for him the way he had cared for her. Even in her tangled-up mental condition, she was using his devotion only to help her get out of a bad situation. She called and he came running. She snapped her fingers and he dropped everything. Pathetic.

In a moment of rare clarity, it dawned on him that after time spent with Trudy, he became a better man. At least, she'd always thought he was a better man than he was, and in a way he couldn't quite explain, he became that man. It wasn't just Billy who didn't deserve Trudy. He didn't deserve her, either.

All those thoughts ran through his head as he sat in the Gingeriches' kitchen, listening to Titus read from the Bible during evening devotions in a slow, monotonous tone. The gray had returned, promising a gloomy, damp day tomorrow. Even the late-afternoon light seemed flat and dull. Micah couldn't focus on anything. He felt anxious about David's arrival, anxious about Shelley, anxious about everything. He knew the Bible said to pray about everything, to worry about nothing. But he just couldn't help it. He was anxious about everything, on pins and needles, and knew he wouldn't feel better until the bishop arrived.

Trudy Yoder, Bird-Watching Log

Name of Bird: *Black-capped Chickadee*

Scientific Name: *Poecile atricapillus*

Status: *Common, numbers are even increasing in places. (Hooray!)*

Date: *January 10*

Location: *Lost Creek Farm*

Description: *Small, with a black cap and crisp white cheeks. Short, thin bill (perfect for cracking open sunflower seeds).*

Symbolism: *The chickadees flock in groups together to forage for food and to evade danger. They represent teamwork.*

Bird Action: *Penny Zook set out a new feeder and the chickadee was the first one to find it. Only took a few minutes.*

Notes: *Chickadees are one of my favorite songbirds. They might be tiny, but they are very smart, curious about everything and everybody in its territory. They mate for life and are doting parents. (What's not to love?)*

Their name says it all. Chickadees have a wide range of vocalizations. Their <u>chicka-dee-dee</u> *is not only a sweet song, but it can also be a warning call to the flock. The number of <u>dees</u> can indicate how serious the threat. (Listening* to it, you can imagine that a cat lurking nearby would sound the highest <u>dees</u>-alert.)

Chickadees don't migrate, so they can be enjoyed all year long. At the Bent N' Dent, I fill a bird feeder at the same time each day. Two chickadees always arrive to supervise me. Together, they chatter at me quite bossily. Amazing, aren't they?

18

Zeke had driven David over to his house to let Birdy know he was heading to Tennessee to bring back Shelley Yoder. "I knew it!" she said, clapping her hands in delight. "I knew there was a reason we were meant to send a team down there." She lifted a finger in the air. "You start packing. I'll get some fresh clothes for you off the clothesline. And then I'll pack some sandwiches for the trip." She bit her lip, as if mentally running through a list. "Don't forget your checkbook. You might need it. You never know what you might encounter. Best to be prepared for anything."

As David quickly packed a bag, he felt amazed at his wife's keen spiritual sensitivity. It wasn't the first time she'd had a hunch in the right direction, and he hoped there'd be many more times to come. He wasn't a man who relied on his intuition, on his feelings. He let time guide for most decisions.

Birdy popped her head around the bedroom doorjamb. "Be sure to let your mother know you'll be away."

David stopped packing and turned to face Birdy. "Did Dok come by today?"

"She did. Said to keep trying to get your mother to eat."

"Did she seem concerned?"

"Concerned? Hard to tell. More like . . . in a hurry."

A beep on the horn outside by Zeke prompted David to pick up his pace.

"I'll finish packing," Birdy said. "Go to your mother. Let her know you'll be away."

He took her up on the offer and went down the hall to knock gently on his mother's door. She was sitting in a chair by the window, which he thought was a good sign. "Mem? Something's come up. I'm going to have to go out of town. I'll be back as soon as I can. Two, three days, at the most." He hoped so, anyway. He didn't really know what to expect.

He expected her to argue, to ask if this was about the church relocation, to remind him that she was not going to budge from Stoney Ridge. She'd moved enough times in her life, she had told him. No more.

Instead, she turned to him with that flat, tired look in her eyes. "When you get back, son, I'll be home."

Well, now that was another good sign. Home was the little house in their backyard. That was very, very good news. David crossed the room to give her a hug goodbye. She took his hand and squeezed it, hard. So hard that David paused. There was strength in that grip. Outside, Zeke honked his horn again. Twice. That man had many gifts but not one of patience. "David," she whispered, and he leaned closer to hear her. "You need a haircut."

Ah, see? His mother was going to be fine, just fine. He kissed her on the cheek, reminded her to eat something, and said a hurried goodbye.

———

Titus and Alice Gingerich's home was as quiet as a Sunday afternoon, except for thunder that rumbled far off in the distance, and except for Hank Lapp who had never known how to be quiet in his life. Micah, Billy, and Hank sat in the kitchen with Edith, guarding Shelley. She'd come downstairs and insisted that she needed to go, that "they" were coming for her. Edith assumed she meant the workers at the clinic, but Micah wasn't sure about that. Whoever "they" were in Shelley's mind, he didn't think they actually existed. To calm Shelley down, he reminded her that her father was on his way. "You n-need t-to b-be here when he c-comes." *Stupid stutter.* It was getting worse.

Shelley shook her head. "I don't know. I just don't know."

Edith stepped right in and saved the day. She cupped Shelley's jaw, forcing her to look straight in her eyes. "Micah's right. Your father's coming all this way to get you and bring you home, where your mother and sister are waiting for you. It's where you belong, honey. It's where you've always belonged."

Shelley settled at that, enough so she decided not to go back upstairs. That was good, Micah thought. When she was alone, her thoughts seemed to go haywire. She needed to be with people.

So they all sat around the kitchen table, all but Alice and Titus, who'd gone to bed right after supper. Probably, Micah guessed, because they were freaked out by their houseguests. For good cause.

Hank told terrible knock-knock jokes, which got Billy laughing so hard he had to hold his sides. After ten minutes of Hank's jokes, Edith threw her hands in the air and said, in a long-suffering air, that she was done for the night. Micah had a funny feeling this was how most of Hank and Edith's evenings wrapped up. When she'd had enough of him.

After Edith had gone to bed, quiet filled the room. The smallest of fires crackled behind the grate of the woodstove. Micah had to fight down the urge to go outside and do something to be useful—anything. Fill buckets with water, split kindling, feed animals, muck stalls. Anything to keep busy during this uncomfortable, awkward time of waiting. Shelley, it was plain to see, was always on the cusp of getting worked up. It came in waves, he'd noticed. Her hands would grow restless, and her feet couldn't be still. She would jump at the slightest sound—the chimes of the wall clock, the hoot of an owl. He dared not leave the room. He didn't know what she might do.

Billy cut into Micah's thoughts with this outlandish remark: "You know, she reminds me of my goats."

The absurdity of that comment nearly caused Micah to burst out with a laugh. Nearly, but he coughed it down. Shelley Yoder? There was nothing about her that was goat-like. Nothing. Now, a lamb, that he could see. Shelley was meek like a lamb. Gentle like a lamb. But a surly, stubborn goat? He didn't see the connection. Billy stared at him soberly, so he swallowed down his amusement and did his best to keep a straight face. "How's that?"

"My goats are real skittish," Billy whispered. "If they get startled or upset, they'll freeze. Their muscles stiffen up. I've found that singing settles them down."

Micah worked to keep the mockery off his face. Billy's fainting goats were a running joke among the Amish, a source of continual amusement. They would topple over in a dead faint at the slightest hint of alarm. In a world in which there was no shortage of troubles, why would any farmer in his right mind want to keep such an animal? Only Billy Blank. He loved those goats.

Years ago, he'd been given a pair by an Englisch boy who'd tired of them as pets. Billy had tended and nurtured and grown them into a small herd. Being a goatherd was now his full-time occupation. He sold goat meat and goat milk at the farmers' market and did pretty well for himself. An admirable accomplishment, Micah had to give Billy that, but it didn't change his mind about fainting goats. They were just ridiculous. "G-Give it a try," he said. "Sing."

Billy cleared his throat a few times, and Micah braced himself. He wondered if Billy's singing might resemble the bleating of his goats—a terrifying sound like an old woman's scream. Billy took in a deep breath, opened his mouth, and out came a familiar church hymn in a surprisingly in-tune baritone voice. Micah was shocked. Hank was wide-eyed. Shelley . . . she watched Billy, and then she joined in, harmonizing with him. Her whole countenance became transformed. The most serene look came over her, like her heart was saying, *This is what I was made for.*

The two sang one hymn after the other, a genuine concert, Hank called it. The singing calmed Hank down so much he fell sound asleep stretched out on a bench against one kitchen wall, snoring like a bear, then like a freight train. His loud snoring had a muffling effect on other small sounds, the ones that made Shelley jumpy, and she curled up on the hickory rocking chair near the woodstove. It wasn't much longer that she nodded off.

Micah paced around the room, looking out the window now and then, hoping for David's arrival. The moon had risen. A full moon tonight, which he hoped would help Zeke Lehman find his way to this remote farm.

Micah paced down one side of the room, turning to make sure Shelley was still there, then paced up the other side of the room. More than once, when he turned, he would see Billy watching Shelley carefully. He didn't even pretend not to be staring at her. He just stared. The look on his face! Er watscht ihr wie'n Katz en Maus. *He watches her like a cat does a mouse.* Mesmerized. Micah could just imagine all that was running through Billy's brain. He could imagine it because he'd done it himself.

Man o' man. Good luck with that, Billy Blank, Micah thought to himself. Didn't hold out much hope for him, but he wished him the very best.

———

Dave Yoder sat in the far back seat of the van and hardly said a word on the long drive, but then again, Zeke didn't give anyone else much of a chance. It was only fair, after Zeke drove them nearly one thousand miles, fourteen straight hours, all the way to Tennessee, to let him air his complaints about the Old Order Amish church of Stoney Ridge. It was good for David to hear them, because he had only considered the conflicts between the churches from his own point of view. Zeke had some valid gripes, beginning with the claim that his church hadn't been warmly welcomed by

David's church. In fact, most Old Order Amish treated them coldly, he said. Right from the start.

There was some truth to that, David couldn't deny. Most of the Old Order felt threatened by the coming of the Beachy church. Right from the start.

Zeke had other complaints too. The reason the Beachy church had talked the tourist buses into changing their routes and skipping some of the Old Order stops was because of timing. At first, the tour bus company tried to make some accommodations to add stops to the schedule. Izzy Schrock wouldn't agree to switching from mornings to afternoon for the tourists because her children napped. And Elsie Fisher didn't want the buses to stop by her house in the mornings because she was busy making soaps. Finally, the tour bus company gave up and switched strategies: one large bus making one daily swoop through Stoney Ridge. "It had nothing to do with trying to stop the buses from frequenting your people's businesses."

Put that way, Zeke had a valid gripe. Increasingly, David felt more than a little embarrassed. Not only should his church have been more accommodating to newcomers—especially those who shared similar roots of faith—but he should've made more of an effort to befriend Zeke, instead of making unfair assumptions.

There were other complaints, so many that the conversation took them through Maryland and Virginia. Around midnight, as they crossed the state border into Tennessee, Zeke brought up the biggest complaint of all, the sticky wicket. It was about the land that led up to Wonder Lake. Zeke was indignant that the permits had been revoked after all that he had done to move the project forward. He splayed his hand in the air and listed them off, finger by finger. "I found a good architect. A reliable contractor. These two know what's required of them by city hall. I wanted to avoid any unforeseen problems. And it was all running along smoothly, everything was going so well . . . until a bird moved in."

"Bird?" David said. "What does a bird have to do with the permits getting revoked?"

Zeke gave him a hard glance. "Have you not been listening to me?"

David had to stifle an eye roll. Listening was all he'd been doing for hours!

"Some bird moved into the area, and suddenly the president of the Audubon Society is involved. Next thing I know, the city is yanking the permits, at least until that bird takes off." He wagged a finger at David. "And my contractor says he's seen some bonneted, barefoot girl go up and down that hill. That's got to be a girl from your church."

"The women in your church wear prayer caps too." David said it meekly, knowing full well that the girl in question must be Trudy Yoder. Who else?

Zeke kept up his rant, until at last he turned off the main county road and stopped talking to pay close attention to his cell phone's GPS directions, and David was grateful for the breather. So many things had been happening without his knowledge or awareness: Micah had gone on a search for Shelley. Somehow, he had found her. Trudy—meek, trustworthy Trudy—had found a way to stop the Beachys from building a church on Wonder Lake. How had he missed so much? Were these two just particularly clever? Or were David's bishop skills slipping?

The latter, most likely.

And before another troubling thought could fill David's tired mind, Zeke Lehman rolled into the dark driveway that led to the Gingerich farmhouse. The kitchen was lit with one or two kerosene lanterns, sending out a soft glow. David thought he could make out Micah standing at the window, waiting up for them.

The door opened and Billy Blank came out to meet them at the car. "Your Shelley's in the kitchen," he said to her father.

Dave Yoder walked toward the house, then picked up his pace and ran up the steps and into the kitchen. David followed behind but stopped at the door. He put a hand on Micah's shoulder, and the two of them watched Dave Yoder cross the room to kneel by the rocking chair where Shelley was curled up, sound asleep. She stirred, then lifted herself up on one elbow. She blinked a few times. "Daadi?"

At that, Dave Yoder's shoulders heaved with relief. He dropped his chin on his chest and sobbed.

What a difference a day made. Trudy Yoder had promised David she would manage the Bent N' Dent entirely while he was off to Tennessee. She would've promised him the moon. After all, he was bringing her sister Shelley home!

Since hearing yesterday's news, her mother hadn't stopped smiling, humming to herself as she bustled around the house. It was like she'd woken from hibernation and was hurrying to catch up on all she'd missed during her long slumber. She was bent on scrubbing Shelley's bedroom, top to bottom. Windows, floor, rugs. Sheets and curtains washed, then carefully ironed. Every dress in Shelley's closet was getting the same loving care. The works.

Trudy did feel a hitch of concern that her mother's hopes were pinned too high. Shelley's erratic behavior leading up to her departure had been disturbing. Would it be any different now?

Still, it was good that Shelley was coming home. It was where she was loved, where she was understood and accepted, where she belonged. Family meant everything to the Plain People. Maybe Shelley was ready to embrace being Plain.

Early this morning, before the store opened, she fed her father's livestock, went to Lost Creek Farm to check on the guests—who, thankfully, had gone out bird-watching. The husband and wife were quite chatty and Trudy had no time to spare this morning. She fed Penny's hens and Micah's horse Junco. Then she practically flew on her scooter to arrive at the Bent N' Dent on time.

Two Englisch men were at the bottom of the steps, waiting for the store to open. As she hurried past them, she heard one of them say, "Can you believe it? A stinkin' cow pond."

Stinkin' cow pond? Trudy's ears perked up.

The men had come for coffee, so she hurried to get a pot started. While the coffee was brewing, she listened to them discuss the endangered hawk found in an eagle's nest. Turned out, one of the men said, it was discovered by the president of the local Audubon Society.

Trudy smiled. Of course. *Help yourself, tattooed woman. Take all the credit. I don't mind one little bit.*

As she poured coffee into to-go cups, she heard one man say that a nanny cam had been set up so people could watch the eagle's nest on their computers. They handed Trudy a few dollars, took their coffee, and left the store, still talking about that stinking cow pond.

Wuh-oh! What Trudy would give to be able to see what was going on in that nest right now. To watch, day by day, as the hawklet grew. To notice its emerging plumage. To observe its eaglet-ish behavior. What a thrill that would be!

And yet she couldn't. She couldn't watch it on the nanny cam because she had no internet access. She couldn't even watch it through her binoculars. There was yellow caution tape all over Wonder Lake, warning everyone away. Including Trudy.

Still, if that was what it took to protect Wonder Lake, to allow the Goshawk chick to fledge, to provide time to come up with a plan to stop the construction project permanently, to keep Micah Weaver here in Stoney Ridge, then that was fine with her.

Micah didn't know how the bishop kept going. After the van arrived, Zeke, Micah, and Billy had gone to the barn to get a few hours' sleep before the day started, but David stayed up with Shelley and her dad, talking. That suited Micah nicely, because he wanted to stay clear of Dave Yoder. As far away as he could. He knew he had made a mess of things, stirring up people's lives, and for all the wrong reasons. The cell phone kept vibrating with texts for the Beachy boy, so he finally turned it off completely and stuck it in the bottom of his duffel bag. He didn't need it anymore.

When Alice Gingerich woke them up with the clanging dinner bell, Micah considered skipping breakfast. He'd had enough people problems to last him for a while, and he was facing a fourteen-hour drive ahead in the back seat of a van.

This, he thought drowsily, nestled in his sleeping bag, was the reason he preferred birds. People were too complicated for him. A whiff of bacon in the fry pan floated from the house. Micah unzipped his bag and rose to his feet. Bacon had that effect on a man.

Still, Micah did avoid Dave Yoder by sitting at the opposite end of the table from him. He knew they probably needed to have a conversation, but he was too hungry and too tired for it now. Happily, his concern was for naught. Not only did Dave Yoder seem equally uncomfortable around Micah and avoided eye contact, but a few hours of sleep did wonders for Hank Lapp. He dominated the conversation, enthusing over the many benefits of McNairy County.

Zeke Lehman listened, a skeptical look in his eyes. "So you're telling me," he said, pointing his fork at Hank, "that there is rich farmland just waiting to be plowed and cows just waiting to be milked?"

"THAT'S RIGHT," Hank said. "It's the LAND of MILK and HONEY. The PROMISED LAND, RIGHT here in TENNESSEE."

Zeke turned to Micah, pointing his fork at him. "Is he exaggerating?"

It was a fair question, because Hank often did. Micah finished chewing, swallowed, and said, "Not t-too m-much."

Lathering a piece of toast with butter, Edith chimed in. "It's a good place for Plain People."

It was a rare occurrence for Hank to have others back him up and he was delighted. "David, THIS is the PLACE for US! Plenty of CHEAP land."

228

Not so fast. At least, that was how Micah read the look on David's face.

"I'll look forward to hearing more about your fact-finding on the drive back," David said in his diplomatic way. "For now, Dave Yoder and I are going to borrow Titus's buggy to head over to The Yellow House Project."

Micah stopped, mid-chew. He wasn't sure that was such a good idea.

Zeke wiped his mouth with his napkin. "David, I'll drive you over there. That'll give me a chance to fill up the van with gasoline, and look around at this"—he lifted his eyebrows in Hank's direction—"this Promised Land."

"Sounds good," David said. His gaze covered each one at the table, landing on Shelley, who sat next to her father, quietly picking at her food. "And when we return, plan on being ready to head back to Stoney Ridge."

If you return, Micah wanted to say. *If*. He didn't know what was true about The Yellow House Project and what was fabricated. If he listened to Shelley, it was a place filled with kidnapped hostages. If he listened to Hank and Billy, it was an insane asylum. All Micah wanted was to get everyone back to Stoney Ridge as quickly as possible. Home never sounded so inviting.

———

Trudy Yoder, Bird-Watching Log

Name of Bird: *Ostrich*

Scientific Name: *Struthio camelus*

Status: *Least concern*

Date: *March 21*

Location: *An ostrich farm (So I am cheating a bit here . . . I went to see them at a farm.)*

Description: *Huge (8 feet tall!), flightless birds with a long neck, a round body, stubby wings, all stacked on top of two long, deceptively spindly looking but-oh-so-powerful legs.*

Symbolism: *In the Bible, Job—after his many afflictions—said he became a companion to ostriches. It wasn't a compliment to the big bird.*

Bird Action: *Viewed safely in a large, penned pasture.*

Notes: *Ostriches are thought to be the world's biggest, heaviest bird. And while they can't fly, they can run. Faster than any bird in the entire world! They can sprint up to 43 miles per hour.*

And they can be dangerous. The farmer told me a story about an ostrich kicking a man with its powerful leg and killing him with one strike. So they are faster than people and they can kill with a single kick—striking terror in its own way.

If that isn't enough to give you the shudders, maybe this will: ostrich eggs are the size of a man's hand! A female will lay as many as forty eggs in a nest, though only incubate twenty or so. She seems to know which ones are viable and ejects the bad eggs right out of the nest.

About an ostrich burying its head in the sand—according to the farmer, that is a myth. Ostriches dig nests in the ground. If an ostrich is seen poking around the ground, it is checking on its eggs or moving them around.

Something to admire: Ostriches look out for each other. They can see great distances with those big eyes and long necks, and will warn the flock of danger. As big and strong as they are, they know they need community. So wise.

19

When the receptionist at The Yellow House Project poked her head into the director's office to announce that two Plain men were here and to explain why they'd come, a Hank Lapp–style bellow spewed out of the door. "WHAT TOOK THEM SO LONG?"

Immediately, David liked her.

Miranda Petersheim, the director of The Yellow House Project, was a heavyset, jowly, no-nonsense woman. Sitting on metal fold-up chairs in the director's small office after introducing themselves, David felt a bit like a pupil receiving a schoolteacher's scolding. Miranda Petersheim looked them both over, sizing them up. Finding them lacking, he gathered.

Frowning, she said, "Do you two even know what The Yellow House Project is?"

"We've never heard of it," David said. "Not until yesterday."

"It's a halfway house for women."

David and Dave Yoder exchanged a look. "You mean," David said, "a place for drug and alcohol addicts?"

"Former addicts. This is a sober living house. It's for women who've completed detox, but they aren't ready to go home yet. Here, we teach them all kinds of life skills. Things they never got before. When they leave our program, they leave transformed. Brighter and lighter. Clean and sober."

The metal chair squeaked as Dave Yoder leaned forward. "My daughter is no addict."

Miranda Petersheim gave him a *look*. The silence that followed was so full of meaning that Dave Yoder shrank back in his chair. "Your daughter," Miranda said, eyes fixed on Dave Yoder, "was found on our doorstep. She said she'd been dropped off for singing lessons."

"How long ago was that?" David said.

"Two, maybe three weeks ago," Miranda said. "She refused to give her name or tell us how she got here. Wouldn't hardly talk at all. Only thing she said was that someone was coming to get her and she needed to wait here until he came. She was insistent about that."

Micah Weaver. David clicked back in his mind and realized that must have been the time when Shelley had first started to contact him.

"We don't turn anyone away," Miranda said. "We're privately funded. No government money. Not a penny. And for someone like your daughter . . . what'd you say her name was?"

"Shelley," Dave Yoder said. "Shelley Yoder."

"For someone like your Shelley, who seemed so utterly vulnerable and abandoned and alone—"

David glanced at Dave Yoder and saw him wince.

"We weren't about to let a little gal like her stay out on the streets, or hand her over to the police. We don't throw women out like tomorrow's trash." She fixed eyes on them both. "Do you have any idea what happens to girls like her on the street?"

David couldn't imagine how it must feel for a father to hear this information, still full of missing details, about his precious daughter. "So, about Shelley," he said, hoping to redirect the conversation.

"It was obvious Shelley had some serious mental health issues going on," Miranda said. "We're used to that. We're even used to women showing up on our front step. We do our best with everyone. We tried to help your girl, but she refused any treatment. She wouldn't talk to our counselors, wouldn't participate in group therapy sessions, didn't want to connect with any other patients, wouldn't give us any information to locate her family. She just kept saying that someone was coming for her, and she needed to be here." Miranda pointed to the door. "Just so you know, she was always free to walk out that door. We keep our doors locked up for security reasons, but no patient is kept here against their will. They are always free to go." The woman lifted her large shoulders. "But when a patient won't cooperate, there's only so much we can do. We have a certain amount of beds in the center and our mission is to get these women back on their feet. We like to think of ourselves as a launching pad, not a holding tank. There was a meeting scheduled for tomorrow to discuss what to do with this Jane Doe." She slapped her palms on her desk. "And now we know. She's yours."

David thought the director looked immensely relieved by that thought. "So you know nothing about who dropped her here?"

"Nothing. But that happens now and then. We're known in these parts for having an open-door policy." She peered at David over her glasses. "Did I mention that we don't receive any government funding?"

"Yes, I believe you did." Oh, hold on. She wanted a donation. And deserved it too. David reached for his checkbook and she smiled.

David signed his name on the check and ripped it out, handed it to Miranda Petersheim, who looked at the amount and her smile widened.

"So Shelley Yoder is Amish?" she said. "I wouldn't have guessed that."

"Well, she is," Dave Yoder said. "She is Plain." He said it conclusively, as if there was no question about it.

234

Miranda ignored him. Her attention was now riveted on David. "I hope you don't mind my saying so, but you people need to do a better job with mental health. Lots of Amish folks in need around here, but they don't want to take advantage of what The Yellow House Project has to offer. We've been trying to get out the word to them. We offer outpatient services, and we invite Amish folks in to hear talks by our counselors. Nothing. No interest."

Not surprising, considering the Swartzentrubers were the dominant Amish in the area. "Some areas," David said, "do better than others. Ohio and Pennsylvania, for example, have facilities just for Plain People in need of mental health treatment. The counselors even speak Penn Dutch, our first language. Perhaps as the Plain population grows in Tennessee, there will be more openness to seeking help."

"I sure hope so." Now her focus zeroed in on Dave Yoder. "There's no shame in it, you know. Seeking help. Getting treatment."

Dave gave her a hard look. "Shelley needs to come home. That's all she needs."

"Now, that's just what I'm talking about. Mr. Yoder, your daughter needs more than just to come home. She's going to need medical care, and counseling. She's got some serious mental health issues. She's not well."

"She'll be fine," Dave Yoder said, "once she's back home."

His response had the effect on Miranda Petersheim of tossing a match on gasoline. She slammed the desk with her fist and glared at Dave Yoder. "Your little girl is sick. You hear me? She is sick." She turned her wrath to David. "And you. You're the bishop! If you think caring for your people is to ignore their mental health problems, to pretend they don't exist, to think that you can pray it all away like magic, then . . ." She tightened her lips into a straight, stern line. "Well, then I don't know what to think about you people."

David lifted his palms like a stop sign. "There's an excellent mental health and rehab facility near us. Shelley will be cared for there."

Dave Yoder stiffened and David was thankful for this director's strong words. It hadn't occurred to him that Dave would be resistant to getting the care that Shelley so obviously needed.

A wave of fatigue hit David, hard. He needed to keep things moving along. They'd gotten the answers they'd needed. "Thank you for all you've done for our Shelley." David rose and shook the director's hand, but Dave Yoder just turned and walked out of the room. "I'm sorry about that. He's upset. But I'm sure he's very grateful for the care you provided for his daughter."

The director held on to David's hand and looked him right in the eye. "That man might need a little mental health treatment too. Usually, when one person in the family is sick, others get sick too."

An image of Shelley's depressed mother popped into his head. "I'll remember that. Thank you again. You've been a blessing. More than you can imagine."

Zeke was waiting out front for them. Dave Yoder was already in the van, back seat, staring out the window. David slowed to a stop for a long moment to catch his breath.

Zeke leaned over to shout out the window. "You okay?"

David lifted a hand. His exhaustion was palpable. But he was okay. Better than okay. A lost sheep had been found.

"You sure you're okay?" Zeke shouted.

Yes, David was okay. He started toward the van and climbed into the passenger seat next to Zeke. "Any luck finding a gas station?" He looked forward to a good long sleep on the drive back to Stoney Ridge.

"I did. While I was filling up, a fellow named Rodney was filling up too. Said he knows you."

"Rodney the real estate agent?"

"Yes. Great guy. We got to talking, and then he offered to drive me around town to get the lay of the land." He turned the ignition, then paused and looked at David. "I'm glad I came on this trip. This place . . . it holds a lot of potential for Plain People."

David turned to look back at The Yellow House Project. "I agree, Zeke," he said. A lot of potential. He couldn't agree more.

———

Trudy heard the door chimes and left the buttermilk donut mix boxes she was unpacking to go see who had arrived at the Bent N' Dent. David had left her in charge but forgot to tell her that it was delivery day. Boxes were piled all around the store, blocking aisles. Each time the store emptied of customers, she returned to the task of unpacking a box to get its contents on the shelves. She had to make her way to the counter, weaving around boxes. "It's you," she said.

"This is where you work?" The tattooed woman looked all around the store, squinting. "The lighting is so dim."

True, especially on cloudy days like today. "How did you find me?"

"Kiddo, I make it my business to know everyone in this town."

"Oh, right." Trudy grinned. "You're planning to run for mayor."

"I sure am. And I'll be counting on you to get your people to vote for me."

Maybe, Trudy thought. *Probably not.*

"Big news." The tattooed woman set a copy of the *Stoney Ridge Times* on the counter. "Didn't take long. It's already international news." She pointed to the headline: "Endangered Northern Goshawk Chick Adopted by Eagles."

Trudy glanced at the paper. "How? How did you get it into the newspaper?"

She gave her that amused half smile. "Connections, kiddo." She tapped the paper. "Read it."

The article took an interesting twist. It tried to answer the question that had been nagging Trudy, the one that wouldn't let go. How did that chick get in the nest in the first place?

While the woman walked around the store, looking curiously at the products on the shelves, Trudy finished reading the article. It said that Maureen "Mo" McIntosh, the local president of the Audubon Society, provided the likeliest theory. Trudy glanced over at the woman. So that was her name? She'd never volunteered it.

"Being highly opportunistic predators," McIntosh said, "the eagle raided a Goshawk's nest and brought a hawklet in its talons to feed its own young. According to my birding team—" (Wait. What birding team? Did she mean Trudy?) "—the eaglets in the nest were well fed. They probably didn't even know what to do with live food. So the hawklet did what hawklets do—it opened its beak and begged for food. The eagle parents responded and fed it morsels of food. Once that happens, the parent-nestling bond began. That bond is particularly strong among raptors."

"McIntosh," the article continued, "considers herself to be an expert in raptors."

Trudy folded the newspaper and set it on the counter. The tattooed woman saw she'd finished the article and walked over to the counter, a pleased look on her face.

"Your name is Maureen?"

"Call me Mo, kiddo." She pointed to the folded newspaper. "Pretty sweet coverage."

"Yes, but we don't really know how the hawklet got there."

Mo frowned. "There's undocumented stories of eagles that raid nests. And some anecdotes in the *Journal of Raptor Research*."

"But we probably will never know. It seems like quite a stretch to make it sound like we know what actually happened."

Mo picked up the newspaper, a bit churlish. She started toward the door and turned when she opened it, pausing to say, "I did say it was the likeliest theory." She left in a huff.

Mo McIntosh had done exactly what Trudy asked for help to do: Stop the construction project at Wonder Lake. Trudy hurried to catch her before she reached her car. On the top steps, she shouted, "Mo! Mo McIntosh! You're probably right. It's the likeliest theory."

Mo tossed her big purse in the back of her rusted out Volkswagen bus and turned to face Trudy. "You just can't know everything in life, kiddo, but you can get pretty close to knowing. At least that's the way I see it."

Trudy hurried down the steps. "Mo, thank you for everything you did."

Mo slipped into her car. "Just remember me, kiddo, when it's time to vote."

Maybe, Trudy thought again. *Probably not.*

Mo turned the key and the old bus roared to life. She backed it up, one arm waving out the sunroof as she shouted, "Toodles!"

Trudy watched the Volkswagen until it disappeared out of sight. *"You just can't know everything in life, but you can get pretty close to knowing."* That remark hit Trudy like a cold slap in the face.

That was exactly what had been bothering her about Micah's role in finding Shelley. She might not know everything that had gone on the last few days, but she felt pretty close to knowing. And here was what she thought she knew: Micah had lied to her. More than a few times.

Trudy Yoder, Bird-Watching Log

Name of Bird: *Eastern Meadowlark*

Scientific Name: *Sturnella magna*

Status: *In steep decline (near threatened!!!)*

Date: *April 28*

Location: *Beacon Hill's lower end pastureland*

Description: *Known by the black V on its bright yellow breast, and white outer tail feathers. (Sooooo cute.)*

Symbolism: *The meadowlark is considered a symbol of hope. In some Christian traditions, it represents the resurrection of Christ.*

Bird Action: *Seen on a cattail near the creek that runs along the farm. Lots of insects buzzing over the creek. A feast. Such a help to farmers by ridding pastures of bugs and pests.*

Notes: *As the name says, meadowlarks are known for their sweet whistle at the start of the day, adding to the dawn chorus. (Can you tell? I just love all larks.) They might be shy, but they're known for being quick thinkers with sharp memories. According to Micah, the species is down 98% in Pennsylvania. (Terrible news.) Our state is at risk of losing something precious if those numbers don't turn around. Fast.*

20

Trudy wasn't sure exactly when her dad would arrive home with her sister Shelley—probably after midnight, he said on the message he left on the answering machine in the phone shanty. "So don't wait up." He didn't leave any details, only that Shelley was fine, just fine, and eager to get home again.

Trudy wondered if her sister was truly fine, or if her dad just wanted everyone to believe that because he so desperately needed to believe it. Shelley's "episodes" were a well-kept family secret. Her dad would minimize them, insisting she was just like Grossmatti, his mother, who suffered the same kinds of spells. "These spells pass soon," Dad would say, "and she'll be right as rain. She's just got a vivid imagination, that's all."

Spells. Vivid imagination. Words that softened Shelley's odd behavior. Trudy remembered the first time when she realized her sister wasn't quite right. Shelley was thirteen, Trudy was almost eleven. The two girls had been mowing the grass and raking the leaves, and Shelley stopped what she was doing to talk to someone. Trudy stopped to listen, thinking her sister was trying to tell her something. Shelley looked right through her in a creepy way, like she was seeing people. Shelley had grown more and more upset, to the point where she started screaming at the invisible people, yelling at them to stop bothering her. Frightened, Trudy ran to the house to get her mother. By the time they got to Shelley, her dad was with her, trying to soothe her and calm her down. Her mom and dad took her into the house and Trudy remained outside, bewildered. That moment was never spoken of again.

Another time Trudy woke in the night to find Shelley barricading the door to their bedroom with furniture. She insisted someone was trying to break into the house. Her parents pretended everything was fine, just fine. But it wasn't.

When Shelley was fifteen, she started to get noticed—both for her beauty and for her singing. She loved the attention. She confided to Trudy about wanting to sing on the radio and said there were people who wanted to help her get started. Trudy thought "these people" were just like the others—figments of Shelley's vivid imagination.

But it turned out that Shelley did have a real live person who wanted to help start her singing career. Jack Spencer, who said he'd be her agent. He booked singing gigs for Shelley in bars in Lancaster. Shelley talked Trudy into helping her sneak back into the house late at night, and reluctantly, Trudy agreed. Later, she found out Shelley had been lying to her parents, saying she was meeting Micah Weaver. *Micah!* What really stung was that Shelley had known how Trudy felt about Micah. Shelley knew she loved him.

Trudy deeply regretted ever confiding her feelings about Micah to Shelley. She felt betrayed. She also regretted her role in helping Shelley deceive their parents. Looking back, Trudy supposed she'd been accommodating to Shelley because it was the first time she felt as if they were sisters. Normal ones. Not like they usually were, where she walked on eggshells around Shelley.

It wasn't long before Jack Spencer talked Shelley into leaving home to go to Nashville to start a singing career. She believed him, hook, line, and sinker. And her dad blamed it all on Micah Weaver! He insisted that Micah had put these grandiose singing notions into Shelley's head. Anyone who knew Micah knew that was ridiculous. He didn't care about singing—he only cared about birds. But her dad wouldn't forgive Micah.

She wondered what her dad would think now, knowing that Shelley had contacted Micah, had asked him to come get her. Would her dad forgive his imagined grudge against Micah? Or would it only confirm to him that Micah Weaver was not to be trusted with his daughters?

The first thing David Stoltzfus did when he arrived home was to take off his shoes so he wouldn't wake anyone. All he could think about was crawling into bed. The grandfather's clock chimed three in the morning, and he was so tired he couldn't think straight. But they'd done what they set out to do. Shelley Yoder was home with her family.

He tiptoed up the stairs, pausing at his mother's room, the door left ajar. He was tempted to check on her, but another wave of exhaustion hit. He was bone-weary, for he hadn't really slept in two days and all he could think about was stretching out flat in his own comfortable bed. Quietly, he changed and slipped between the sheets, taking care to not disturb Birdy. She heard him though, or sensed him, and snuggled closer to him in the bed. He put his arm around her.

"Everything go okay?" she asked. She didn't sound at all tired, which surprised him.

"Everything went fine. I'll tell you all about the trip in the morning."

"David . . ."

He yawned. "Birdy, I'm too tired to talk." Suddenly, a thought occurred. His eyes opened wide. His mother's door was left ajar. His eyes opened. "What's happened?"

"We can talk in the morning."

Now he was wide awake. "Something's wrong."

Birdy turned on her side to face him. "David . . . your mother passed away."

His mother's door wasn't shut because she wasn't there. *"I'll be home,"* his mother had told David. She hadn't meant that the Grossdawdi's Haus in the backyard was her home. She had meant Heaven.

Shelley and Dad had arrived at the house in the wee hours. Trudy heard the car drive up and went to wake her mother, but she was already up. Up and dressed and eager to welcome her lost daughter. Her dad led Shelley into the house and Mom let out a sob, then ran to embrace her, pulling her close. For a brief moment, Shelley allowed herself to sag into her mother's body, but when she tried to draw back, Mom wouldn't let her go. Or maybe she couldn't let go.

"Mem, genunk!" *Mom, enough!* Shelley said she was tired and went straight up to her bedroom.

The look on Mem's face! So disappointed. So hurt. "It's late," Trudy said, trying to appease her. An awkward, brief hug was all the acknowledgment Shelley had extended to Trudy. "It's been a long day for Shelley and Dad. Everything will be better in the morning. You'll see." She looked to her father for confirmation, assuming he'd add reassurance. But he didn't.

Her dad looked pained. "Ich geh noch em Bett," he said in a flat voice. *I'm going to bed.*

Trudy watched as her mother followed her dad up the stairs. They both seemed suddenly old.

David hardly slept. He should've been here for his mother's last breath. He missed it by hours. Just hours! He wondered if it might have made a difference if he'd been home last evening.

Exhausted, he knew he needed to be careful of where this futile thinking took him, but he indulged himself and let his thoughts fly loose. He had failed his mother. He'd been so busy, so distracted, he'd hardly had time for her.

It was the same for the church. He had failed his church. Looking back over the last few weeks, he saw clearly now that he had let everyone give him advice about this relocation. He'd taken suggestions from everyone—all with the intention of keeping unity in the church. Even Birdy. Especially Birdy. He accepted her advice unequivocally.

And then things started moving fast. Micah brought up Tennessee. Andy Miller could get them there. Suddenly, David was telling God the plan, expecting his blessings. He'd never asked the Lord if this was the right step to take. Not once.

In the blink of an eye, Micah had called David, panic in his voice. Shelley Yoder had been found. She wasn't well. She needed to get home. Zeke Lehman offered to drive them. Once again, David was telling God the plan. Not asking. Telling.

Maybe, had he asked, the Lord might have slowed things down, provided a sense of perspective. Maybe there could've been another way for the team to return home.

And if so, David might have been home for his mother's death. If so, maybe his mother would have rallied. Hung on until she turned the corner and started feeling better. Had she felt abandoned by him? Is that why she gave up? Could depression be that powerful?

Look at Shelley Yoder, he thought. *Look where her tangled-up thoughts took her.*

Was it possible that his mother had just willed herself to die?

No, he reminded himself. God alone appointed the time of one's death. "And as it is appointed unto man once to die," said the book of Hebrews. "There was a time to be born and a time to die," wrote King Solomon. Now, more than ever, David knew he needed to lean heavily on the truth of Scripture. On the hope of eternity in which he would see his mother again, in the presence of the Lord.

When he heard the first birdsong at dawn, David gave up on sleep and went downstairs to make coffee, pausing at the door where his mother had died, just hours ago. Her body was already at the undertaker's and would be returned later today for the viewing.

In two days, the funeral would be held.

By midmorning, the death message would be out and their house and yard would be filled with helpers, drawn like bees to the hive. They would go right to work without anyone telling them what to do—lawns would be mowed, edges trimmed, windows washed, the house swept and dusted and scrubbed. Furniture would be moved out of the kitchen and great room, to make space for the benches that would be delivered by wagon. Great quantities of food would be organized, both for the viewing and for the day of the funeral—sandwiches, cupcakes, fruit salad.

By this afternoon, pall bearers would start digging a new grave in the Amish cemetery. Travel plans would be underway for those distant friends and relatives to arrive in time for the funeral. The ministers would take David's role in the services, allowing him to grieve with his family. And after his mother's coffin had been lowered into the ground, after the final fellowship meal was over, everything would be returned to its proper place.

And life would go on.

These rituals, they were comforting. No decisions needed to be made because they'd already been made, centuries ago.

But the grieving, that was still a lonely chore.

Only because David had insisted, Birdy described the discovery of his mother's body. Around five in the evening, Birdy had brought dinner to Mom. She seemed the same as she'd been, Birdy said. Tired. Her voice was weak. She didn't like what Birdy had made for dinner. The boys were too loud. The usual.

An hour later, Birdy went to get her dinner tray but thought Mom had fallen asleep. So she tiptoed back out and returned an hour or so later, after getting the boys to bed. That was when she realized Mom had died. Peacefully. No sign of struggle. Like she'd just fallen asleep. She mentioned that several times.

Birdy called Dok right away, and she drove over to confirm the time of death. Dok contacted the undertaker to come get the body, and she had called their other brother, Simon, to give him the death message. Simon said he hoped to come to the funeral, but he wasn't sure he was up to the trip. That sounded like Simon. His brother was fragile.

Not his sister, though. Birdy said Dok never missed a beat. "She was utterly professional. Calm and matter-of-fact," Birdy said. "In a way, you wouldn't have thought this was her mother."

That sounded like Ruth. His sister was pretty tough. Like their mother.

Deep down, David wondered all that Dok might be thinking and feeling about Mom's death. They'd had a complicated relationship, so he suspected that grieving might be complicated too.

As for him, grief felt raw. It had sharp edges.

He'd had the closest relationship to his mother. More than his brother Simon and much more than his sister Ruth. Even as a boy, his mother tended to lean on him for support. And while she wasn't an easy mother to have, he hadn't been ready to let her go.

He thought of a phrase that his friend Amos Lapp used to say. *"We don't grieve as those who have no hope . . . but we do grieve."*

He thrust forward on his elbows nearly to the middle of the kitchen table, put his head in his hands, and for the first time since he was a boy, he wept.

Unable to sleep last night, Trudy had made cinnamon rolls, her sister's favorite. But as sweet as the kitchen smelled, as tempting as the rolls were, Shelley hardly ate. Trudy tried to hide her concern. Shelley seemed so painfully thin. Her wrists looked bird-brittle. She had come downstairs in a favorite purple dress that Mom had freshly washed and ironed, but it just hung on her body like a big sack. She didn't eat much, she didn't say much. She didn't volunteer any information about where she'd been, or what she'd done, or why she hadn't bothered to send word. Her father acted like everything was back to normal. A quiet breakfast, morning devotions, then he went out to tend the farm like he did every morning, pretending it was just an ordinary day. But it wasn't.

Mom knew. She hovered over Shelley, not touching her but never far from her. She kept asking if she'd like something to eat or drink, was she warm enough or too cold? Trudy could see Shelley's anxiety level rising as Mom grew more desperate to connect with her. Shelley moved around the house like a bumblebee looking for a flower to land on.

Trudy tried her best with Shelley, but she didn't make it easy. Trudy offered to pin her short hair up so that it could be hidden under a prayer cap, but Shelley said she didn't like being fussed over. Trudy told her about the new farm animals that had been born since she left, offering to go show her around, but Shelley just wanted to stay in the house. That was what she said, but she also looked anxiously out the window every few minutes.

Finally, Trudy brought out an embroidery project Shelley had been working on when she left home. "I thought you might want to pick up where you left off."

Shelley winced. "I don't know, I just don't know."

"I'll help," Trudy said. "We can sit together. I'll work on one end and you can work on the other."

Shelley shrugged, shook her head. "I don't know. I've forgotten so much."

"It'll all come back to you. You'll see." Trudy persisted and Shelley tried, but she couldn't sit still. Her fingers moved clumsily, her toes were restless, she fidgeted in her chair, and she kept peering out the window as if she was expecting someone. Or afraid of something? Worry would darken her features, then in the blink of an eye she would go from fretting to calming herself, humming quietly.

The whole thing gave Trudy a sick sensation in the pit of her stomach. She wasn't sure what to expect with Shelley's return, but she hadn't expected *this*: Nothing had changed.

And suddenly it all seemed so wrong. Everyone was trying to help Shelley fit back into her Plain life, and that seemed to be the last thing her sister wanted or needed. A terribly discouraging thought kept buzzing, mosquito-like, around Trudy: When Shelley kept repeating "I don't know, I just don't know," was she talking about being home? Or was she thinking about leaving?

The sound of a whistle made Shelley freeze. Then something welled up inside of her and she burst out of the chair like a surprised bird. She gazed out the window and a wide smile broke over her face. Curious, Trudy joined her at the window. There came Billy Blank, striding up the long, winding driveway, hands in his pockets, whistling away. Shelley bolted outside to meet him, leaving the door wide open. Mom watched them from the kitchen window, the two standing together in the yard. She patted her hands over her heart and sighed a happy sigh. "Glaabscht du sell?" *Can you believe that?*

Trudy saw Dad appear at the barn door and stop abruptly when he noticed Billy and Shelley, deep in conversation, not far from him. He turned toward the house and saw Mom and Trudy at the window. A look of delight filled his face, mirroring Mom's. He tucked his chin the way he did when he seemed pleased, and went back into the barn.

Everything was the way Mom and Dad wanted it to be. Trudy had her doubts. About Shelley, about Micah.

Trudy was thankful that her sister was home again, grateful for the lengths that Micah had gone to in finding her. Appreciative to the bishop for making that long trip to bring her home again, where she was loved and accepted.

But Trudy couldn't shake how hurt she felt by knowing that Micah had withheld information about Shelley from her. Her sister had been calling him, asking him for help, and Micah had never said a word. She couldn't stop her thoughts as they connected the dots. Her brain felt like a runaway horse, galloping through recent memories.

Micah's abrupt and complete lack of interest in the chick in the eagle aerie.

That morning when the team was leaving for Tennessee and he acted so cold to her.

That time when she was helping him change sheets at the guesthouse. He had said he was on the chase for a hard-to-find bird. A jinx bird, he said. Now it was so clear: he had meant Shelley.

In the morning, after an overdue and lavishly steamy shower because the Swartzentrubers had no indoor plumbing, Micah took the cell phone back to the Beachy boy.

The boy looked at Micah suspiciously. "I thought you wanted it for the whole month."

"I did. I don't."

"I'm not giving your money back."

"Keep it." Micah was frugal by nature, but he was happy to get rid of the cell phone. It created endless distractions, 99 percent of which were unnecessary.

The Beachy boy looked his phone over. "Funny thing . . . I missed it a lot at first. Took a while to get used to not having it. Then I kind of liked it. Sort of nice to not feel like everybody could find me, day or night." He clicked the button on and waited for it to come to life, then smiled as the dings for text messages started loading up.

Micah rolled his eyes. He wouldn't miss that thing. Not at all.

After leaving the Beachy boy, he planned to head to Wonder Lake to see what was going on up there. David had said something about a significant development occurring but said he couldn't talk about it in front of Zeke Lehman. When Micah started up the ridge behind Lost Creek Farm, he quickly realized what David had meant—there was a ribbon of yellow caution tape sealing off the trail. A stern sign was posted: ENDANGERED SPECIES NESTING SITE. DO NOT TRESPASS.

What? Micah grinned. What?! So *this* was what Trudy had been trying to tell him on the phone. Not for the first time, he wished he hadn't cut her off so dismissively.

Why couldn't he have said, "Trudy, I do want to talk to you. I want to tell you everything that's been going on. To explain why I've acted like such a jerk lately. But right now, I'm in a panic. My heart is pounding, my hands are sweating, my stomach is tumbling. I've created a huge mess and David is the only one who can fix it. Please go get him. Please, don't be mad at me. Just go get David!"

Instead, he'd been short with her, abrupt. Hurt her feelings. And she'd only been trying to tell him about what had been discovered at Wonder Lake. He hit his forehead with the palm of his hand. *Idiot!*

An endangered species. It *had* to be that hawk chick. But which genus? His mind ran through a list of hawks—some were under threatened status in Pennsylvania, but there was one that had been moved fairly recently to endangered status. Which one? Northern Goshawk! That was it. So that was how Trudy was able to stop the building.

His grin bloomed into a full smile. Trudy Yoder was a genius. Absolutely brilliant.

He pivoted and ran as fast as he could to the Yoders' farm, cutting through pastures and cornfields. He slowed as he reached the outskirts of the Yoders' farm. Slowed, then stopped. Buggies were lined up in the driveway, with more arriving. Amazing, how quickly word spread in a community without cell phones.

Maybe he shouldn't interrupt as everyone was welcoming Shelley home.

Maybe he didn't want to see Shelley anyway.

He definitely didn't want to see Shelley's dad.

The farmhouse door opened and out came Billy Blank. Good grief! That guy was like Hank Lapp. He was everywhere.

Micah waited until Billy reached the road, then he ran to meet him. "What's g-going on?"

"Hi there, Micah." Billy beamed, like he hadn't seen him in ages. It had just been a few hours. "Did you hear about the bishop's mother?"

"What?"

"She died. Birdy found her last evening."

Man o' man. He felt for David. The last forty-eight hours had been tough on him, and then to come home to that news. "Is D-David at the Yoders'?"

"No. None of the Stoltzfuses are here. They're all home. The viewing starts this afternoon, I heard. Funeral on Saturday."

Micah tipped his thumb in the direction of the farmhouse. "So w-who's up there?"

Billy turned and looked at the farmhouse. "Let's see. Trudy and Shelley, their folks. Fern Lapp, Hank and Edith Lapp, Luke and Izzy Schrock—"

A buggy drove past and Mose stuck his head out of the window. "Micah! I hear you saved our Shelley! Everyone's talking about it."

Micah's eyes went wide.

Billy grinned. "It's true, Micah. You're a real hero. It's all over town."

No. No, he wasn't. Not at all. "Who t-told?"

"Hank, of course. He told folks all about the phone calls from Shelley, and how you tracked her to Tennessee, and rescued her. Hank says you can track anything."

Micah's head spun toward the farmhouse. He should've been the one to explain everything to Trudy, before she heard it from anyone else. "Billy, c-can you g-go get Trudy for me?"

"Sure. Absolutely. But it'll have to wait until I get back from feeding my goats." He paused, and a goofy look came over his face. "She sure is something, isn't she?"

"Trudy?" Yeah. Yeah, she sure was.

"Trudy's fine. Smart. Real smart. But I'm talking about Shelley. Man! She can sing the birds right out of the tree." He went off whistling down the road, not a care in the world.

Micah watched him go, annoyed.

When the next buggy pulled into the Yoder driveway, and Micah saw Teddy Zook behind the reins, he asked him to send Trudy out. Quietly, he said, so others didn't know he was waiting out here for her.

Teddy laughed. "Don't want the big hero's welcome, eh?"

Not hardly.

Micah paced up and down the road, slipping behind trees when buggies drove up. He didn't want to talk to anyone but Trudy right now. There was a lot he had to explain, and he reminded himself to listen too. His sister Penny told him that, often. *You can listen so well to birds,* she would say. *Try listening to people in the same way.*

Ten minutes later, Teddy came out of the farmhouse to find Micah. "Sorry, pal. Trudy said she's too busy to talk to you."

Trudy Yoder, Bird-Watching Log

Name of Bird: *Yellow-bellied Sapsucker*

Scientific Name: *Sphyrapicus varius*

Status: *Low concern*

Date: *February 27*

Location: *At home, along a stand of birch trees*

Description: *Of the woodpecker family. Bright red patch on its head, yellow belly.*

Symbolism: *The woodpecker testifies to the existence of God and his might. If you've ever listened to the hammering of a woodpecker against a tree or some other hard object, then this isn't hard to imagine.*

Bird Action: *Drilling a sapwell—hole it had made in one of many young birch trees recently planted by my father.*

Notes: *They might be called yellow-bellied, but don't be fooled into thinking they are cowardly. To me, the Yellow-bellied Sapsucker is a symbol of courage. It's the only woodpecker in the Northeast that's completely migratory (maybe because they need lots of trees for tapping). Most woodpeckers stick around their known territory, happy to rely on snags filled with insects. Not the Yellow-bellied Sapsucker.*

It spends half its time drilling tidy lines of sapwells in young trees to lap up the sap with its sticky tongue. (To the constant aggravation of my father.)

21

Trudy knew better than to believe everything Hank Lapp said, but she could tell there was some truth in his gripping tale of how Micah Weaver had rescued Shelley Yoder from the clutches of an experimental insane asylum. Not the complete story, not even close, but there were some thin shreds of truth in it.

These last few days, Trudy had made every effort to avoid Micah because she just couldn't bear the thought of seeing him or talking to him. She was pretty sure she'd break out in tears. More than sure. She knew she would because that was what she did at Tillie Yoder Stoltzfus's funeral on Saturday. Each time she caught sight of Micah, she started crying. Everyone thought she was crying for Tillie, and Trudy let people think just that, though the truth was she'd never been terribly fond of Tillie.

Frankly, the woman terrified her. Whenever Tillie had come into the Bent N' Dent, she would tell Trudy to drop what she was doing to reorganize the store shelves. She'd run a store in Ohio all her life, she would say, and she knew what worked and what didn't. She would pick her way through the store, complaining nonstop about the mess, the dust, the peanut shells left by the old men who tossed them into the woodstove and missed.

Trudy thought David should be the one to decide what went on the shelves and where, but she didn't dare say so to Tillie. You just didn't contradict her. No one did. Not even the bishop.

The last time Trudy had seen Tillie was two months ago, the day before the fall that broke her hip. She'd come into the store just as Hank Lapp had been trying to pop corn kernels on top of the woodstove. Hank had distracted himself with telling a long story and burned the popcorn. The entire store reeked with that acrid burnt smell. And somehow, according to Tillie, it was all Trudy's fault. She could still hear Tillie's shrill staccato voice, almost as if she were standing right next to her. "You are responsible for the store in my son's absence. Are. You. Not?"

Trudy felt sad for the bishop. It must be hard to say goodbye to a parent for the final time. But she had to admit that she wasn't going to miss those soul-piercing glares from Tillie Stoltzfus. Those were the thoughts that ran through her head during Tillie's long funeral. Those, and how to evade Micah after the funeral service, when the women served the meal to the men. She made sure she served a table far, far from Micah. She always knew where he was, even without looking. She could just sense his whereabouts.

The next day was an off Sunday, so she didn't have to worry about seeing Micah at church. That made life a little easier. She figured it was just going to take time to stop thinking about him. After all, he'd occupied her thoughts—her heart!—for years now. Falling in love with him had been so easy. Falling out of love was much harder.

On Monday, as her shift ended at the store, she came out to get her scooter and there he was. He'd been sitting on the ground next to it, waiting patiently. He rose to his feet, wiping his hands on his pants. "Trudy, I found out about the G-Goshawk chick. You did a g-great job. Very . . . clever. Amazing."

She bent down to pick up her scooter. "Thanks." And then, "Bye."

"Hold it. Can't you give me a m-minute?"

A week ago, she would've been elated by the question. No longer. Chin tucked, she said, "I . . . just don't want to see you."

"I know, but I n-needed to see you."

257

She met his gaze.

She knew this moment would come eventually, so she'd already carefully chosen her words. "Micah, I thank you for bringing my sister home again. Our whole family is grateful." She put her hands on the scooter handles.

"Trudy," he said, his voice hammered thin. "Please. Wait." He put his hand right on top of hers to keep her from leaving, and it nearly made her falter.

Nearly. She kept her eyes down. If she looked into his warm brown eyes, she'd buckle. She hadn't planned on telling him all that she'd been feeling, but the words tumbled out, one after the other, and she was fighting tears so she spoke as fast as she could. "The way you went about it, keeping everything to yourself, not telling me the truth when I asked you for it. If you would've just talked to me, I could've explained that Shelley wasn't well. I would've told you how my parents didn't want anyone to know so we kept it a secret. But you never shared any of this with me, Micah. She's my sister, my only sister, and you never thought to tell me she'd been trying to contact you. What's worse is that you lied to me."

"I d-didn't." He had a look on his face as if she struck him. "I just . . . didn't tell you the t-truth."

"Why?"

"What if I d-didn't find Shelley? I d-didn't want you to get your hopes up."

This . . . this was her breaking point. Sudden anger boiled up in her. How dare he! She yanked her hand out of his grip, as if his touch felt scalding. "Can't you just be honest with me for once?"

His head snapped up, startled by her harsh tone. "Be honest?"

"You didn't want to say anything because you still have feelings for Shelley."

"I might have. I d-did. But I don't. Not anymore." He rubbed his face with his hands. "I learned my lesson."

A lesson. That was what Shelley was to him? Nothing more than a schoolboy's test? *She's not the girl you wanted her to be,*

258

Trudy wanted to shout at him. *She never was. I tried to tell you but you didn't listen.* "Well, I learned a lesson too. I accepted that you cared more about birds than you cared about me, but I didn't realize that you cared about Shelley more than me too. Maybe that's why you spent time with me in the first place. Like maybe I reminded you of her or something like that."

Micah shook his head. "No. Not at all. You're completely d-different from Shelley. You don't even seem like . . ." He stared at his boots like he didn't know how to finish that sentence.

"We don't even seem like sisters. I've heard that my whole life." She put one foot on the scooter. "You lied to me, Micah. Maybe not out-and-out deception, but as close as you could get to it. That's what's so hard for me to understand. I thought we were friends."

He shifted, seemingly surprised by her declaration. Then he met her eyes, his expression soft. "Best friends."

She turned away. "I was never your best friend. I was your birding friend. There's a difference. A big, big difference. And you don't even know what that difference is."

Her words did the trick. He looked as shocked as if she had struck him, his ears colored pink and red streaks started up both cheeks. It made her feel a little better to have spoken her mind. A little better, but not much. Tears were threatening, she could feel them clot her throat. *Don't you dare cry, Trudy Yoder,* she told herself. *Not now. Do. Not. Cry.* Before a single tear could escape, she scootered away. Once she whipped around a bend in the road and knew she was safely away from him, hot tears streamed like ribbons down her cheeks.

Micah just wanted things to be nice between them, to be back the way they were, and that wasn't good enough. Not anymore.

Trudy Yoder, Bird-Watching Log

Name of Bird: *House Sparrow*

Scientific Name: *Passer domesticus*

Status: *Low concern (though their population has been declining worldwide for many decades. Distressing!!!)*

Date: *July 16*

Location: *Near the trash bins at the Bent N' Dent*

Description: *Small, brown bird with short tail and wings*

Symbolism: *Represents the concern of God for the most insignificant living things. (Love this so much!)*

Bird Action: *Taking a dust bath out by the hitching post. It had scratched an indentation in the ground and kicked with its claws to throw dirt over its feathers, just like it was taking a shower. Adorable!*

Notes: *Drab-looking, little sparrows are truly amazing in their own way. Their constant presence and familiarity make them easy to overlook, but it's the very reason why they're so remarkable. They're extremely adaptable birds and are on every single continent except Antarctica. But that's not even the best part about sparrows! It's this: They work together. If one sparrow figures out an answer* to a problem (like, finding a food source), the rest of the group learns from that sparrow. They just seem to know, instinctively, that they are better together than apart. <u>Amazing</u>.

People could learn a lot from sparrows.

22

It was autumn but warm, a day of colorful leaves and pale sky. Penny and Ben finally returned to Stoney Ridge this afternoon, full of stories to tell Micah about the birds they'd seen in Canada. The three sat at the kitchen table at Lost Creek Farm, sharing cups of coffee. Penny kept looking around the kitchen, as if she couldn't believe she was really home. She seemed happy. Really, really happy. Ben, too. He lingered much longer than Micah would've thought, telling stories of rarities and dips, until his attention shifted out the large bay window. Shifted and stayed. When Micah saw what Ben was peering at, he noticed that the Nyjer seed bird feeder was empty.

Argh! Of all the feeders! Trudy always chided him about empty feeders. Nyjer, in particular, because it attracted songbirds. Tufted Titmouses were one of her favorites that counted on the feeders. Micah would explain that birds didn't become dependent on feeders, that they always preferred natural food over a bird feeder, and that they never relied on feeders for more than half their food intake.

"Still," Trudy would say. "Still, they come here and they expect to find the feeders full."

So faithful Trudy was. Man o' man. He missed their talks. He missed her.

Micah rose in his chair to go fill the feeder, but Ben waved him back in his seat. "I'll take care of it. I want to check a few things in the barn too." He grabbed his hat off the wall peg and went out the door, whistling.

"Sit," Penny said, refilling Micah's coffee cup. "So, you're a local hero."

Micah groaned. "Hank?"

"We saw him after we got off the bus."

Hank Lapp was *everywhere*.

"He told me that Shelley's getting treatment now."

Micah gave a nod. At the firm insistence of Dok Stoltzfus, reinforced strongly by the bishop, Shelley Yoder was checked into the Mountain Vista rehabilitation facility for a complete medical and psychological screening. Micah heard about it from Billy Blank, who visited Shelley each day.

"Hank told me about Wonder Lake. About Trudy's role. I can't believe what she managed to do, all on her own! I hope she stops by today. I brought her back some maple syrup."

Micah looked out the window at Ben, as he filled up the feeder. "Trudy . . . doesn't c-come by anymore."

"Oh, Micah," Penny said, her voice sinking. "What have you done?"

He let out a shaky sigh. He didn't really want to tell Penny more, but he did need someone's perspective. A female someone. He just didn't understand Trudy.

So he swallowed down his embarrassment and told Penny everything. How he had kept Shelley's phone calls from Trudy because that seemed in everyone's best interests. Yes, Shelley's, mostly, but he didn't want to get Trudy's hopes up. Nor her parents'. "But Trudy's convinced I lied to her." Then he told her about that parting remark she made to him, the words that kept echoing through his mind: *"I was never your best friend. I was your birding friend. And you don't even know the difference."* He felt as if he'd been punched in the stomach.

As he finished the story, a look of disappointment covered Penny's face. Great. Just great. His heart sank. "What did she even mean by that?"

"She meant . . . you won't see your part in it."

That wasn't true. Or was it?

Penny leaned her elbows on the table, resting her chin on the backs of her hands. "Micah, what do you like about Trudy?"

"Like?"

"Yes." She reached out and nudged his shoulder gently. "You spend hours together. You spend more time with her than anyone else. There must be qualities about Trudy that you enjoy."

What did Micah like about Trudy? He took his time pondering that question. Her brown hair had these little frizzy curls along the nape of her neck that never quite made it into her bun. And when they met up to go birding pre-dawn, she still had a sleepy look that he thought was kinda cute. She had a pair of the nicest lips he'd ever seen, and once or twice, he found himself staring at those lips.

What did he like about her? She was one of those people whose expressions were a window to her every feeling. Her eyes acted like a weather vane, pointing to her feelings. He knew exactly what she was thinking because she didn't hide anything. She just seemed so . . . real.

What else? She took an interest in everything, asking questions, offering comments. She was the first person he wanted to tell about an accidental bird sighting, even before Ben. Even Penny.

And she made him laugh, a lot. Especially with the way she phrased things. He called them Trudy-isms. The way she would gasp in surprise when she saw something unexpected or something that delighted her—colts chasing each other around the pasture or kittens curled up on a haystack—it was as if her whole being was filled with awe. With joy. He felt happy when she was around.

Maybe this was what he appreciated most of all about Trudy, something he found astonishing: She never noticed his stammer.

Maybe she was just being kind, but he didn't think so. He honestly thought she never seemed to notice it. And then he would start to forget about it and, in doing so, somehow his stutter lessened. It was nice to not have to think about it when he was talking with someone.

Penny traced the top of her coffee cup, waiting for an answer.

He gulped down a sip of coffee, feeling foolishly self-conscious. His face grew warm. He urged himself, but he couldn't get the words out of his mouth. Taking up a pen to write down thoughts came with fluidity, as naturally in his mind as songs to a bird. But voicing them aloud was sheer torture. Feelings, especially. He felt clumsy, fumbling, haltingly slow.

Penny patiently waited.

He struggled to force out the words as if pulling the stingers of bees from his arms. "She's . . . funny. Loyal. K-Kind to everyone. Dependable. Faithful, as in . . . full of faith. Super s-smart but she doesn't think she is. She never g-gives up on people." He let out a sigh. "At least, most people."

Listening thoughtfully, Penny's eyebrows lifted. "Hmm."

"What?" Why were women so vague? Why couldn't they just speak clearly?

"None of what you just said, Micah, has anything to do with birds."

Einem den Staar stechen. *To open a person's eyes.* Micah felt as if he'd been sitting in a darkened room and someone swiped the curtains open to reveal a bright, sunny day. It was like a thunderclap sounded. Penny was right. She was absolutely right. He felt struck to the very marrow. He loved being with Trudy, it was that simple.

Leaning back in the chair, Penny sipped her coffee, but Micah forgot his. All his attention was riveted on his sister's belly, where she had rested a hand on her roundness. Micah was faced with another shock. Was he that blind? How could he have had no idea? Sad to say, he might be one of the most oblivious men on this planet. Right up there with Hank Lapp and Billy Blank.

His sister was going to have a baby.

———————

When David saw Penny climb out of her buggy and walk to the store, he had to bite his lower lip to keep from smiling. Clearly, Penny was with child. Soon to deliver, he surmised. She had a certain waddle to her gait, with one hand on the small of her back. The Plain People never spoke about pregnancy. Such a condition was considered immodest. An outdated tradition, David believed, that probably had its roots in superstition. If you acknowledged the coming of a baby, you might tempt fate. That was far from the Lord's view of a developing fetus. Fate had nothing to do with a baby. Just the opposite. Each one was wonderfully and fearfully made, already known by its Maker.

If it were up to David, he would like to tell Penny that he couldn't be happier to see that she and Ben, who married late in life, were going to be blessed with a child, the start of a family. He'd like to tell her that she could count on his prayers for this precious new life to arrive safe and sound. That he couldn't wait to welcome this already loved child into the fold.

But it just wasn't done.

Instead, he went down the store steps to greet her and guide her over to the picnic table. Here, they could speak privately. He knew she had come to give a report on Vermont as a possible place to relocate. The truth was, he hadn't had much free time to consider the topic of relocation. Too many other things needed attention. Like his mother's funeral. Like getting Shelley Yoder settled into the Mountain Vista rehabilitation facility for treatment.

"So," David said, "tell me all about Vermont."

"I will. But first, I just wanted to let you know how sorry Ben and I are about your mother's passing. Sorry we missed the funeral. We didn't get the death message in time."

At the mention of his mother, tears pricked David's eyes. He was still getting used to her absence, still forgetting that she was really gone. Still regretting that he was not home when she died. "Thank you." He cleared his throat. "Now, about Vermont."

"The fall foliage is spectacular. We're not even at the peak yet and it's . . . well, just glorious. Everything you can imagine and then some."

David could imagine. He'd seen pictures on wall calendars. "Go on."

Penny fished a folded paper from her pocket and looked it over. "Let's see. We came down from Canada to an area called the Northeast Kingdom. It's very remote, very isolated. And very beautiful. A stark beauty. We noticed plenty of vacation homes that were already closed up for the winter. We found the Amish settlements near Browington. Three of them. But there's only one Amish school."

"In each town?"

"No. Only one Amish school in the entire state. And I think you know that the settlements are Swartzentrubers."

"What's the population like?"

"Actually, Vermont is declining in population."

That wasn't a deterrent to David. It meant there was land to buy and room to expand.

"There's a bank, a post office, a store. Basic necessities."

That, too, appealed to David. Small towns, underpopulated, with opportunities to engage local economies.

"Where do the farmers sell their produce?"

"Farming?" Penny's voice had a smile in it. "Not much farming, not like you'd see in Pennsylvania."

"No hayfields?" Farmers here cut and baled hay all summer long to provide their livestock with nutritious feed through the long winters.

"Well, yes. We saw the telltale sign of stubble in fields. But not the variety of crops that you'd see here. There weren't many plowed fields. The soil was very rocky. I did meet one family that grew watermelons, but they had to do it on a south slope."

"South for the sun."

"Yes. I heard it was a difficult climate to sun-dry hay. Most of the farmers dried it in their barns." She shifted on the picnic bench, as if a little uncomfortable, reminding David of Birdy in her last trimester. She couldn't get comfortable.

"The Vermonters have a term for anyone out of state. They're called 'flatlanders.' We spoke to one flatlander who said he'd developed strategies for extending the growing season and getting the most out of his garden." She paused, wrinkling her brow. "But I can't remember what those strategies were."

"So . . . what crops do the farmers grow?"

"Cows, mostly. Dairy farming is big. Cows dot every hillside. Lots and lots of rolling hills. There's even a joke that Vermont cows have two legs shorter than the others, so they can stand evenly on a hillside." She read through her list.

That would be good news for Vern and Mose. "Then there must be a processor that buys the milk."

"Yes, but here's something else. A number of the working dairy farms had on-site creameries." She leaned forward, her eyes dancing. "Vermont is known for its cheesemaking. Famous for it. We stopped by one artisanal cheesemaker that had cheese-maturing caves. Jasper Hill Farm. Oh David, you would've loved their Moses Sleeper cheese. Or Willoughby. Just out of this world." She closed her eyes as if reliving the moment.

This, too, reminded David of Birdy. She had odd, intense cravings during her pregnancies. Once, in the middle of the night, she sent him to the Bent N' Dent for a jar of Spanish olives.

"Apparently there's a growing demand for locally grown beef. One Plain farmer we spoke to was doing it on a small scale. He thought it had a future." She shifted on the hard bench again as she glanced at the list. "Oh, I nearly forgot. Maple syrup! Everywhere we went, we saw woods full of maple trees. Even those Swartzentrubers are using modern equipment to tap the trees. Instead of taps and old buckets, they draw the syrup with sleek plastic lines running from tree to tree. I brought a bottle of dark maple syrup for Birdy, but I forgot to bring it today. Dark maple is considered an inferior grade on the marketplace, but I found it had the most intense flavor."

"She'll enjoy that." Vermont was starting to sound appealing. "Any drawbacks?"

"Well, I'm not sure if it's a drawback, but it is something to keep in mind. There's a reason the leaves turn color in September. The winters are long. Dark. And bitterly cold. While we were there, we had one morning with hard frost on the roofs. That was early September."

Ah, see? So that was why Vermont farmers chose dairy over crops. This would be a serious drawback to relocating to Vermont. Most church members wanted land to farm. It was in their DNA. It was the very reason they felt squeezed out by the Beachy group. "Anything else?"

"Good birding. Very good birding. Not so much with variety, which was a disappointment to Ben. But definitely with quantity. Migrating birds stopped everywhere as they made their way down from Canada to wherever they spend the winter months."

David chuckled. "I'll add good birding to the list of benefits."

"Are things becoming clear?"

"Yes," he said. "Very clear." But he didn't reveal anything more. Not yet. Something else was brewing behind the scenes, and he wanted to see how it all played out before he said or did anything more about relocating the church.

The door to the store opened and Trudy came out with a box in her arms. She was helping Fern Lapp carry groceries to her buggy. Typical of Trudy, she was chattering away to Fern, something about birds migrating at night. Stars. Magnets. David smiled. "Do you understand what she's saying?"

"I do," Penny said. "Bird migration is a fascinating mystery." Moving carefully, she pulled herself to a standing position. "You should ask Trudy to explain it to you. She's a wonderful teacher."

David watched as she waddled away to go say hello to Trudy and Fern. *"She's a wonderful teacher."* Trudy Yoder.

David's gaze shifted to Trudy. The best employee he'd ever had, bar none. Thoroughly dependable, conscientious, loyal, intelligent, well liked. It would be a loss for the store, but that was part of the cost of being in a community. Everyone sacrificed for the good of the whole.

He smiled. He'd just found the new schoolteacher for Stoney Ridge.

Trudy kept asking the bishop to repeat himself. "You want me to do *what*?"

"Teach school," David said.

Had she done something wrong? She squinted. "So . . . are you firing me?"

David laughed. "Farthest thing from my mind. It'll be a tremendous loss to the store to have you go. It pains me to say so, but you're needed more at the school than at the store."

She couldn't get her head around it. The bishop was asking her—no, he was telling her and you never said no to a bishop—to become the new teacher for the school. *Me*, she thought. *Me?* "But why?"

"I think you'd make a fine teacher. An outstanding teacher, I have no doubt. Your enthusiasm is contagious. Why, just look at how you were able to change the story for Wonder Lake. Incredible! You're just the one to fill pupils' minds with curiosity about the glories of creation. I, for one, can't wait to see how you'll start influencing all those children."

Was she dreaming? She'd just been given a boatload of compliments by the bishop.

"So, would you be willing?"

Would she be willing to give up her beloved job at the Bent N' Dent to teach school? Her mind started spinning: She'd always enjoyed field trips as a pupil. It would be nice to have more outdoor excursions. And maybe do some science experiments. The teacher she'd had in school didn't like science. Too many uncertainties. But that was exactly what Trudy loved about science. The mysteries. So many mysteries to explore in nature!

The bishop was waiting patiently for an answer.

Slowly, Trudy nodded. "I believe I would."

David smiled, pleased. "I'll go ask your father for permission. I think he'll be happy to hear that a teacher's salary is much more than an employee for the store. Even the top employee."

No, Trudy thought. No, she didn't want the bishop to ask permission from her dad. It was time she started making decisions for herself. "If you don't mind, I'd like to tell him myself."

David studied her for a long moment. Then he smiled. "I don't mind a bit."

———

Trudy Yoder, Bird-Watching Log

Name of Bird: Northern Bobwhite Quail

Scientific Name: Colinus virginianus

Status: Common bird in steep decline (nearly gone in Pennsylvania!)

Date: Years ago. (I can't remember when.)

Location: In a wildlife museum

Description: Stocky little member of the quail family, the Bobwhite Quail is smaller than a crow but larger than a robin. It has chestnut and black-and-white-striped plumage with a distinctive crest on its head.

Symbolism: In the Bible, quails are an indication of God's provision. Quails rained down from the skies on the Israelites (during a mass migration, most likely, which would be typical of the Old World Quail found in the Middle East) to give them the sustenance they desired while they wandered in the wilderness.

Bird Action: None. It was stuffed.

Notes: Quails were desired for their meat in the book of Exodus, and that desire has not waned through time. Once plentiful in North America, the Bobwhite Quail's numbers are now in steep decline. Quails are well camouflaged, with markings that help them blend in with grasses and shrubs. But their habitats are disappearing.

Bobwhite Quails travel in coveys. They run from bush to bush, their little feet spin in a panic. When frightened, they duck into a cover. They eat seeds and leaves and bugs. Quails are not imposing or threatening, they aren't fast or strong, which only makes me feel very protective of them. Their sweet song is missing in Pennsylvania. Let's hope it will make a comeback. Nature is full of surprises. (So is life!)

23

It was one of those perfect days in mid-October. The canopy of leaves that enveloped the country road were a riot of bright colors, there was a crispness to the air, the sky was bluer than blue. Micah thought back to Interstate 81 on the way to Tennessee and wondered what it might look like today. He wondered, but without a yearning to see it. He remembered the thought that had passed through his mind. Was October just as beautiful in Stoney Ridge?

He had his answer. It was. And thankfully, he was noticing, fully appreciating it. Micah was heading to the Bent N' Dent one afternoon to pick up some things for Penny. As he turned onto the lane that led to the store, Billy Blank was driving a buggy in the opposite direction. He waved to Micah in that way he had, like he couldn't believe his good fortune at bumping into him. How could anyone be so cheerful all the time? It wasn't normal. Before he could finish the thought, Billy hopped out of his buggy and crossed the street to greet him, his hand extended.

"Where've you been?" he said, pumping Micah's hand. "I haven't seen you around."

"Migration," Micah said. "Lots of b-birders coming through. How's Sh-Shelley?"

"She's doing great. Just great. I'm heading there now. Want to come?"

Micah shook his head like a wet dog. No way.

"Another time, then. I'm sure she'd like to see you. You're our big hero, you know."

Micah looked out the buggy windshield. "Billy . . . d-doesn't it b-bother you that Shelley's not . . . q-quite right?" He turned to Billy. He wanted to know his answer. He really did.

Billy considered his question for a long while. He looked placid, almost philosophical. A word Micah would never have thought he'd slap on Billy Blank.

"Shelley's just Shelley," Billy said in his Billy way, upbeat and lighthearted, as he thumped Micah on the upper arm. "Gotta run. She's expecting me." He hurried back to his patiently waiting horse and buggy.

In the side mirror Micah watched Billy waving to him as the buggy rolled down the road. *"Shelley's just Shelley."*

And didn't that just say it all? Micah thought he had never in his life seen anyone so content as Billy Blank. So accepting, so unquestionably loyal. Micah wished he were more like Billy. He couldn't believe he was thinking such a thing, but he was.

He let out a deep sigh and flicked the horse's reins. At the store, he was relieved to find the store entirely empty—no customers, no one working the register—but for the light shining from David's office.

Micah went to his open door and knocked on the jamb. "Busy?"

David looked up, surprised to see him in the doorway. "Come in," he urged, smiling a remarkably warm, patient smile. "I'm working on a sermon. It can wait. I'm happy to have an interruption." He tossed his pen down on the pad of paper.

Micah remained where he was. "Trudy's a g-good choice for a teacher."

"She's surpassing all expectations."

In four words, the bishop had just nailed Trudy Yoder. She was underestimated by just about everyone. *Myself, included.*

David clasped his hands behind his head, amusement lit his eyes. "The pupils spend more time out in the woods looking for birds than they do in the classroom. No wonder they love her."

Micah had to smile at that. Good for Trudy. The outdoors was the best classroom, and nature provided the best lessons for life.

"Only complaint I have about Trudy as the new teacher is trying to replace her here. I'm still on the hunt, if you happen to know of anyone needing a job."

Micah wasn't the one to ask. He'd kept a low profile these last two months. Too uncomfortable. Everyone badgered him about the Tennessee trip, wanting details about how he tracked down Shelley Yoder. Thanks to Hank Lapp and his protégé Billy Blank, the tale grew bigger with every telling.

"Any chance you might be interested in working at the store? Part-time, of course. I know you're busy."

Me? No way. Not a chance. Too much interaction required with people. "Can't."

"I'm glad you dropped in." David dropped his arms and leaned forward. "There's something I've been wondering about, ever since Shelley was found."

A slight tension tightened Micah. It was almost as if David could see it, or sense it, because he quickly added, "About birding."

Micah felt his shoulders relaxing. "Shoot."

"I learned something interesting recently about bird-watching from my wife. If a rare bird she's interested in has been spotted in a certain area, she'll rise before dawn and head out to that area. Then she finds a place to sit quietly and she waits, and waits, and waits. She knows she can't make the bird magically appear, but she also knows that if she puts herself in that certain area, practices the right amount of quiet and calm, the bird might show itself." David paused. "Is that what you do? Is that how you find your rare birds?"

Micah nodded. "And l-look for its food source. That's pretty m-much all that's on a bird's mind." Food and reproduction, but he'd never say that to the bishop. Too embarrassing.

"I suppose, in a way, that's how you found Shelley. You put yourself in a certain area."

Micah stiffened. He looked down at his scruffy boots. "F-Folks keep trying to m-make me a hero."

"Everyone's pretty impressed that you were able to track Shelley down. You didn't have much to go on, after all."

The bishop's eyes were on Micah in that way he had, of seeing into a man's soul. Made Micah so uncomfortable that he finally blurted out, "I'm not a hero."

"No?"

"No."

David pointed to the chair across from his desk. "Why don't you sit down?"

Settling into the chair, Micah took in a deep breath, let it out. "I t-talked you into sending the team to T-Tennessee because I knew Shelley was there. I was d-determined to find her."

David didn't seem surprised by that. "Why do you think it would be wrong to want to find Shelley?"

"Not wrong. Not exactly. But . . ." This was the gut-wrenching part. Hard to say what needed to be said. "I p-put what I wanted ahead of what was b-best for the church."

David tipped an eyebrow Micah's way. "Tell me more."

"I wanted to find her . . . because . . ." His eyes started stinging. "I had f-feelings for her. Strong ones. I c-cared for her before she left, q-quite a lot. When she ran off like she d-did, I thought I was d-done with those feelings. But when she started c-calling me, it churned everything up. But after I f-found her . . . I could t-tell right away that . . ." He pointed to his head. He didn't know how to describe her anymore.

A benevolent expression filled David's eyes. "She wasn't well."

Bull's-eye. Turning his face to the door, Micah tried to hide the fact that he was swiping at his eyes with the back of his hand.

"Must've been a shock," David said. "I can't imagine how you felt when you realized Shelley wasn't the girl you thought she was."

Micah sat there with brimming eyes. One tear after the other started streaming down his cheeks. Embarrassing. And yet, it was okay. "Nothing was what it s-seemed. Even the way I thought about Sh-Shelley before she left . . . I d-didn't know her. I'd made up my m-mind about her without really knowing her. I'd c-created an illusion. N-Nothing," he repeated, "was what it seemed."

David didn't respond for a long moment. "You know, Micah, I've found that to be a rather common occurrence. In just about every area of life. We make up our minds ahead of the facts."

Micah wiped his eyes with the back of his sleeve. "I feel . . . like I t-tried to f-fool you." Others too. Trudy, especially.

"That makes us even." David leaned back in his chair. "I might have fooled you too."

Hold it. What? Micah scrunched up his face in a question.

"I sent you on that trip because I had confidence that you'd find out the information that we needed for unity in the church. And you did." He smiled, ever so slightly. "Boy, did you ever." The smile left his face. "But I knew this would be a difficult trip. I wanted to test you."

"Why?"

"Because you are a young man on the verge of adulthood. I've seen you take one step forward into manhood, then step back again. You took on the shoe repair shop because it was needed. That was a step forward."

Micah knew there was something to come. He braced himself. "But . . ."

"Your birding skills are pretty remarkable, and I know you get a great deal of enjoyment out of your work. But your gifts were given for the benefit of God's church. You were able to locate Shelley because of those gifts. However, do you remember how you responded after I told you about the construction project planned for Wonder Lake? You planned . . ." David held out an open palm, letting Micah fill in the blank.

"To leave." Micah wondered if Trudy had told David, or if he had just figured it out for himself. He was savvy like that. As if he had a direct phone line up to God.

"That," David said, "struck me as a step backward, away from manhood. A big one. So when you came to me with that folder, full of information about Tennessee, I sensed it was time for a test."

His mouth started to form an *oh*, but the word never made it out. Tears threatened. His throat felt clogged, his eyes stung. He smothered his face with his hand. "And I," he said, "failed the t-test." Not just failed. He'd taken a giant step back from manhood. He'd panicked after finding Shelley, called David to come quick, to fix this mess he'd made. As soon as David arrived, Micah took still another step backward. In a somber mood, he'd offered nothing at all to the team. No support. No words of encouragement. No help navigating the route. He didn't even try to keep Hank Lapp occupied the way Billy did, sandwiched between Micah and Hank in the far back of Zeke's van. Shelley and her dad sat in the middle seats, David and Zeke were up front. During the entire drive home, Micah kept his eyes closed, pretending to be asleep. In reality, he never slept a wink. As hard as he had tried, he couldn't wipe his mind clean of all thought, not enough to sleep.

It struck him now that he had returned to Stoney Ridge a far more immature man than a mature one. His heart sunk even lower. Man o' man, had he ever failed David's test.

Once again, David took his own sweet time to respond, giving Micah plenty of time to tally up his shortcomings. "Failure can be the greatest teacher. And the best lesson of all, the one that redeems all our failures, is realizing that God charts the road we take."

"Meaning . . . ?"

"God has the big picture in mind. You might have had an ulterior motive for influencing me to send the van to Tennessee. But God's purpose was larger than yours or mine. I think he used your tracking skills to bring Shelley home again. This is where she needed to be, without a doubt. But God is the hero in this story."

Yes. Yes, that was exactly what Micah had needed to hear. To remember. That was what kept bothering him whenever someone called him a hero. He wasn't. God was the hero in this story.

David leaned forward to rest his elbows on the desk, looking straight at Micah. "And maybe it was time you needed to come to terms with a few things too."

I'll say. Like putting birds before people. Like putting Shelley before Trudy.

"If you think I'm going to ask you to confess to the church, then you're mistaken. This is a conversation that belongs between you and the Lord, Micah."

Now tears were streaming again and he couldn't hold them back. Part of Micah thought that David was too easy on him. He deserved time on the sinner's bench for what he'd done. But another part of him felt washed clean. After confessing, the healing comes. It was a phrase Micah had heard David say many times. Today, he felt it.

David handed him a box of tissues. "Zeke Lehman dropped by a few minutes ago to tell me some news. Big news. You ready for it?"

Micah mopped his face and cleared his throat. "Ready."

"Zeke said he was so impressed with the potential in Stantonville that he's moving his church there. He put in an offer on a large parcel of land and it was accepted."

Rodney the real estate man hadn't wasted his time. "What d-does that mean for our church?"

"Keep this to yourself for now . . . but I think it means that the Lord has given us a number of clear messages to stay put. Bringing Shelley back home, for one. And she's getting the help she needs, with her family and church surrounding her. Now that Zeke Lehman has made a decision to move the Beachy church, it seems like another sign from the Lord to stay right where we are. There's going to be a lot of farmland available in Stoney Ridge."

"I suppose so."

David's eyebrows rose. "Including Wonder Lake."

Micah's heart leaped. He slammed a palm on the desk. "I want it."

David grinned. "I thought you might be interested."

"I'm serious. I need to b-buy that land."

"Do you have the money?"

"I have savings. If I don't have enough, I'll figure s-something out. I just need that land."

"Okay. I'll do what I can to keep you in the loop after the news is official."

"Whatever it costs, I want that land." No stutter.

"I'll make sure you've got the first stab at it."

The phone rang and David reached out to answer it. Before he did, he gave Micah a smile. "All in all, I'd say that things have worked out for everyone."

Maybe, but it didn't feel that way to Micah. He felt shaken up like nothing before in his life. For the first time, he knew what it meant to be broken.

Later that day, on the buggy ride home, David dreaded a long night ahead to write Sunday's sermon. Normally, by the middle of the week, the Lord would give him an idea, something specific, a sense of what the church members might need. This week, he'd felt empty. He'd felt this way ever since his mother had passed. Like the well had gone dry.

A red cardinal dashed past him on the road, breaking his bleak line of thought, making him think of Micah. The visit this afternoon was a poignant one, and he was thankful the store had been empty. Had anyone else been in the store, Micah's reserved nature would've sent him home rather than get him talking. Confessing. It was touching to see the Lord at work in a young man's heart. God had plans for Micah Weaver, David sensed.

The horse shook his head, jolting David. The sermon, he reminded himself. Get back to writing a sermon.

But his mind couldn't seem to stop drifting off to reflect on Micah's visit. On mulling over the way bird-watchers seek out their bird. By learning to appreciate the stillness as well as the bird.

How had he not thought of this before? It was such a parallel of how a person should seek stillness before the Lord. Put oneself in the right place, the right posture. Let the mind and body quiet. Learn to appreciate the stillness.

How many times did the psalmists commend the benefits of being still before the Lord? Too many to count. The one that stuck in David's mind was from the Forty-sixth Psalm: "Be still and know that I am God."

When was the last time David had been still before the Lord? He hadn't given his best to God these last few months, maybe even longer, and that was a dangerous habit. A corrosive one. He thought of a forgotten metal garden rake that Birdy had left out in the rain for too long. It had grown rusty. That was what had been happening to his soul. He couldn't even think of the last time he had risen early to have a quiet time of prayer and supplication before the Lord. It used to be part of his regular habit, as vital as food. It *was* food, after all. Spiritual nourishment. It was time to correct that.

He thought of all the time and energy he'd spent on relocating the church: he'd read books, he'd spoken to bishops who had moved, he'd listened to his church members' opinions, he made lists of pros and cons. He'd put a lot of weight on Birdy's enthusiasm to relocate. Quite a lot. But had he spent time being still before the Lord over the entire issue? Asking, then waiting patiently for an answer?

No. He really hadn't. To be fair, maybe he had asked, but he didn't wait for an answer. He just plowed forward.

The whole notion of relocating the church had emerged during an especially busy stretch—not only busy with the church but at the store. Busy at home with his mother's failing health.

Thankfully, God was faithful even when he was not. The Lord

used unusual circumstances to bring good for the church, in so many ways. Shelley was home, getting the help she desperately needed. The fact that Micah found her at The Yellow House Project brought her mental health concerns out in the open, into the light. Secrets were terrible. It only made everything worse—for Shelley, for Trudy, for the Yoder parents. The entire Yoder family was now in counseling at Mountain Vista rehabilitation facility.

And the Beachy church had come to the unexpected conclusion that they preferred Stantonville to Stoney Ridge. Zeke said his church was expanding so rapidly that they needed more space. He said the trip to Tennessee opened his eyes, and there was no looking back.

Birdy had been the phone call that interrupted his conversation with Micah. She needed something from the store, and he told her about the Beachy move.

Her surprise took him by surprise. "I wonder how long that will last."

"You don't think they'll settle in Tennessee?"

"Do you know the bird Cedar Waxwing?"

"Let's see. Tan bird, black mask, red tip on its feathers." He was getting better at this.

"Exactly." There was a smile in her voice. "Cedar Waxwings are always on the move. They stay in an area only as long as the fruit lasts, then wander again in search of the next meal."

She might be right. The Beachy church hadn't stayed long in the place before Stoney Ridge, and they'd only been here a year. But at least David and Zeke and the two churches were parting on good terms, which meant a great deal. To David, while the differences between the two churches remained, the friction and conflicts were resolved. They would part as friends, hoping the very best for each other. And David knew that pleased the Lord.

The Beachy relocation also meant that the Old Order church was no longer feeling squeezed out. Just the opposite. With church members able to buy the land for their children from the Beachys, they would have all the land they needed. Maybe even more than enough. For now, anyway.

David knew full well that the notion of relocating the church could have gone a different direction very quickly. Most likely, had it kept going, it would've resulted in a church split. Dave Yoder would never have left Stoney Ridge, not without Shelley, and he had significant influence among other men. The Lord in his graciousness had protected the church from David's inadequacies as a leader. At the same time, the Lord had used those same inadequacies to find Shelley and bring her home to her family, to get the help she desperately needed.

A masterful stroke by the Lord God to keep the little Amish church of Stoney Ridge united. David smiled. "Yet he abideth faithful."

The horse slowed as it reached the steep driveway that led up to the Stoltzfus house. At the top of the hill, David hopped out of the buggy and tied the reins to the hitching post. He paused for a moment, eyes lifting to the sky. The sunset was particularly beautiful tonight, gauzy clouds pierced by sun rays. That wonderful feeling of awe at creation filled him, leaving him with a certain springy keenness. Joy. Something he hadn't felt in months and months. Tomorrow, he thought, would be a good day to take his two little boys out fishing. A little chilly, perhaps, but they would dress warmly. It would be a fine day for an outing.

Once again, he reviewed the steps birders took to find their bird.

You can't make the bird appear, but put yourself in the right spot if it does make an appearance.

Practice being quiet, calm, and patient.

Learn to appreciate the stillness.

How good was that, all that? He laughed out loud. There was a sermon in this.

Epilogue

It was Christmas Eve. Trudy grabbed her coat, scarf, and gloves to head to the barn. She had told her dad to stay reading the newspaper by the fire, that she'd feed the animals in the barn tonight. As she went down the front porch steps, she was hit in the face by a bitter gust, so sharp it made her gasp. Another clear night. No snow yet and none in the forecast, which meant the cold would be even colder.

Folding her arms tightly against her chest, she set out, braving the windy walk across the crunchy frozen grass to the barn. About halfway there, she heard a noise and turned to look at the house. A buttery glow filled the downstairs windows. Smoke from the chimney dotted the sky. She could see her mom hustling around the kitchen to prepare for tomorrow's big meal, full of energy and happiness. She could see her dad at the table. In the background, she could make out the outlines of Shelley and Billy Blank as they played a game of checkers near the woodstove.

Shelley had come home for Christmas. She'd spent the last few months as an inpatient at Mountain Vista rehabilitation facility. She'd started taking medication, something her father had objected to but the bishop had intervened and insisted. He said to withhold medication for Shelley was like not giving insulin to a diabetic, and that finally changed her father's mind.

Dok Stoltzfus, who kept a close eye on Shelley's treatment, stopped by yesterday to say she was pleased with Shelley's progress. When her dad asked when Shelley could stop taking meds, Dok snapped. Really snapped! "Never. Never ever ever. Over time, the medication might need adjusting, but your daughter will need medical help for the rest of her life to avoid a psychotic break with reality. Do you understand me? For the *rest* of her life."

Her father withered. He visibly withered!

Trudy figured her father was the reason why the facility wasn't quite ready to release Shelley. She'd been able to come home for Thanksgiving Day, and this time, for Christmas, she was staying overnight. But they expected her back tomorrow evening.

But there was a good side to dwell on: Bit by bit, little by little, Shelley was getting better. Something was easing in her spirit. Trudy could see the improvement because she'd been visiting her sister at the Mountain Vista rehabilitation facility most afternoons, as soon as she finished teaching school. A job, to her surprise and delight, she loved passionately. Almost as much as she loved birds. The best days of all were when she combined the two and took the pupils out birding. Bliss!

More often than not, just about the time Trudy was leaving the facility, Billy Blank arrived to visit Shelley after tending to his fainting goats. The two seemed to have a connection, strengthened through their singing. She didn't know if Shelley was in love with Billy, but she knew that her sister felt safe and secure around him. Maybe that was enough? Trudy wasn't sure that Shelley was fully capable of love. At least, not the kind of give-and-take relationship that true love required.

Then again, Trudy thought, what did she know about true love? Obviously not much.

Now, Billy Blank. He seemed to have a knack for true love. Billy didn't seem at all put off by Shelley's mental illness—not like Jack Spencer certainly did. Billy seemed to make Shelley happy, and that made Trudy glad. She wanted her sister to be loved. He had the right combination of qualities to love Shelley: abundant patience and blind devotion.

Now that Trudy gave it some thought, she did think Shelley made Billy happy too. It was hard to tell because Billy was always happy. Another thing they had in common: Shelley liked his fainting goats. No one in Stoney Ridge considered Billy Blank's fainting goats as anything more than the butt of jokes. But Shelley understood their fearfulness. The goats, she said, were quite wise. They realized there was so much to be afraid of in this life.

She'd even given Billy the idea of making cheese from goat's milk, and now, it was all the two talked about. They had big plans to start a goat cheese business.

Nearly at the barn, she paused, tipping her head back to look up at the velvety darkness. A thin thumbnail moon hung in the sky, allowing the smattering of stars to shine brightly, to sparkle like lightning bugs. In the new year, she decided, she would teach her pupils all about bird migration. It took place during the night, as birds used stars to navigate their path. She let out a happy sigh. There was so much to learn about in this life!

An owl flew past her, so close she could hear the whir of its wings. For a split second, she thought of asking Micah to help her identify it, so she estimated how big it was, and how large its wingspan. But she caught herself and dismissed the thought. Bad habit.

Inside the barn, Trudy hung her lantern on a nail. With a flashlight, she first checked to see if the water in the horses' buckets had frozen. Once, she'd been woken in the night to a mournful wailing. She followed her dad to the barn only to find a panicky mule with its tongue stuck to the bucket. Mules were always doing silly things like that.

The door creaked open and shut and she turned, expecting to see her father. Instead, Micah stood near the lantern light. Trudy stilled, her heart pounding. She'd hardly seen him these last few months since Shelley had returned. She'd gone out of her way to avoid him, but then, he didn't seem to try very hard to find her.

Just as well. Micah had hurt Trudy, deeply, and she just couldn't snap out of it. Even tonight, she waited for him to say something. She wasn't trying to give him the cold shoulder, the silent treatment. She just didn't have anything to say to him.

"Merry Christmas, Trudy." He held up an envelope.

"What's that?"

"Something for you. It's taken a while to get everything in order."

Curiosity rose up, but she held back and didn't take a step forward. "There's no need to give me anything for Christmas, Micah."

"Oh, but there is." He took the lantern off the wall and crossed the aisle, still holding out the envelope to her. He drew a breath. "This is something meant for you."

Micah was much taller than she was, so she had to lift her chin to look at him. There was tenderness in his brown eyes. He swallowed visibly. "Please, Trudy. Open it."

Curiosity overtook her. She took the thick envelope from him and unsealed it. She stared at a sheaf of official-looking papers. "What is it?"

"It's the deed to Wonder Lake. Look there." He pointed to a section of fine print. "It's in your name."

Her mouth opened and closed. "My name?" She looked up at him, confused. "But how?"

"As soon as I found out that Zeke Lehman was putting Wonder Lake up for sale, I made him an offer he couldn't refuse."

She didn't understand. "Micah, I don't have that kind of money." And she knew her dad would never consider buying it. He'd dropped his grudge against Micah, but he wasn't exactly friendly toward him.

"It's a gift."

288

"But . . ." She cocked her head, bewildered. "But you don't have that kind of money."

"I did," he said with a grin. "Not anymore."

She couldn't wrap her head around this. "Why? Why would you put it in my name?" was all she could think of to say.

"Because you deserve it."

Trudy stood perfectly still, perfectly stunned, eyes fixed on Micah. Every nerve ending in her body went on high alert. She couldn't even breathe.

He lifted his eyes and caught her gaze, and she couldn't put it into words, exactly, but something shifted in that moment between them. "There's something I need to say to you." He took another step toward her. "Trudy, you *are* my b-best friend," he whispered. The next words came soft and unhurried. "And you're my best girl." He swallowed. "The only girl for me." He reached out to cup her shoulders with his hands, his touch light and careful, yet she felt the heat from his hands burn all the way through her coat. "I'm asking you to f-forgive me. I'm . . . begging you for another chance." The ragged edge of his voice nearly undid her. His expression was so earnest, so plaintive, so intense, for a second, she thought he might cry.

Her heart and mind started to turn and spin and race and she had to blink to slow them down. Was this real? Was Micah Weaver actually standing inches away, her heart beating only a few inches from his, looking at her in that way she'd always dreamed he might? His eyes swept down her face, landing on her lips. When his eyes lifted again to meet hers, they were on fire, a trick of the light coming from the lantern behind her.

She took so long processing her thoughts that Micah took another step closer, his warm, minty breath swirling around her. "Tell me, Trudy. Tell me what you think."

What did she think? She was starting to like that question. "What do I think?" she repeated. Her smile must have given her away. Before she could finish, Micah pulled her against him and planted a kiss on her lips that made her forget all about feeding horses or filling buckets with water or how cold it was in the barn or that her family was waiting on dinner for her over in the farmhouse. In that tender moment, she even forgot about birds.

Discussion Questions

1. The plot of *Lost and Found* revolves around seeking. The Amish church of Stoney Ridge wanted to find a place to thrive. Micah Weaver was looking for Shelley Yoder. The little hawk chick was seeking security in the eagle's nest. In what ways were they all misguided?

2. There are a few different themes in this novel: Micah's realization that things aren't always as they seemed, Billy Blank's ability to accept people just as they are, David's conviction that, in his desperate attempt to keep unity among church members, he asked for everyone's opinion *but* the Lord's. Was there a theme that resonated most with you? Which one and why?

3. Early on, readers learn that Micah Weaver viewed Trudy Yoder as an LBJ (Little Brown Job), a sparrow. Being described as a plain, common bird wouldn't appeal to most women, but it didn't seem to bother Trudy. In fact, she seemed delighted. Why do you think she took it as a compliment?

4. For several reasons, Trudy grew up in the shadow of her sister, Shelley. There's one line in the book that sums it up: "Shelley might have left home, but home hadn't left her." Did you grow up feeling like a favored child, or an overlooked child, or did your parents make a point of treating their offspring equally?

5. After Micah had rescued Shelley from The Yellow House Project, she made a comment that had an effect on him like being struck by a bolt of lightning. Were you, like Micah, surprised when she told him that the hawk wasn't really a bird? How did that aha moment suddenly make other things clear?

6. What were some of the lessons Micah learned when he realized Shelley Yoder wasn't the girl he thought she was? Or the girl he wanted her to be?

7. Did you feel any sympathy for Shelley? Did you like her at all? How did you feel about the direction things seemed to be going with Billy Blank?

8. Trudy Yoder found great delight in birds. Variety, appearance, behaviors, instincts, and choices. Symbolism, too. What are your thoughts about the Christian tradition of giving such meaning to birds?

9. David Stoltzfus was a man with many responsibilities. Husband, father, son, shop owner, bishop. He was a good listener too. In *Lost and Found*, with the important task of considering a church relocation, he listened to everyone *but* the Lord. When have you had times in your life when others' voices—even those whom you love and trust—are louder than God's?

Author Note

You might be wondering about the Beachy Amish and the Swart-zentrubers, nearly opposites on the progressive/conservative spectrum of the Amish. They have much in common—roots in Anabaptism, theologically adhering to the Dordrecht Confession, including nonresistance and foot washing. Each church is governed by a deacon, ministers, and a bishop, all chosen by lot.

First, the Beachy Amish. Let's roll back the calendar to 1927. A dispute about shunning rose in an Old Order Amish church in Somerset, Pennsylvania, led by Bishop Moses M. Beachy. One group preferred a milder discipline for those who chose to leave the Old Order church to transfer to another Anabaptist church. The faction broke off and became known as the Beachys.

Unlike the Old Order Amish, the Beachys own automobiles, do not use Penn Dutch, and gather in meetinghouses. Their church has an emphasis on evangelism and mission work, and they believe in the assurance of salvation. Currently, they allow filtered internet in their homes, but no television or radio. Similar to the Old Order Amish, they wear the garb—women wear prayer coverings, married men have horseshoe beards.

Although they are called the Beachy Amish, they're associated with the Mennonites. Some don't even consider them Amish.

Let's jump to the other side of the spectrum and take a look at the ultra-conservative Swartzentrubers. The year is 1913. Again, a dispute over shunning arose in an Old Order Amish church in Holmes County, Ohio. Once again, the disagreement had to do with how to handle those who left the church. This time, the more conservative faction—those who favored a severe discipline—splintered off to become a subgroup of the Old Order Amish, known as the Swartzentrubers (named after a bishop who succeeded the original bishop of the schism). They have the most restrictive use of technology and have flatly rejected modern conveniences—no indoor plumbing, no hot water, no community telephone, no power mowers, weed-eaters, milking machines. More controversially, no reflective triangles on their buggies, no indicators, no side mirrors. They're not even permitted to ride in a car unless it's an emergency. Mostly farmers, they live in over a dozen states, preferring more remote, isolated areas than most Old Order Amish, creating what is called a "wall of silence" with outsiders.

There have been all kinds of schisms and splits from the original group, but the Swartzentrubers are the largest and most well-known subgroup of the Old Order Amish. This is the group that continues to practice the custom of bundling (an old-fashioned form of courtship). Consider this anecdotal, but when you read of an unusual story about the Amish in the media, it usually has to do with the uber-strict Swartzentrubers.

In 1944, a Swartzentruber church moved to Ethridge, Tennessee. Today, it's the largest Amish settlement in the south.

And that brings me to *Lost and Found*.

When I first tossed out the plotline of relocating the Amish church of Stoney Ridge, my editor Andrea Doering gave it a quick thumbs-up. "I like it," she said. "America is on the move." That remark stuck with me as I worked on this book because she was so right. In 2020, according to the US Census, nearly 10 percent of

Americans relocated. That figure strikes on a personal level too. Over the last year or two, I've had numerous longtime friends move away. Lots of reasons—they're in search of a lower cost of living, less traffic and crowds, more like-minded people. Two couples sold everything and are currently roaming the United States in a pickup and trailer, searching for a place to call home. In a nutshell, these friends all want a change. And the change, they believe, will bring them a better life. I wonder. I hope so, and I wish them well, but I'm not quite sure there is a better life to find, or if we're meant to make our lives better.

In this story, Bishop David Stoltzfus realized there were two things at stake in considering a relocation for the church: Leaving Stoney Ridge, and all that would mean. Staying put, and what would need to change. If relocating your home is something you're thinking about, both points seem worth a good, long ponder.

The last thought I'd like to leave you with is this one:

Wherever you are, or wherever you go, one truth you can count on is that God is the One who never changes. He is the Alpha and the Omega, the First and the Last, the Beginning and the End (Revelation 22:13).

Satisfy your sweet tooth with a trip to Cape Cod Creamery

COMING SOON

1

"I'm skipping dinner and going straight for the pints."
—Unknown

Fingers hovering over the phone, Brynn Murray hesitated before texting her best friend. Was Dawn the right person to go to? Brynn had met Dawn as a freshman in college, and she'd never known her to do anything wrong, stupid, embarrassing, or rash. All those adjectives could describe the last twenty-four hours in Brynn's life. Add to the list mortifying, humiliating, impulsive. What happened last night was, by far, the worst thing she'd ever done, so out of character. So shameful.

How would Dawn react? From the start of college, Brynn and Dawn had been dubbed the Sensible Sisters. They never did anything crazy, nothing close to foolish or irresponsible. Their majors, and then careers, reflected their rational, logical, left-brain-dominant personalities. Dawn was a CPA, Brynn was a civil engineer.

Until last night. Brynn had committed a regrettable, out-of-character, reckless act.

How to untangle it? How to make it all go away? She needed help. Desperately.

Brynn looked up from her phone to see why the long, snaking

line to get through TSA was barely moving. There was only one TSA agent checking IDs and boarding passes, and he looked as old as Methuselah. Behind him, only one screening machine was open. She blew out an exasperated puff of air and looked down at her phone. She needed Dawn's help.

Brynn
Something terrible has happened.

Dawn
What? Are you OK?

Barely OK.

Can I call you?

No! Don't call!

If she were to hear Dawn's voice, if she had to try to explain herself, she would burst into tears. And once the tears started, they'd never stop.

I just can't talk. I can hardly think straight.

Where are you?

Standing in a TSA line.

Airport? Change your ticket and come to Cape Cod.

But . . .

Don't overthink. Just come! We'll sort it all out.

Not this time, Brynn thought. This wasn't something that could be easily sorted out. But she did step out of the interminably long TSA line to return to the ticket counter. There, she switched her flight to Boston to a flight that would go straight into Hyannis on the Cape.

She knew she was running away from her problem. She knew that what happened last night would require some legal action, but all she could think about was escaping to the beach. From somewhere deep inside her, she felt a frantic longing to face the ocean, to hear the crash of the waves against the shore. To sense their eternally soothing reminder that everything was going to be okay.

She squeezed her eyes shut, defeated. She had absolutely no idea how to get back to being okay.

———

When Dawn picked Brynn up at the airport, it was obvious something was seriously wrong. Brynn always looked like she'd stepped right out of *Vogue* magazine, even on a sleepy Sunday morning in a college dorm. She sent her blue jeans to the dry cleaners. She leather-conditioned her purse and shoes. And her personal grooming was impeccable: French-manicured nails, long dark straight hair cut every six weeks, bangs trimmed every three weeks, makeup perfectly applied. Even the wings on her eyeliner looked professional.

But this girl? She was unrecognizable to the Brynn whom Dawn had roomed with all through college and into their midtwenties. Brynn had no makeup on, or if she had, it had been washed away with tears. Her hair was pulled into a messy bun, and it wasn't the stylish kind of messy. Her socks were mismatched, her T-shirt had a coffee stain, her beautiful dark doe-eyes were puffy and red.

Dawn couldn't imagine what had happened. Brynn was a civil engineer who worked with tough construction types. Somehow, as small and slender and feminine as she was, she handled them well. But in the back of Dawn's mind was a fear that someone had hurt her, had taken advantage of her, and that worry made her stomach turn over. Then flip back. Brynn was one of Dawn's most beloved persons in the world. She was the sister she'd never had. Brynn's parents had divorced, several times, and were absent more than present. Since the age of eighteen, she'd spent every holiday with the Dixons. If anyone had laid a hand on her, Dawn would hunt him down and—

Hold it. She was letting her imagination run wild with dreadful possibilities. Dawn didn't see any bruises, any signs of physical injury. Still . . . *something* had happened to Brynn.

On the way to the airport, Dawn had promised herself that she would let Brynn talk when she was good and ready. So as hard as it was to stay silent, Dawn held her tongue. She hugged Brynn, opened the car door to help her in, put her suitcase in the back, and drove away from the small Hyannis airport, all wordlessly.

In Yarmouth, as Dawn flipped on the blinker to turn onto Highway 6, Brynn finally spoke up. "Could we go to the beach first? I don't think I can face anyone right now. Especially your mom."

Dawn flashed her a sympathetic smile. "You bet." She knew of a quiet beach in Chatham that wouldn't be overrun with children and dogs. July was the most crowded time on the Cape, and today was a picture-perfect day. The population of Chatham swelled fourfold in the summer. Good for an ice cream shop, not so good if you were trying to find a quiet spot on the beach to sob your eyes out.

Dawn knew all about *that.* A few years ago, she'd come to Cape Cod to nurse a broken heart. Her fiancé, Kevin, had broken off their engagement just weeks before the wedding. Dawn had felt the same desperate longing to sit on a beach and watch the waves come in, to absorb the tranquil sounds of the ocean. Time healed her heartbreak, aided by her mother's impetuous purchase of a run-down ice cream shop. And somehow, both time and the dire needs of the ice cream shop brought Kevin back into her life. Two years later, they had worked through their problems and were happily married. So happily that they'd been trying to start a family.

Trying—without success—for six months. She hadn't found the right moment to tell Kevin that she'd made an appointment with a fertility specialist. She'd known that her mom had trouble conceiving, and she'd always feared infertility might be a problem for her too. Because of that niggling fear, she didn't want to let any more precious time slip away.

Brynn sniffed, wiping her nose with her sleeve (soooo unlike her), and Dawn rummaged through her purse with one hand to find a tissue packet to hand to her. When she saw the sign for Harwich, she exited onto Pleasant Lake Avenue, then drove up Queen Anne Road until she came to a narrow lane that led to the beach. Easy to overlook because it seemed like a long driveway with sand along the edges. A perfect hidden spot.

Most people assumed that Cape Cod beaches were one long sandy strip, one wide ribbon. Just the opposite. The beaches were narrow strands, separated from each other by inlets, ponds, bays, jutting dunes covered in wild roses. More like a chunky necklace than a wide ribbon.

Dawn parked the car along the side of the lane, and the two walked down to the beach. She let Brynn decide where to plop down. There were a few people clustered on the beach but no children, no leashless dogs, and the tide was heading out. About a third of the way down, Brynn dropped to her knees. Dawn followed her lead, crossing her legs, settling into the sand, and patiently waiting. She breathed in the salt-scented air, watched the waves as they crashed, admired a bobbing sailboat in the distance, looked at the seagulls circling overhead, noticed the angle of the sun, counted a few puffy clouds floating in the sky. Waiting, waiting, waiting for Brynn to start opening up. Dawn had never been good at waiting. She lasted a full two minutes before turning to Brynn.

"Okay, spill it. What in the world happened to make you so upset?"

Eyes squeezed shut, Brynn tensed up, and suddenly the dam broke. Big, choking sobs. Shoulder-shaking gasps. Struggling breaths. Dawn rubbed her back in circles and let her cry it out. In between sobs, Brynn mumbled something.

"You did *what*?" Too harsh. Dawn had just triggered another crying jag.

When that jag ebbed, Brynn repeated herself, more clearly.

Dawn's mind could hardly grasp what Brynn was trying to tell her. She leaned back, elbows digging into the sand, gobsmacked. "You got *married* . . . to a stranger?"

Acknowledgments

Special thanks to these two people who put in extra time with research help: Hayden Fisher, who also happens to be my daughter-in-law. Hayden is nearly at the finish line with her PsyD in clinical psychology. She is a gifted therapist. Any blunders made in describing the mental illness and unusual behavior of Shelley Yoder are all mine. My daughter, Lindsey Ross, has an uncanny ability to do a "flyover" read of a drafty first draft and see what's missing. Thank you both for your insights. You made this story better.

Thanks to the Revell team: Andrea and Barb, Karen and Hannah, Michele and Brianne, and so many others who are excellent at your job so I can focus on mine.

And you, my readers. Thank you for your enthusiasm about my books and for sharing them with your friends, library, and book clubs.

Above all else, my deepest gratitude goes to the Lord for allowing me this wonderful career in writing. My hope is to strive to be worthy of the calling.

Suzanne Woods Fisher is an award-winning, bestselling author of more than thirty books, including *The Sweet Life*, *The Moonlight School*, and *Anything but Plain*, as well as the Three Sisters Island, Nantucket Legacy, Amish Beginnings, The Bishop's Family, The Deacon's Family, and The Inn at Eagle Hill series. She is also the author of several nonfiction books about the Amish, including *Amish Peace* and *Amish Proverbs*. She lives in California. Learn more at www.SuzanneWoodsFisher.com and follow her on Facebook @SuzanneWoodsFisherAuthor and Twitter @SuzanneWFisher.

Welcome to Summer on Cape Cod

"This story is uplifting and inspirational, emphasizing what is important in life. The small-town setting, humorous banter, colorful characters, and healing make for a wonderful story."

—No Apology Book Reviews

"Readers will be won over by the delightful leads, and the nuanced treatment of Lydie's ADHD and crisis of faith brings depth to the narrative. This is another winner from Fisher."

—*Publishers Weekly*

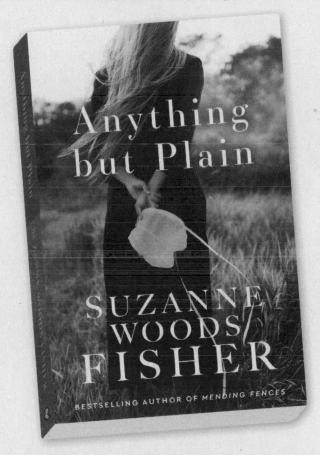

Impulsive and unreserved, Lydie Stoltzfus has always felt like a disappointment—a square peg in a round hole in her quiet Amish community. Leaving Stoney Ridge seems like her best move—even though it would mean leaving Nathan Yoder behind.

"*A Season on the Wind* overflows with warmth and conflict, laced with humor, and the possibility of rekindled love."

—AMY CLIPSTON,
bestselling author of *The Jam and Jelly Nook*

A rare bird draws Ben Zook back to his childhood home, the Amish community of Stoney Ridge—and back to Penny Weaver.